God, he hated innocents!

He was hoping she'd be some cold-blooded harpy, a worthy opponent. He wasn't counting on someone with the wounded eyes of a fawn and the body of a—

He'd better stop thinking about her body. He wasn't in any shape to be doing anything about it, anyway, so why torment himself? He'd better stop thinking about her doelike eyes, too. He'd seen eyes just that vulnerable on a woman who was trying to kill him.

She didn't stir when he pushed her door open at a few minutes past six in the morning. She was sound asleep, wearing an oversized white T-shirt that was pulled up to show a flat, tanned stomach above her plain white cotton panties. Not a woman with a taste for exotic underwear, he thought. Which told him one of two things. Either she was shy, retiring. Or she was here to do a job....

Dear Reader,

We've got a terrific lineup of books for you this month, something I hope you've come to expect from Silhouette Intimate Moments. Starting off with a bang, Anne Stuart makes her second appearance in the line with *Now You See Him*.... This is a hair-raisingly suspenseful look at the struggle of Francey Neeley to recover from the heartbreak and betrayal inflicted on her by a man who turned out to be a coldhearted terrorist. Complicating her life is the arrival of Michael Dowd, a man who may or may not be the good guy and romantic savior he seems. You'll be turning pages long into the night once you pick up this book!

Two of our "February Frolics" authors are back this month, too. Rachel Lee makes her third appearance with *Defying Gravity,* while Rebecca Daniels offers *L.A. Midnight,* a sequel to her first book, *L.A. Heat.* Both of these talented writers have created characters who will find their way into your heart forever. Finally, Barbara Faith's *The Matador* is a story of love regained and a family rebuilt, when a long-estranged couple find the power to overcome their differences in the face of what may be a life-ending injury to *the matador.*

In coming months, more of your favorite authors will be appearing, including Nora Roberts in June, and Marilyn Pappano and Paula Detmer Riggs in July. And that's only a taste of what's to come, so be here every month for the best in romance today, especially for you from Silhouette Intimate Moments.

Yours,
Leslie Wainger
Senior Editor and Editorial Coordinator

ANNE STUART

Now You See Him...

SILHOUETTE·INTIMATE·MOMENTS®

Published by Silhouette Books New York

America's Publisher of Contemporary Romance

SILHOUETTE BOOKS
300 East 42nd St., New York, N.Y. 10017

NOW YOU SEE HIM...

ISBN: 0-373-07429-8

First Silhouette Books printing May 1992

All the characters in this book have no existence outside the imagination of the author and have no relation whatsoever to anyone bearing the same name or names. They are not even distantly inspired by any individual known or unknown to the author, and all incidents are pure invention.

Books by Anne Stuart

Silhouette Intimate Moments

Special Gifts #321
Now You See Him... #429

ANNE STUART

was first published at age seven in *Jack and Jill* magazine. She wrote her first novel in 1974 and has since published in a variety of genres, including Gothics, Regencies, suspense and contemporary romance. She particularly likes the spice of danger mixed with the emotional turmoil of romance. She currently lives in the mountains of Vermont with her husband and two children.

Prologue

"They're going to kill him!" Caitlin Dugan pushed past Frances Neeley's partially open door into the Greenwich Village apartment.

Francey knew Caitlin better than she wanted to and was far too accustomed to her fits of melodrama. She simply continued toweling her hair, wishing she hadn't gone to the trouble of getting out of her bath to come face-to-face with Caitlin's hysteria. "What are you talking about?" she asked patiently, planting herself in Caitlin's way. She didn't want the woman to see the apartment, or it might precipitate an even greater crisis.

Her converted loft was set for seduction. Francey and her distant cousin Patrick Dugan were going to make love that night, after weeks and months of careful courtship. He'd finally been able to break down her resistance, her natural reluctance to surrender. And for some reason it had always seemed like a surrender. But finally, tonight, she was ready. Once Patrick returned from the demonstration they were going to celebrate in truly memorable style, he'd promised her, kissing her before he left. And she'd told herself that she'd waited long enough—if she really loved him, there was no reason to wait any longer. Was there?

But Caitlin was an oddly possessive sister, jealous where she had no moral, Catholic right to be. She wouldn't like the notion of Francey and Patrick going to bed together. She wouldn't like the notion of anyone coming close to her brother. And her expected protest would only strengthen Francey's lingering doubts.

But Caitlin was uninterested in either the apartment or Francey. "They're going to kill Patrick!" she shrieked. "Did you talk to anybody? Tell them anything you shouldn't?" She grabbed the lapels of Francey's terry-cloth bathrobe in her sharp little hands, yanking at her. "Did you turn him in, you traitorous bitch?"

Francey shoved her away, wiping the angry spittle off her face. "You must be absolutely crazy," she said, disgust and pity mixed. "I don't have the faintest idea what you're ranting about. You know as well as I do that Patrick's at the anti-British demonstrations while the Queen speaks at the UN And why aren't you there, for that matter? Don't you care about a free Ireland?"

"Don't give me that. Patrick hasn't gone to waste his time shouting slogans. The time for that passed decades ago. Why the hell do you think he borrowed your car? He wouldn't need a quick getaway from a simple demonstration." The green eyes in her narrow, pointed face were bright with contempt.

"What are you talking about?"

"Patrick's gone to kill that royal bitch. Then maybe they'll pay attention. But some dirty sneaking traitor has ratted on him, and he's going to be shot down like a dog."

Horror overcame Francey's shocked disbelief. "No!" she said, unable to push her doubt away. With sudden clarity, she realized that beneath Patrick's rich Irish charm was a streak of fanaticism that ran deeper than she'd ever wanted to admit. "But he's coming back here...."

"Of course he is," Caitlin scoffed. "He's coming back to screw you, get you to marry him and then get back into Ireland using you as a cover. You must have said something, told someone, you stupid idiot...."

"I didn't talk to anyone," she said numbly. *This isn't happening,* she thought, pulling the robe more tightly around her. *It can't be....*

"Get your clothes on."

"Why?"

"You're coming with me. Maybe we have a chance to save him. You love him, don't you?" she demanded, her voice full of contempt. "You were about to go to bed with him, you wanted to marry him and donate all your money to the bloody cause, didn't you? Get dressed!" she shrieked.

It took Francey less than two minutes to pull on jeans and a baggy sweatshirt, ignoring the silky lingerie she'd bought in preparation for tonight, ignoring the perfumed scent of her bathwater. Even if she hadn't wanted to go, she would have had no choice. Caitlin was fierce and dangerous, and Francey was no match for her kind of dirty street fighting.

She didn't recognize the car Caitlin had waiting outside. She didn't bother to ask where it came from—she didn't want to know the answer. They drove through the New York streets like any New Yorker—with speed and desperation. The streets surrounding the UN were blocked off, as usual, and Caitlin simply left the car standing in the middle of Forty-eighth Street, grabbing Francey's wrist and dragging her toward the huge modern complex of buildings.

They could hear the noise of the demonstration from a distance. There were television cameras everywhere, noise and light and confusion. In the swirling mass of angry demonstrators there was no sign of Patrick, no sign of his broad, smiling face, his charming green eyes, his warmth. He couldn't be a murderer, Francey thought. Caitlin must have been doing drugs. She must have finally flipped. She must...

"There he is," Caitlin breathed, stopping short, her Irish lilt rich with satisfaction. "They haven't seen him yet. There's still a chance."

Francey peered into the shifting crowds, squinting against the glare of the television lights amidst the mass of media equipment. "Where? I don't see him."

"Maybe we'll still be able to pull this off. Move over there and keep your mouth shut. We'll watch and see what happens."

The hard prick of a knife against her baggy sweatshirt left Francey with no choice but to go along. "He can't really mean to kill her?" she said, stumbling slightly as she searched for a thread of normalcy beneath all this horror.

"Oh, can't he just? And you'll get to witness it, or you'll get this between your ribs, and trust me, I've done it often enough to know what I'm doing. I'll make it deadly, and I'll make it hurt."

Francey didn't doubt her for one moment. "Aren't you going to try to warn him? He won't get away with it...."

"It won't matter. He'll die gloriously, a worthy death for any Irishman, to die for the cause."

"He's your brother, for God's sake! How can you watch him die?"

"He's not my brother. Oh, he's some sort of kin—all Dugans are related to each other. He's my lover, and has been since I was thirteen." Caitlin pushed her face against Francey, and there was a look of pure hatred on her pale, Celtic face. "It was my plan to have him seduce you and get all your wonderful American money. He was going to come to me afterward and tell me all the details."

Francey didn't move. "I don't believe you."

"Believe me. He's not your distant cousin, darlin'. He's not some charming Irish expatriate. He needs your money, he needs your protection, and he doesn't give a damn about the spawn of Sean Neeley and the rich American bitch he married. Screwing you was the frosting on the cake.''

They were huddled against a building on First Avenue, across from the UN, across from the demonstration. The motorcade that was pulling up could signal only one thing, and the sudden increase in activity from the crowd, the television crews, and the security people was ominous.

"There he goes," Caitlin breathed, and if she hadn't said anything Francey would never have seen him. It happened so quickly. She could just make out Patrick, the lithe, strong body she'd ached for, blending in with the scaffolding on one of the light platforms. But no one else was looking in his direction, not even Caitlin, momentarily distracted by her anticipation. Everyone else was concentrating on the Queen's arrival.

It was Francey's only chance, and she took it without stopping to think. She shoved hard, knocking Caitlin off balance. The knife went skittering away on the sidewalk, and Caitlin's slender body went tumbling in front of a slow-moving limousine. But not slowly enough.

"Watch out!" Francey screamed, not sure who she was warning, Patrick or the security people, Caitlin or the driver of the limousine.

It didn't matter. Her call signaled the onset of a blood-bath. Patrick began spraying the crowded plaza with bullets, a look of monstrous delight on the face she'd thought she loved. He was so intent he didn't notice another figure climbing a scaffold near him until it was almost too late. Something must have alerted him, for he turned the gun in time to mow down the man who'd almost reached him. But not quite soon enough. As the man lay writhing on the scaffold his hand moved, and Patrick went plummeting off his own platform, into the crowd below. As he fell, Francey could see the blood spurting from the hole in the middle of his forehead, in his beautiful, soulless face.

She started screaming then, the sound swallowed up by the hysteria around her. She simply sank onto the sidewalk, wrapped her arms around her legs and continued to scream until her voice dried up, her mind shrank, and everything went mercifully blank.

Chapter 1

Francey let her long toes wriggle into the hot white sand.
They were her one beauty, she thought dispassionately.
How many people could say they had beautiful toes? And
considering that she'd lived most of her life in chilly northern climates, few people had had the chance to appreciate
the one gift nature had given her.

Here on the tiny island of St. Anne in the blue Caribbean she seldom wore shoes at all, and when she had to, she
made to do with leather thongs. Still, no strange men were
falling all over her, rhapsodizing about her toes. Which was
just as well. She wasn't going to be ready to have any men
falling all over her for quite a while. If ever.

She'd been lucky so far. In the time she'd been staying in
her cousin's secluded villa, he'd sent very few people to in-
trude on her healing process. A couple of elderly women
who'd just lost their husbands, a college student breaking
away from drugs and an unhealthy relationship, a middle-
aged woman facing cancer with remarkable courage. All
broken birds, traveling to the peace and serenity of Daniel

Travers's rambling colonial cottage. All of them eventually left, their healing processes begun. All but Francey, who stayed behind, walking alone in the sand, waiting for her own healing to start.

But today her luck had run out. Arriving on the evening flight from Boston was the first man Daniel had inflicted on her, and there was nothing Francey could do but accept with much grace as she could muster. After all, she had no place else to go. At least, no place that she could face. The whitewashed walls of the villa, the wide boundaries of Daniel's land and private beaches, were all the world she cared to deal with. And if she had to share that world with another one of Daniel's charity cases, then share it she would.

It wasn't as if she weren't a charity case herself. Not financially, of course. Her personal fortune, while not in the league of Daniel Travers's, was respectable enough to keep her from having to worry. But emotionally she was as dependent as a welfare mother, and Daniel knew that.

Besides, the new arrival wasn't likely to make many demands. Michael Dowd was a semi-invalid from somewhere in the south of England, a man who was recovering from a near fatal auto crash. The hospitals had done the bulk of the work over the past few months. Now he just needed sunshine and rest, something the villa could easily provide. It was named Belle Reste for just that reason, and Francey could no more resent the intrusion than she could welcome it.

She would have to leave for the plane soon enough, using the absurd, pink-awninged Jeep Daniel had provided, but until then she was going to treasure the last moments of her solitude.

Maybe she should have pushed it. Maybe she should have forced herself to face the debacle her life had become, forced herself to deal with it. She'd been coasting on a mindless, dreamless breeze, the dark shadows left behind in New York. She'd thought there was no hurry, but Michael Dowd was about to prove otherwise. The presence of any man was going to force her to deal with things she would rather keep ignoring.

She could always abandon him to his own defenses, rent a house of her own. The tourist season hadn't geared up yet, and she'd made a few connections during her infrequent visits to town. Something would turn up.

But she couldn't do that to her cousin Daniel or the ailing Michael. Providing a haven for emotionally destitute souls was one of Daniel's many charitable activities, and Francey had taken full advantage of it. The least she could do would be to provide the kind of healing environment she'd been enjoying. She didn't know whether Michael Dowd could stay alone, but she suspected he needed someone keeping an eye on him at the very least, if not outright nursing.

The villa was big enough that he wouldn't have to get in her way. And he was hardly likely to be making a pass at her in his current condition.

She threw back her head and laughed, squinting up into the bright sunlight. Who the hell did she think she was? In the best of times, with the healthiest of males around, she was hardly irresistible. Even the forced proximity of Belle Reste wasn't likely to turn an invalid into a ravening beast.

Maybe she had been alone too long. Maybe she needed to get used to the company of men again. Someone weak and harmless would be a perfect start. He would probably be querulous—most sick men were—and no threat at all. She could cosset him with custards and fresh fruit, and outwalk or outrun or outswim him if he grew to be too much of a pain. He would probably talk about his girlfriend or his ex-wife or both, and he'd probably whine. All in all, there was absolutely nothing to worry about, she told herself.

Nevertheless, she was going to savor every last minute of her solitude. She was going to drink in the hot sun, the cooling breezes, the rich scent of the ocean and the tropical growth around the villa. She was going to sit and drink fruit drinks and think about absolutely nothing at all until she had to face the mountainous drive to the airport. And from the moment she picked up her unwelcome house-guest, she was going to be the perfect hostess.

But for now she was simply going to vegetate in the bright, glorious sunlight and hope the sun would bake more of the pain away.

"I don't want her hurt." Daniel Travers was a man in his prime—just under sixty, with a bull-like body, a high complexion, bright blue eyes and a deceptively hearty demeanor. He was a great deal more astute, and more dangerous, than most people credited him with being, and that was part of his great value.

Michael Dowd wasn't under any delusions, however. He knew just how far Daniel Travers was capable of going, and he knew enough not to antagonize him more than he needed to. Goad him far enough but not too far, and you got the best results.

"I'm not planning on hurting her," Michael said, leaning back against the leather seat of the Rolls. There was one thing to be said for Travers—he knew how to live well. At least this current assignment involved Rolls-Royces and a villa in the Caribbean. Better than a hovel in Northern Ireland anytime. "I just want to find out what she knows."

"She's gone through extensive debriefing...."

"You know that's not worth a damn if it's not done right. She was in shock, all her defenses in place, not knowing whom to trust. Now she's had a long time to recuperate, with no one bothering her, no one asking unpleasant questions. She's had a nice, peaceful vacation, and she should be just about ready to open up to someone who knows how to ask the right questions in the right way. Particularly someone as harmless as I am."

Travers's bright blue eyes slid over to him, doubtful, and Michael almost laughed. In his current condition he was no threat to anyone at all. He was pale, skinny, and he couldn't walk without the aid of a cane. At least it was better than the wheelchair he'd been inhabiting for longer than he cared to remember. But it was going to be a while before he was back at full strength, maybe longer. Before that wary expression in Travers's eyes would be justified.

Travers shook his head. "I don't think you'd be harmless if you were in a coma," he said. "That's why I'm warning you. Don't hurt her any more than she has been already. Find out what you need to know, and then I'll get you out of there. I have a dozen places at my disposal if you want to finish your recuperation."

"I've finished my recuperation," he said savagely, hating his weakened state. "I've just about gone off my nut these past few weeks. There's no end to the things I can accomplish, even while I'm still so knocked up. As soon as your cousin tells me about her friends, I can move on to another job, and no one will ever bother her again. I'm not that interested in pumping a lovesick female for information, but I'm sick of sitting on my butt watching other people ball up things I've been working on for years."

"That's between you and Ross Cardiff," Travers said stiffly. "I wouldn't presume to give you advice."

"The hell you wouldn't," Michael said with a ghost of a smile. "Particularly when it comes to your precious cousin. Don't worry, old man. She'll be safe as houses with me."

"Considering your expertise in explosives, that's hardly a sterling recommendation," Travers said. "Just remember, you're a dangerous young man. But I can be a dangerous old man, when me and mine are threatened. I'm letting you go to Belle Reste because I want this settled once and for all. Tread carefully."

"I can't do much else, now can I?" Michael countered, lifting his metal cane in a negligent gesture. "Don't worry," he said again. "When I leave St. Anne, your cousin won't even know her brain's been picked clean."

"For your sake, you'd best hope so," Travers grumbled as the Rolls pulled up beside a small private jet.

Michael didn't bother to answer. Private citizens like Daniel Travers were one of the few things that made his job easier. He didn't know what motivated the man—patriotism, civic duty, or sheer boredom—and he didn't particularly care. All that mattered was that Travers put his considerable resources at the disposal of certain select branches of the secret service organizations of various countries, Travers's own and Great Britain among them. All the man asked for in return was a vicarious taste of the excitement and the knowledge that he'd struck a blow for democracy or whatever he was after.

Michael suspected he was deeply disappointed by the recent easing of relations with Eastern Europe. Travers still managed to cheer himself up with thoughts of Middle Eastern terrorists and the subversive branches of the IRA, but even South Africa seemed to be mellowing. If things continued as they were, Daniel Travers would be out of a hobby and Michael would be out of a job.

He doubted it would happen, though. He didn't trust any of it. Not the lessening of repression in Eastern Europe, not the free elections in Latin America, not the hopeful steps in South Africa. Thirty-seven years of life on the edge had made him an extremely cynical man, and a few examples of media manipulation and feel-good public relations weren't going to convince him that the intrinsic nature of the world had changed from bad to good. As long as there were people left alive, he and others like him would be needed. And the nastier, more unpleasant the job, the more often he would be the one to be called.

He hadn't been exaggerating—the past few weeks had been holy hell. He'd been pretty well shot to pieces, and a body takes time to heal, particularly one that had gone through this sort of thing too many times. He didn't like drugs, and his mind instinctively resisted painkillers, even when his body craved them. The pain had been the only thing that had kept him going when he'd first emerged from three weeks in intensive care. The pain, and the hatred.

Normally the idea of weeks in the sun, lying there doing nothing but swelter, would be his idea of hell, especially after such a long stretch of forced inactivity. But he wouldn't be inactive. While he lay in the sun and tried to marshal his strength, his energy, he would be finding out exactly what Frances Neeley knew. And just how deeply she'd been involved.

Of course, he hadn't confided those suspicions to Daniel. If the old man thought Michael suspected his young cousin of conspiracy, he wouldn't let him within a thousand miles of her. And Daniel could do just that, spirit her away on that ocean liner of a yacht he owned and head out into international waters where there'd be no reaching her.

So Michael had pretended to believe in the woman's innocence, keeping his own opinion in reserve. Word on the street had been divided. Some said she was sleeping with Dugan, some that she was just another victim. He intended to find out the truth as soon as possible and then head back to England to clean up the mess Dugan had left behind. See if he could find out who'd been pulling the strings, giving the orders. Who headed up the dread sect of the IRA known only as the Cadre. With Frances Neeley's information in hand, there was no way they could keep him on the sidelines, much as Ross Cardiff wanted to.

He was going to the Caribbean with a very simple goal in mind. To get stronger. And smarter. And meaner. Even though he knew that most people simply wouldn't consider that possible.

He wondered if he was going to have to sleep with Daniel Travers's plain, pale cousin to get what he wanted from her. And he wondered if he was going to have to kill her.

Francey had never liked the way the pink Jeep handled. It tended to pull to the left, particularly when she was enthusiastic with the brakes, and she had grown a little too accustomed to power brakes, power steering, power windows and the like. The old Jeep was not much of an improvement over a push-pull railway cart, and she'd been half tempted to rent a more reasonable car to get around the mountainous little island.

Two things stopped her. One, she didn't go out often enough to make the hassle worthwhile. Daniel had regular deliveries of food and staples arranged, and just about every need was taken care of by a silent army of workers who came and went with smiling faces and almost invisible presences.

The second reason was less practical but far more devastating. She simply didn't want to drive on the left-hand side of the road. She had too many memories of Patrick teasing her about her future, trying to drive on the left-hand side of the road when they went back to Ireland. She had too many memories of Patrick.

One of those almost invisible workers had just checked over the Jeep that morning, so at least she could reassure herself that the silly vehicle was marginally safe. The gas tank had been topped off, the bright pink paint was newly waxed, the awning clean, the vehicle swept clean of sand. She could only assume that whoever had checked the car was equally well versed in its underpinnings. The only sign that marred the spotless paint was a greasy thumbprint on the hood, proof that someone had known enough to at least check the engine.

One of the great blessings of Belle Reste was its remoteness from the rest of the small, busy island. One of its greatest disadvantages was its distance from the tiny airport, most of it over hilly, twisty roads. People also tended to fly in during the evening hours, making the trip even more hair-raising, but Francey navigated the narrow roads with her usual aplomb. She liked driving. And she hadn't yet gotten to the point where it mattered terribly if she lived or died.

Daniel's private jet had already landed by the time she drove the stubborn little Jeep into the airport confines. She slammed the vehicle into Park and jumped out, absently noticing that the brakes were a little spongier than usual. The moment she caught sight of the man making his way carefully down the flight ramp she held her breath, oddly startled.

Even in the electric light she could see that his color wasn't good. He was deathly pale as he moved down the stairs, leaning heavily on the handrail and a cane, and his eyes seemed too big for his face. He was tall and as thin as a scarecrow, his rumpled white suit flapping around his long legs, and his face was narrow and lined with pain beneath a shock of incongruous auburn hair.

A thousand confusing emotions swept over her as she leaned against the mesh of the fence, watching him as he reached the tarmac and moved slowly forward. She didn't quite know what she was feeling, whether it was déjà vu, the odd sense that this had all happened before, or something else. Some strange, psychic knowledge that the sick-looking man walking slowly across the empty runway was going to matter to her very much. Was going to make the difference between life and death. And that he might mean death.

She shook her head, forcing such morbid thoughts away, and the movement caught his eye. Across the deserted tarmac he looked at her, and while she knew that he wouldn't be able to see that well across the artificially lit distance, she suddenly felt uneasy. As if she'd been caught spying.

Opening the wire gate, she started toward him, forcing a welcoming smile onto her stiff face. "You must be Michael Dowd," she said when she reached him. "I'm Frances Neeley, better known as Francey." And she held out her hand.

It took him a moment to laboriously shift the cane, then reach out his own thin hand. His grasp was weak, ominously so, and for a moment she forgot her own concerns in worry over him. "I'm Michael," he agreed, and his voice was surprisingly warm, strong and unnervingly British. During her brief time with Patrick Dugan she'd learned to think of British accents as those belonging to the enemy, compared to Patrick's charming lilt.... No, she wouldn't think of that.

"How was your trip?" she asked, pushing away her instinctive doubts. "How are you feeling? The Jeep's just over there—you won't have far to walk. Unless you'd like me to see whether I could find a wheelchair."

"No wheelchair," he said flatly. "I've already spent too much time in them since the car accident. And I feel like hell."

Querulous, Francey thought with a trace of satisfaction. A pale, weak, querulous man. A pain in the butt and nothing worse.

And then he looked down at her and smiled, and the charm he was exerting was a palpable thing, something she could no more resist than she could stop her heart from beating. "I'm a pain in the butt, aren't I?" he said, reading her mind. "I promise you I won't spend my time here whining. I'm just done in."

She found herself smiling back, up into eyes that were very, very blue. "That's all right," she said soothingly, falling into her natural role of caretaker. "We'll get you home to Belle Reste and get you settled. By tomorrow you'll be able to lie out in the sun and feel a lot better."

"If you say so." His expression was wry. "Lead the way to the Jeep. I'm assuming that pink monstrosity is yours."

"Daniel's, not mine. Where's your luggage?"

"Lost," he said succinctly. "The airline people said they've managed to track it down, and someone will be bringing it over in the morning. In the meantime, I can borrow something of Daniel's can't I?"

"Of course." She held out her arm, to give him some extra strength to lean on, and for a moment he simply looked at her, his eyes distant and unreadable.

"Thanks," he said, taking it and leaning heavily. "I need all the help I can get."

It was a slow process to reach the Jeep. By the time she got him settled she was breathing heavily herself, and she glanced over at him as he lay back in the seat, his eyes closed, his color pale, his chest rising and falling beneath the too-big suit. "Are you sure you're all right? We don't have much in the way of hospital facilities here on the island, but they might be able to help—"

"I'll be fine," he said without opening his eyes, and his voice sounded slightly fainter.

Whatever doubts she'd had about him vanished the moment she realized how very sick he was. She'd been able to be a remote, gracious hostess to the other lost souls Daniel had sent her. Michael Dowd was another prospect altogether. For the first time in months she found someone whose needs superseded her own. Someone to concentrate on, ignoring her own helpless pain. From the moment she'd felt his weak clasp and looked into his pain-lined face, she'd known he wasn't really a threat at all. He was simply a sick man, someone she wanted to help.

She drove with uncharacteristic sedateness through the narrow streets of the town, then headed up into the hills toward Belle Reste with only a decorous increase in speed. Driving was one thing she really enjoyed, and during the past few months of penance and mourning she'd been denying herself that pleasure. Now, suddenly, she felt like stretching her wings, but she knew that with an invalid beside her she had to be as demure as an old lady. Maybe tomorrow she would see about renting a car after all. A small sporty convertible, something with a little power beneath the hood. Her new houseguest would probably enjoy going for drives once his strength increased a bit.

The road to Belle Reste was a series of three hills and three valleys, with the villa lying at the end of the final valley on a spit of land jutting out into the warm Caribbean. With Francey keeping a sedate pace and a companionable

silence as her passenger rested, they made it through the
first hill and valley, up the next hill, and were heading
downward again when the car began gathering momentum.

Francey pushed her sandaled foot down on the brake,
but instead of slowing down the Jeep seemed to move even
faster, and she glanced down, wondering if by some odd
chance she was pressing the accelerator instead.

The brake was all the way to the floor. Pumping was utterly useless—the speedometer was climbing past its well-
bred thirty-five to something beyond fifty. Suicide, on
roads like these.

Don't panic, she told herself, still pumping the useless
brake pedal. Keep steering and try to downshift.

The gears ground noisily as she tried to push the stick
shift into third, and the speedometer climbed to fifty-five.
Her passenger turned his face toward her, opened his sleepy
eyes and said in a tone of complete unconcern, "Brakes
failed?"

She couldn't help it—his mundane tone made her want
to laugh. "It seems so."

"You've tried pumping them, you've tried shifting
down," he observed casually. "What about the emergency
brake?"

"It never worked." She allowed herself a quick glance
over at him. She would have expected him to look even
worse, paler, now that death stared them in the face. Instead his color had improved, and his eyes had something
that might almost be called a sparkle in another man, another situation.

"Then you're simply going to have to drive like hell," he
said. "Or we're going to die."

The speedometer had reached sixty. They were only
halfway down the hill, and coming up was a series of S-
curves worthy of the Grand Prix of Monte Carlo. "Maybe
in a Ferrari," she muttered, "with decent tires. We have
maybe a snowball's chance in hell of making it."

Michael Dowd laughed. "Well then, Francey, it's been nice knowing you."

"Nice knowing you, Michael," she muttered, concentrating on the steering. The speedometer was edging toward seventy, the S-curves were approaching, and Francey Neeley didn't want to die. Patrick Dugan was dead, cut down in a hail of bullets, and she didn't want to run the risk of ever seeing him again, even in some nebulous afterlife.

She took one last glimpse at her passenger before they headed into the curves. At least he didn't seem to mind dying. That should have made two of them. But she didn't want to die. She didn't want to take the easy way out, the coward's way out. There was too much left to do, to accomplish.

"For heaven's sake put your seat belt on!" she shrieked at her passenger, just noticing he hadn't bothered to fasten himself in.

"Will it make a difference?"

"Humor me. We just might make it. If we get through the next section there's a stretch of rocky beach. I might be able to steer this thing into the water."

"I don't fancy drowning any more than I do crashing."

"Shut up and let me drive."

She almost made it. Not by slowing down, something that was beyond the Jeep's capabilities, but by speeding up just at the curve of each turn. She was cursing beneath her breath, a steady litany that had to take the place of the prayers she'd forsaken months ago, and by the time they entered the final S-curve she knew she was going to make it. The curve was ending, the beach was up ahead, all she had to do was steer across the stretch of rocky beach....

She hadn't counted on the moped with the teenager on board, driving too fast and blithely ignoring her oncoming Jeep. She stared in horror at the accident about to happen, momentarily paralyzed, and then Michael reached over and yanked the wheel sharply.

They went sailing past the teenager, past the stone abutment, past the rocky beach. Gripping the steering wheel, Francey closed her eyes and prepared to die.

Chapter 2

The Jeep banged down on the rock-strewn beach, its deadly momentum slightly blunted as it hurtled toward the water. Francey was beyond fear, beyond rational thought, as the water loomed ahead. Bracing herself for the impact, she was astonished when the Jeep came to a stop almost immediately once it hit the ocean. Water sprayed up around them, drenching her, and for a moment she didn't move, letting the water settle around them in the sudden, deafening silence.

Then she reached over and turned off the engine that had already stopped, pulled out the key and turned to her passenger.

Michael Dowd was looking a great deal healthier than he had less than an hour ago when she'd picked him up at the airport. He'd fastened his seat belt sometime during those last frenzied moments, and his baggy white suit was drenched. "You're one hell of a driver, you know that?" he said in a conversational tone. "Where'd you learn to handle a car like that?"

The water was lapping over the side of the Jeep, over her sandaled feet. "I had lessons from a bootlegger." She smiled at the almost forgotten memory.

"Bootlegger?"

"I used to spend summers in the Smoky Mountains when I was a teenager. One of my stepfathers was a congress-man from a fairly rural district, and his biggest supporter made his money from the sale of illegal whiskey. Someone suggested his son teach me how to drive."

"He did a good job," Michael said. "What else did he teach you?"

She glanced at him, startled. "Not as much as he wanted to. I was seventeen, but I was strong-minded."

"I can believe you. What next?"

She glanced around her, at the water lapping up around them. With a resigned sigh she climbed out into the hip-deep water. "I need to push this thing out of the water. You stay put while I see what I can do...."

But he'd already unfastened the seat belt and climbed out the other side. "You can't do it alone."

"But you're in no shape..."

"One and a half people are better than one," he said flatly. "And I'm in no shape to spend hours sitting in a Jeep in the middle of the ocean. Let's go."

She knew it would have been a waste of time to argue. The moon had risen sometime during their wild flight, and the silvery color danced off the ocean waves, gilding his pale face. He was right; she needed to get him warm and in bed as fast as possible. But they couldn't leave Daniel's Jeep in the middle of Martinus Bay. Not without checking what had happened to the brakes.

It was easier than she would have thought, given the push of the water against the Jeep. By the time they rolled it onto the rocky beach, water was pouring out of the engine, and a group of people from the nearby village had joined them, helping push.

She was in the midst of explanations to her curious helpers when her eyes sought out Michael. He was off to one side, talking to a man she'd never seen before, a huge black man who looked more like a football linebacker than the fishermen on St. Anne who'd come to her rescue.

Michael's instincts were lightning fast. His eyes met hers, seconds after she glanced his way, and he started toward her, leaning heavily on his cane. "I've got us a ride home."

"This is a small island—most of the villagers don't own cars. You did get a ride in a car, didn't you? I can't say I fancy a ride on a motorbike. Or a mule."

"Sort of a car," he temporized. "A delivery truck, to be exact. Cecil has offered his services." He gestured toward the linebacker, who smiled and nodded, flashing his white teeth in the moonlight.

"Who is he? I've never seen him before."

"Neither have I," Michael said wearily. "Do you know everyone from around here?"

Francey couldn't fight her guilt. Here she was quibbling over strangers when Michael was almost dead on his feet. "Of course not," she murmured. "I just thought I would have noticed him if I'd seen him before. He's awfully big."

"Shall we take the ride or not?" Michael swayed slightly, and his color had bleached back to a sickly white.

"We'll take the ride," she said, taking his arm in hers and helping him over the uneven rock-strewn beach. She could feel him tremble slightly from the exertion, and she held his arm more tightly against her, close to the side of her breast. He was harder, more muscular, then she would have thought beneath the baggy suit. At one point in his life, before the car accident, he must have been a fairly strong, well-built man.

The delivery truck was a silver Ford in surprisingly good shape. The three of them squeezed into the front seat—no mean feat, considering the sheer size of Michael's new acquaintance, Cecil, but apparently the back was padlocked and filled with whatever it was Cecil delivered. There was

no identifying sign painted on the truck, and somehow
Francey couldn't figure out a polite way of asking. Reaction was beginning to set in. Her own limbs were trembling
when she climbed into the front of the truck, and for the
time being all she wanted to do was crawl into bed. Once
she made sure Michael was comfortably settled, she reminded herself.

She felt very tiny, squashed between Cecil's impressive
bulk and Michael's bony frame. Leaning her head back, she
shut her eyes, waiting to be transported home. When
nothing happened, she opened them again.

"Where do you live?" Cecil asked in a pleasant voice
with just a trace of island lilt. He must have spent most of
his life off-island. Playing football?

"Sorry," she said briefly, giving him directions. St. Anne
was a small, social island—everyone knew everyone's
business outside the rush of tourist trade. Cecil should have
known where she lived, just as she should have been able to
identify him.

It didn't matter, she thought, closing her eyes again.
She'd been through too much in the past couple of hours
to make sense of anything. In the calm, clear light of day,
after a good night's sleep, she would be able to place him
and these nagging inconsistencies would make sense.

Like where had their huge black savior come from? Like
why Michael Dowd, instead of being terrified by their near
brush with death, had merely been exhilarated by the experience. Like why the brakes had failed on a vehicle that
had just been checked.

But for now all she had to concentrate on was holding
together long enough to get her frail companion settled for
the night. Then a good strong dose of Scotch and she might
be able to sleep herself. After she gave in to the strong case
of shakes she was busy fighting.

Cecil was damned good; Michael had to grant him that.
He'd objected to having him around at first, saying he

could handle things better without backup. The more people who were involved in a situation, the more likelihood that things would get cocked up. But right now Cecil's buddies would be stripping the Jeep, and if they didn't come up with a severed brake line, then he'd been in the wrong business for the past fifteen years.

Of course, that might be the case anyway, even supposing he was right. A job where you routinely got shot at, threatened, beaten up, a job where you lied, cheated and sometimes even killed, wasn't the sort of job to lead to mental health. Maybe he was reaching his limit. Hell, there was no maybe about it.

But he wasn't ready to quit. Not until he tied up a few loose ends, including Frances Neeley's little chums. He'd learned there was a problem with loose ends, though. No matter how many you tied up, more appeared, ready to strangle you. Sooner or later he was going to have to simply walk away from it. Or the next time the doctors wouldn't be able to pull him back from the edge of death.

Cecil dropped them off at the front veranda of the villa with a flash of teeth and a subservient bob of his head. Michael frowned, wondering whether Cecil might not be carrying things a bit too far, but he pressed something that looked like a high-denomination bill into his meaty hand. Frances would assume it was a tip, not a carefully coded request for information. Unless she was even brighter than she looked.

And she looked pretty damned bright, Michael thought as he limped up the wide front steps. He'd had nothing to do during those last long weeks in hospital but research Ms. Frances Neeley and Daniel Travers's villa on St. Anne. He'd come to a great many conclusions, some snap judgments, some carefully thought through. As usual, he was going to have to alter most of them.

She didn't rush to help him. She'd noticed his reluctance to accept assistance, and she was waiting for some imperceptible sign. She'd chosen wisely both times she'd taken his arm before, and she chose wisely now in letting him navigate the steps on his own. She had a certain intuitive caring that wasn't going to make this task any easier.

"I think you need a drink," she said, when he reached the front door, pale and sweating from exertion. "I've got lemonade and iced tea up in the fridge. And then I think you need a bed. Or would you like it the other way around?"

"A drink first. And something a little stronger, if you've got it."

Francey smiled. It didn't reach her eyes, but there was still a compelling warmth in it. "I'm planning on Scotch myself. Will that do?"

Might as well start now, Michael thought. "You don't have any Irish whiskey, do you?"

He didn't feel guilty at the way her face blanched, the stricken look that wiped the smile off her lips. Not when it was partly her fault he was in this damnably weakened state in the first place. "I don't know," she said. "Daniel probably has some stashed away. I'll go look...."

"Don't bother. Scotch'll do fine." He almost made the mistake of heading for the living room, and he caught himself, cursing beneath his breath. Maybe Cardiff was right. Maybe he wasn't ready for the field, if he was going to make mistakes like that.

"Are you all right?" Francey's voice was anxious, her own earlier pain dismissed.

"Fine," he said tightly. "If you'll just steer me in the direction of the living room . . . ?"

She glanced at him curiously. "The way you were heading. Unless you'd rather go to bed first. I could bring you the whiskey . . . ?"

"Not yet," he said. "Let's have our drink first. It's not everyone who gets so intimately acquainted in the first hour. I think we need time to unwind."

The smile was back, and it was beginning to warm her eyes. Nice eyes, she had. Brown, soft, vulnerable. Not the kind of eyes to be involved in something as nasty as this. "That sounds nice," she said, then disappeared in the direction of the butler's pantry.

Of course, he wasn't supposed to know that was where she was going, he thought as he limped into the living room, turning on lights as he went. He would have to be very careful not to make the sort of mistake he'd almost made earlier. He knew the layout of this place down to the last electrical outlet. He knew where he was going to sleep, and he knew where he needed Frances Neeley. The question was, how to get her there without arousing her suspicions.

The living room was regulation island decor. Wicker furniture with chintz cushions, straw matting on the floor, a huge fireplace that was used on the rare, chilly evenings. Beyond the black picture windows he could hear the pounding of the surf on the private beach below. He would have thought twice about turning on all those lights—they would be perfectly illuminated for anyone approaching from the north, and a sniper would have no trouble at all picking them off. Except that the northern approach was only by sea, and while some marksmen might manage an accurate shot while standing on a deck, the pitch and roll of the ocean would make that unlikely. And no one was going to risk making a mistake. Not at this point.

Of course, they'd already made one. Michael had assumed Frances was safe. Four months had passed, and no one had bothered her. His people had been watching her from a careful distance, but no one had approached her, no hint of threat to her well-being had surfaced.

Maybe they'd sabotaged the brakes to get at him. Maybe they'd simply found the right time to kill her. Or maybe they were being efficient, two for the price of one, and they'd just been waiting for him to come and pick her brain.

They couldn't have known for sure it would be him, though they could have suspected it. His enemies in the

IRA weren't fools. He had a reputation for thoroughness, and for cold-blooded revenge. If they knew him at all, and they did, they would know he wouldn't get up from a hospital bed after Patrick Dugan had nearly finished him for good and simply go about his business.

He intended to find out exactly who and what had been involved in that abortive assassination attempt. How things could have gotten so close, who were Dugan's compatriots. And where an ordinary American like Frances Neeley fit into the nasty equation. Was she part and parcel of the Cadre's plot? Or another one of their many innocent victims?

It would make things easier on him if she *was* involved. There was something about her that got under his skin in ways he didn't like. But he had to keep an open mind. If he condemned her simply because he didn't want to feel anything, then he was going to be useless in the field. And despite what he'd said to Travers, he had no intention of taking a desk job. Ever.

She was probably sleeping in the only bedroom on the lower main floor. The one with access from the beach. He was going to have to put a stop to that. The safest rooms in the rambling old place were the row of four bedrooms on the second storey, overlooking the water. The rocky ledge kept boats and invaders at a distance, and the balconies were high enough to keep all but the most determined assassins away. And he had more than enough experience to boobytrap them so that no one could get close.

If worse came to worst, he could maneuver Francey Neeley into sharing his bed. He'd hoped he would be able to work the arrangements around gradually. But the death-defying ride in the brakeless Jeep had disabused him of any such notion. They weren't wasting any time in trying to get rid of one or both of them. And he couldn't assume they would be given even one night's reprieve just because the first attempt had failed.

He knew enough about her to recognize that her own glass of whiskey was taller and darker than she used to drink before she ran into Patrick Dugan. His own was on the weak side, but he didn't complain. He needed to use the next few minutes carefully, building her trust, then move in for the kill before she realized what was happening to her.

He let his hand tremble slightly as he reached for the glass. "Two car wrecks in six months is a bit more than the old ticker can take," he said in a weak voice.

Her face immediately creased in concern. "Oh, I'd forgotten. You'd just been through a car crash. That must have been doubly awful for you. I'm so sorry...."

"Not your fault. You saved our lives," he said with a brave grin. Just the sort to melt a woman's heart, and this woman looked the sort whose heart melted easily. He drained his glass, despising himself for one brief instant. "Still, I'm not used to so much excitement. In my line of work we consider things to be quite thrilling if we have a bat fly into the house."

"We have bats here," Francey said, taking an impressively big gulp of her drink. He was beginning to wonder whether she'd become a lush in the past six months, but her shudder and grimace of distaste told him otherwise. She was using it for medicinal purposes, to dull the pain and terror. He could have told her that would only work for a while. "What is your line of work?" she asked brightly, and if he were any other man he would have believed her interest.

"Math and soccer master at a boy's public school in Somerset. A place called Willingborough. Have been for twelve years."

She blinked, staring at him. "Somehow I wouldn't have pictured you as a schoolteacher," she said slowly.

Sharper than he'd expected, particularly since he knew he was putting up a good front. All gangling limbs and innocent smile and curly red hair. He could even have managed to drum up a few freckles for her if they'd let him out into the sunshine sooner. "Why not?"

"Your face," she said. "And there's something about your eyes. Something almost...ageless. Ancient. Dangerous." She gave herself a little shake, and he was reminded of a silky cocker spaniel shaking water from its thick coat. "I think I've had too much whiskey. Sorry."

She'd only had three drinks. If she finished that glass she would be flat on her bum, and while that would solve the problem of where she slept, he wasn't in the mood to haul her dead weight around the huge old house. Assuming he had enough strength left after the last few harrowing hours.

"It must be the young hellions I'm in charge of," he said easily. "They age a man before his time."

She laughed at that, as she was supposed to, and he hoped she'd forgotten her sudden astuteness. He knew the expression that lurked in the depths of his blue eyes. It wasn't ancient. It was dead.

Most people didn't look that closely. He wondered whether Frances Neeley was particularly intuitive. Or whether she had reason to doubt.

She was yawning, and he knew he was going to have to work fast, before she shunted him off to the wrong bedroom. "Where were you planning to put me?" he asked, wishing he dared ask for another Scotch, knowing it wouldn't be a wise idea. In his weakened condition he couldn't drink as much as usual, and he'd already learned he had to keep his wits about him.

"There's a nice bedroom at the east end of the house, with stairs leading down to the beach. I thought that would be perfect for you."

He shook his head. He'd guessed she would try to put him there. He could wind up with his throat cut by dawn, and the tide would wash away any trace of footprints in the sand. "Would it be too much trouble if I slept on the west side of the house? That is, if there are bedrooms there? I have a thing about sunsets."

He could see the doubt in her eyes, but she was unfailingly polite. "Of course. The rooms there aren't as nice, and you can't get to the beach very easily, but the balconies overlook the water. I'll just make up the bed...."

He reached out and caught her wrist just as she was about to dash away. It was a slender wrist, with its own strength. He had enough strength to hold her, but he did so lightly, deceptively. He didn't want her realizing that his limits weren't that overwhelming. "I'll take care of it," he said.

She made one faint, futile tug on her wrist, and then let it rest in his hand. "You're dead on your feet."

"So are you. I can manage. Where are you sleeping?"

That startled her, and he let her go, not wanting to encourage any conclusion jumping. "In the back of the house."

Right again, he thought. He summoned up his sweetest, most self-deprecating smile. "I don't suppose you could hear me if I happened to call you?"

"It's too far away," she said, her doubt immediately replaced by concern. "Do you think you might need help in the night?"

He shrugged with just the right amount of rueful unconcern. "I'm certain the attacks have passed. During the past few months I sometimes got a breathing spasm, and I wouldn't be able to get to my respirator. But I haven't had one in quite some time, and I'm sure I'd be able to manage."

"What's quite some time?"

"Five days," he said blithely. "What about an intercom system? A telephone ... ?"

"There are three bedrooms on that side. I'll move down," she said firmly.

He almost batted his eyes at her, but decided that would be carrying it too far. "I couldn't ask you to do that."

"You haven't. I've offered. And I insist. Let me get you some warm milk and a touch more whiskey, and then we'll get you settled for the night."

He came up with a wan smile. She was a very motherly soul, was Frances Neeley. He didn't like to be mothered.

If she wasn't involved in this mess, except as a victim, he had the sudden fantasy of finding her once he'd regained his full strength and showing her just how little he needed a mother. Except that he knew he couldn't do that. Couldn't jeopardize his cover. She'd swallowed it completely, and he would be a fool to let his ego shatter that.

An hour later she had him tucked up in bed, wearing a pair of Daniel Travers's silk pajamas. He hated pajamas. The glass of warm milk was beside his bed, and he wondered if she would have the nerve to give him a maternal kiss on the brow before leaving him.

She didn't. "I'll leave my door open a crack in case you need me," she said, looking down at him with an anxious, doting expression. The problem was, she looked even worse than he did by now. The night's activities had taken their toll—she was pale, limp and swaying slightly, and the sooner she fell into bed, the better off they'd all be.

"You'll hear me if I need you," he promised. "I've got good lungs."

"I thought you had respiratory problems?" she asked, with that sudden unnerving astuteness.

"They don't keep me from screaming bloody loud. Good night, Francey. Thanks for taking such good care of me."

"My pleasure," she said.

He waited a good ten minutes before leaving the bed. She would be asleep by then—she'd been almost asleep on her feet as she stood over his bed. Stripping off Daniel's silk pajamas, he lay down on the rush matting and began his sit-ups.

He couldn't do more than forty-five. Which was better than the twenty-five he'd managed last week. The push-ups were up to forty, but by the time he was finished he was sweating, trembling with the effort, almost ready to throw up. He collapsed on the matting, breathing heavily, and wondered how damned long it was going to take to get his body back in working shape.

Too long. It would be solid months before he was back to his normal weight, back to full strength. Francey Neeley's part in tracking down Patrick Dugan's confederates would be long over by then. He would never see her again, and she'd remember him as a skinny, frail, slightly effete British schoolmaster. Mr. Chips meets James Bond.

Maybe he'd better cut back on the slightly effete part. There were times when the only amusing aspect of a grim job was his playacting, but he had the feeling that Francey's clear brown eyes would see through anything less than subtle. He'd been able to convince people he was gay when it was a necessary part of his cover, but somehow he didn't think he would be able to convince Francey.

Perhaps it was because of his inexplicable reaction to her. She hadn't been at all what he'd expected. He'd seen the photographs—clandestine photos of her and Dugan, family snapshots provided by Travers. She'd looked rather ordinary. Shoulder-length brownish hair, plain brown eyes, large mouth, small nose, heart-shaped face. In reality she was more. So much more that he was having a hard time forgetting that he'd been forcibly celibate for months. Which must be a record, since he'd lost his virginity at the tender age of thirteen. It must simply be a monumental case of horniness.

Still, he'd come to St. Anne ready to distrust her, ready to pin her down and get what he wanted from her through fair means or foul.

He still didn't trust her. But he was willing to give her the benefit of the doubt. There was stark, empty pain in her eyes. Pain that might simply have come from her lover's death. Or a pain that had come from a betrayal far deeper than that.

Those eyes saw too much, though. It was a good thing he'd thought to borrow one of Travers's suits. His own were slightly baggy, but this oversize one had made him look like a scarecrow. Enough to soothe even the most nervous female's anxieties.

Though Francey didn't strike him as a nervous female. She drove like a bootlegger, all right. Or an IRA driver. He didn't trust how good she was; it didn't fit.

Still, someone had definitely been trying to kill at least one of the passengers in the Jeep. Which immediately put her on the side of the hunted.

At least he'd been able to fool her for now. She had a frail schoolteacher in her adjoining bedroom, one barely able to walk on his own two feet. That much was true, he thought in disgust. But he was able to hold his own a hell of a lot better than she suspected, including pushing that damnably heavy Jeep out of the water.

Tomorrow he would begin to work on her. Slide under her unsuspecting guard and see exactly how much she knew about Patrick Dugan and his confederates. And then he would decide what to do with her.

Chapter 3

At the moment there was only one question troubling Francey: Exactly what was going on with the man sleeping in the room next to hers? Something didn't ring true about him, about his arrival, and yet she had nothing to go on but her instincts. Instincts that had failed her badly in the past few months.

She shoved the pillows behind her back and stared out into the dark night. The noises from the room next to her had stopped, and she could only assume Michael had finally managed to drift off to sleep. If only she could be so lucky.

She'd heard him climb out of bed. She'd lain very still, listening to the quiet thuds, the faint groans and wheezes, from the room beyond, and it had been all she could do not to run in and check on him. It had sounded as if he were having one of his spasms, and for all she knew she would find him dead the next morning.

But something kept her tied to the uncomfortable bed, something she couldn't begin to understand. She wasn't going to leave this small bastion of safety to check on her housemate unless he called for help.

And he wouldn't do that unless he had to. She'd seen his self-contempt, his hatred of his weakness, and she knew he hated other people's efforts even more than he hated his own. For all his charm, his wonderful smile and easy ways, he wouldn't take kindly to intrusions and maternal caring. She'd almost kissed him on the forehead when she tucked him in, then wisely resisted the impulse. He wasn't a sick little boy. He was a man, and he was probably already feeling emasculated.

There was one thing troubling her, one tiny niggling little problem. When Daniel had called and told her about Michael during one of the infrequent phone conversations the terrible phone service allowed them, she had accepted everything he'd told her without question. The man asleep in the room next to her was simply an ailing boys' schoolteacher from England, a harmless, weak soul.

So why didn't she trust him? Why did she have the sudden unnerving suspicion that he might really be one of Patrick or Caitlin's friends, sent to wreak justice or revenge or whatever?

It hadn't been her fault that Patrick had died. It had been his, and his alone, his mind clouded with dreams and a cause that went beyond idealism into murder, and she would have been a ready sacrifice. Would he have killed her? She would never know.

She didn't even know whether Caitlin had lived or died. For that matter, she didn't care. That night of horror had begun to fade into a bloody blur, and the weeks and months preceding it were simply part of a nightmare. Every time she thought of Patrick's hands on her, his mouth on her, teasing, taunting, arousing, all the time knowing he was using her, laughing at her, going to Caitlin and telling her all about the foolish, besotted American, her stomach began to churn. And Caitlin, Patrick's willing accomplice, had lost any claim to what Francey had thought was her boundless compassion.

She climbed out of bed very slowly, the cotton sheets sliding against her skin as she moved silently to the balcony window. She slid it open a crack, but everything at Belle Reste worked so well that not the slightest noise penetrated the thick cocoon of the night. Only the soothing rush of the ocean beyond broke the stillness.

Tired as she was, she wasn't going to sleep. She should go back downstairs and find her unfinished glass of whiskey. She should go in search of the pills the doctors had prescribed for her. But she already knew that sleeping pills and tranquilizers and Scotch whiskey couldn't keep the demons away. And they were hovering close around her tonight, so close she could feel the flutter of their black wings.

She discounted her immediate worry. Michael Dowd couldn't be IRA. If he were, he would have killed her already—there was no reason to delay. He wouldn't have been a fellow potential victim in the sabotaged car. He had to be an innocent, one who nearly lost his life because he'd happened to get in the way of people who wanted Francey dead.

She would try to call Daniel tomorrow, see if he could get Michael safely away. Maybe she would go, too. Tonight had been a revelation on several fronts. She'd discovered that she didn't want to die. And she'd discovered that all her hormones hadn't shriveled up and vanished. Michael Dowd might be a frail semi-invalid, but he had the most erotic hands she'd ever seen. And the feel of his arm through the loose jacket against the side of her breast had jump-started something that she'd thought had died.

Leaning her forehead against the glass, she stared out into the inky darkness. The moon had set by then, and the stars were bright overhead. Everything was still and peaceful.

Everything but the ominous shadow of a huge, hulking figure she saw prowling along the side of the house.

* * *

Those sadists at the hospital who called themselves nurses woke him up at six every morning, whether he'd had a good night or a bad one. Michael's body had gotten used to it, and it was going to take a concerted effort on his part to change back to his usual slothful ways. He had every intention of making that effort, but not right now. For now he needed the extra time in the morning to prowl around. He had exceptionally good hearing, and he could make out the regular breathing of the woman in the bedroom next to his. She wouldn't be awake for a good long while.

It was no wonder. He'd listened to her move around after he'd gone to bed, even caught the hurried movements of a momentary panic. He'd taken a glance out the window, noting that Cecil had been fool enough to get himself noticed, and waited for Francey to come screaming into his room.

She didn't.

She didn't place any phone calls or go out to confront her intruder herself, thank God. She had the sense to stay put. At least, this time it showed good sense. If the person prowling the beaches of Belle Reste had been the one who'd severed her brake line, then she might have been signing her own death warrant by staying in her bedroom.

God, he hated innocents! He'd been hoping she would be some cold-blooded harpy, a worthy opponent. He hadn't been counting on someone with the wounded eyes of a fawn and the body of a . . .

He'd better stop thinking about her body. He wasn't in any shape to be doing anything about it anyway, so why torment himself? He'd better stop thinking about her doe-like eyes, too. He'd seen eyes just that vulnerable on a woman who was about to kill him. They hadn't looked any different after she'd died.

Francey probably thought she hadn't made a sound last night when she got out of bed and walked over to the sliding glass door of the balcony. She hadn't counted on his hearing. He could move far more silently than she could, and she didn't stir when he pushed her door open at a few minutes past six in the morning.

She was sound asleep, wearing an oversize white T-shirt that was pulled up to show a flat, tanned stomach above her plain white cotton panties. Not a woman with a taste for exotic underwear, he thought. Which told him one of two things. Either she was shy, retiring. Or she was here to do a job.

He shut the door silently behind him as he padded downstairs. She'd switched on the security system he knew the place came with, and he just as easily switched it off, signaling to Cecil as he patrolled the beach.

The ease with which Cecil jogged up to the front of the house didn't help Michael's feelings of charity.

"She saw you last night," he said without preamble.

"Hey, mon, I do my best."

"Hey, *mon,*" Michael mocked him. "You grew up in Stepney, not Jamaica. You can drop the accent when you're around me."

"Better never to break cover," Cecil said innocently. "You know that, mon."

Michael ignored the provocation. "What about the Jeep?"

"Very professional job. Brake line was severed, and for good measure the fuel line was fiddled with. Gas was spraying all over the engine, and it would have ignited if you hadn't driven into the water."

"I wasn't driving. She was. She seems to have hidden talents."

"You sure she's what she says she is?" Cecil asked.

"I'm not sure of anything, including my own mother. I'm taking a wait-and-see attitude. Got any leads on who might have done it?"

"Any number of people. The people we placed here when she first arrived have narrowed it down to five or so, and we'll wade through them as best we can. I don't want to ask too many questions, get people too excited. This is a peaceful island, one that's not big on secrets. People are already talking about the Jeep going into the water. They all know and like the girl—they can't believe it was carelessness on her part. If I can keep the local police at bay without confiding in them, we'll be in better shape."

"They're going to try again," Michael said flatly. "They haven't tried anything before, so my arrival must have tipped their hand. Now that they've made their move, they're going to keep on until they get it right."

"Of course they are, mon. We just aim to keep them from succeeding."

"You need to try a little harder. Did you bring the luggage?"

"Out on the front porch. Including the hardware we brought in. It's your usual stuff. Can't imagine why you like a Beretta, mon. There's better stuff out nowadays."

"Newer, not better," Michael said. "You'll be back with a full report later? With a reasonable excuse?"

"Sure, mon." Cecil was better at vanishing than he was at maintaining a discreet surveillance. In a moment he was gone, leaving Michael in the empty doorway, staring out into the bright early-morning sunlight. He waited just long enough, and then turned, favoring his leg just a bit more than necessary, to face the woman who was standing a few feet away from the stairs.

"Good morning," he said easily, using his automatic charm. "I hope I didn't wake you. I don't sleep very well these days."

She was wearing a terry robe; her brown hair was rumpled, and her face was creased with sleep. "What did he want?"

Not the warmest greeting, but he'd already known she wasn't as gullible as he'd hoped. "Cecil? He brought my bags from the airport."

She took a couple of steps toward him, pushing a hand through her hair, and he could see the distrust at the back of her eyes. He wanted to wipe that away—for purely practical reasons, he told himself. "Did he?" Her voice was skeptical.

"He's quite a character, our Cecil," he said, leaning against the open doorway. "He got the Jeep towed to his cousin's repair shop last night, then he took off for the airport to bring the bags. He says he was wandering around here half the night, looking for a way in, but the place was locked up tight." He shook his head, a wry smile on his face. "Are most people around here so devoted to duty?"

"He was here last night?" she asked carefully.

You know bloody well he was, Michael thought. "I'd asked him to pick up my luggage, but I assumed he'd wait until morning. I didn't expect him to be wandering around on the beach during the small hours of the night." It had actually been before midnight, but he wasn't supposed to know that.

Francey considered for a moment, and he could see her thin, tense shoulders start to relax beneath the robe. She shoved her hands into her pockets, and he wondered if they were shaking. "You know, I thought I saw someone out there last night," she said ingenuously.

"You did? Why didn't you call me?" He really wanted to know the answer to that question. Why hadn't she turned to him for help?

"I didn't want to bother you. You'd been through enough in the past twenty-four hours. Besides, crime is practically nonexistent on St. Anne. Whoever was out there probably didn't mean us any harm. And if they did, this place comes equipped with the latest in security systems. They couldn't have gotten in."

The security system Daniel Travers had installed was already out-of-date and any operative worth his salt could have gotten past it, but he wasn't supposed to know these things. "That's a relief. Not that either of us has any enemies. Do we?"

Once again her face turned pale beneath her tan, and he wondered if she were simply better than he expected, or if she really was that vulnerable. "No enemies," she said in a slightly raspy voice. "Not that I know of."

"Cecil says his cousin will have word on the Jeep by this afternoon. He'll stop back and let us know."

"Can't he call?"

"No phone."

"Of course." She shook her head at her own stupidity. "Coffee or tea?"

Or me, he thought irreverently. "Coffee in the morning, tea in the afternoon," he said. "Unless it's tea bags. Then I'll stick with coffee the whole time." He started toward the kitchen, moving slowly. He'd left his cane behind, and he had to do a creditable job struggling along without it. It was more of a prop than a necessity most of the time, but after the rigors of his day of travel and night of grand prix driving, he could have used the support. "I can make it."

"You'll do no such thing," she said, suddenly bustling and maternal once more. "You go out on the veranda while I make a pot of coffee and something to eat. You need to take it easy, build your strength back." She'd already turned away from him, heading back through the butler's pantry into the kitchen, and he watched her go, wryly aware of his own conflict.

By the time he got his bags up to his bedroom, managed a shower and a change into a pair of his old, baggy khakis and a loose white T-shirt, he could smell the coffee wafting upward. He took his cane this time and headed downstairs, moving a little more slowly than he had to. One problem with this hot climate was the skimpy clothing. There was no way he could hide a gun in what he was wearing, and assuming he stripped down to shorts or a bathing suit, he would even have to ditch the knife he had strapped to his calf. He didn't like the idea of being out there at the end of St. Anne without proper protection. But until he knew how far he could trust Frances Neeley, he wasn't going to be anything more than an invalid schoolteacher. One who certainly wouldn't be carrying his efficient-looking Beretta.

"There you are," she said when he limped out onto the veranda. "I was worried about you." She'd managed to change into some flimsy sundress, one that exposed long, tanned legs and arms and the slight swell of her breasts. He usually preferred busty women. Maybe it was time to change his tastes.

She made good coffee; he had to grant her that. She made good bacon and eggs, too, even if he'd let them sit too long. She also made good conversation, and, even more, she knew when to be peacefully quiet. All in all, an estimable woman. If she wasn't an IRA murderer.

She yawned, stretching her bare legs out in front of her, and he found himself watching her feet. He'd never seen a woman with beautiful feet before in his life. Of course, he hadn't spent that much time looking below their knees. Maybe she wasn't that extraordinary.

He was on his second cup of coffee, feeling marginally better than he had in months, when her dreamy voice broke through his abstraction. "I wonder what that boat's doing?" she murmured, snatching the final croissant that he'd been resisting for the past few minutes.

Michael narrowed his eyes to squint into the bright sunlight. The boat looked ordinary enough to him. Large, slightly rusty, equipped with fishing paraphernalia, it looked like a commercial fisherman's boat. "Fishing?" he suggested lazily.

She shook her head. "Not there. Any of the locals know that the currents run too fast by the point. I can't imagine who could be out there."

Michael set his cup down very carefully. It wasn't one of theirs. He knew exactly which boats Cecil and company employed, and none of them was a deceptively rusty trawler like the one lurking just beyond the point. Once he looked closer he could see the telltale signs of sophisticated elec-

tronic surveillance equipment, probably the kind that could
pick up every word they were saying. Not to mention the
name of the damned boat. *Irish Fancy*. He could imagine
just what their fancy was.

"I expect they're just testing new waters," he said with
deliberate laziness. The deck they were sitting on wouldn't
be an easy target for snipers. The ocean beyond the point
was particularly choppy that morning, and their watchers
would have to spray the balcony with a machine gun to ensure hitting their targets.

He dropped his coffee mug on the terrace, watching as it
rolled toward Francey. "I'm sorry," he said, making a
suitably abortive effort to retrieve it. It ended exactly where
he wanted it, under her chaise.

"I'll get it," she said with a smile, getting down on the
deck and reaching for it. No sudden hail of bullets, no telltale whine, Michael thought, ready to roll on top of her in
an instant if need be. Whoever was out there, they were
simply watching, waiting. For another accident, perhaps.
Or maybe they really only wanted one of them. But which
one?

He stared down at the boat in the distance. He could see
the sunlight reflect off glass. Someone's binoculars were
trained on Belle Reste, but that came as no surprise. What
was surprising was this wait-and-see attitude.

"What are you looking at?" Francey was on her knees
beside his chaise, her head just above the railing of the
balcony. They could probably manage a perfect shot if the
seas would just calm for a moment.

Catching her arm in a loose grip, he came off the chaise
with clumsy speed and hauled her after him, hoping his in-
firmity would disguise his sudden wariness. He pulled her
into the kitchen, limping more heavily than he needed to.
"Let's get out of here," he said breathlessly.

"What?" She stared up at him, her high forehead wrinkled in confusion.

"Show me the island. I'm feeling a little stir-crazy."

"Michael, you just got here." Her voice was the soul of patience. "If you're housebound already, how do you think you'll feel in another couple of weeks?"

I'm not going to be here in a couple of weeks, he thought with a certain amount of savagery. "I've been in hospital since yesterday, Francey. Belle Reste is absolutely beautiful, but I have a sudden craving to be out and about. Free, for the first time in months. I don't suppose it makes any sense. . . ."

"Of course it does." There it was again, that damned maternal soothing. "I'm just surprised you trust my driving after last night. We have one major problem, however. No car."

"I don't know of a driver I'd trust more," he said, completely honest for once. "Can't I rent a car? Have it delivered?"

"I never thought of that."

"Why don't you get some shoes on, comb your hair, do whatever you need to do?" Michael suggested. "If you point me in the direction of the phone, I'll make arrangements."

"I don't think it's going to be that simple."

"I do," Michael said, knowing that Cecil was already prepared. "Trust me."

She looked at him for a moment with those doubting brown eyes of hers, and then she nodded. "All right," she said. "It won't take me long."

He waited until she left the room before he dialed the number that would be patched through to Cecil's cellular phone. And he wondered whether she trusted him any more than he trusted her. He'd thought he'd fooled her completely. Now he was beginning to wonder.

Michael was as good as his word. Francey dawdled as long as she could, fiddling with the makeup she hadn't touched in months, brushing her hair back, then forward, then giving up on it entirely as it simply began to curl in the humidity. She stared at her reflection in the mirror of the downstairs bedroom. She didn't know why she'd chosen that sundress. In all the time she'd been on St. Anne she hadn't worn it—the colors were too bright, the flowers too cheerful. But she'd put it on this morning, and now there was no way she could revert to the old T-shirt and cutoffs she'd been favoring.

It must be his accent, she decided. Maybe she was just a sucker for a voice from the British Isles. Her stomach cramped at the involuntary thought, but she faced it sternly. There was only so long that she could hide from what had almost happened, and that time was coming to an end.

She had been attracted to a murderer and a liar. A terrorist. She hadn't known it, of course. But the fact of the matter was, if fate and the British secret service hadn't taken a hand, she would have gone to bed with him that night. And probably ended up another victim in a few months' time, after he'd bled her bank account dry.

Not that Michael Dowd was anything like Patrick Dugan. They both had charm, of course. But Patrick's fanaticism had burned deep within him, shedding an intense light on those around him. Michael Dowd probably reserved his emotions for algebra and soccer matches. Anyone who could face their close brush with death last night with such equanimity had to be a pretty cold fish.

She couldn't figure out why she found him attractive. Maybe months of seclusion were finally taking their toll. Maybe it was the first healthy sign of life stirring in her pain-deadened heart. Or maybe she'd really gone crazy.

He was waiting for her by the front door. He was wearing a loose linen jacket and a pair of sunglasses, and his cane was hooked over one arm. "Madame, your chariot awaits," he said, opening the door for her with a flourish that made her smile.

Chariot, indeed. Parked directly in front of the broad veranda steps was a bright red sports car, complete with right-hand steering wheel and convertible top. She glanced at Michael. "Did you ask for this in particular?"

He shrugged. "I just said I wanted something red and fast and racy. You like it?"

"I like it," she said, moving down the stairs. "Who dropped it off?"

"The rental agency," he said easily, and she wondered why she doubted him.

She glanced over at the point, where the mysterious fishing boat had been anchored. It was gone now, and the bright azure sea was empty.

"Shall we take her for a little spin?"

These brakes could have been tampered with, too. He could be carrying a gun beneath that baggy linen jacket, and the moment they were someplace secluded, he could put it against her head and . . .

It was too beautiful a day for such macabre, paranoid thoughts. It was shocking to her, how far her normal trust had been eroded by one twisted encounter. The man standing beside her, frail and weak as he was, was the farthest thing from a hired assassin as anyone could find. She was definitely going a bit looney tunes.

"Let's go," she said firmly, heading for the driver's seat, leaving him to limp his way after her as best he could.

She drove in silence at first, very slowly, testing the brakes at every possible chance. They were tight, secure, and she wondered if there was any other way to sabotage a car.

"I hate to complain," Michael drawled, "but you're giving me whiplash. Stop jumping on the bloody brakes and see what this baby can do."

She glanced at him, startled, but he seemed merely bored at the thought of possible danger. The road stretched out ahead of them, one of the few straight stretches on the curvy island of St. Anne. The sun was shining down on them, gilding his curly auburn hair, and death and danger seemed to belong to another time, another place. The accident last night had been an unlucky fluke. Fate wouldn't be so unkind, two days in a row. Without hesitation she pushed her foot down hard on the gas pedal, and the car shot forward with a satisfying burst of power.

Chapter 4

Michael slid down further in the bucket seat of the sports car, mentally thanking Cecil for his unorthodox choice. While it would never blend in with the crowd, the tiny island of St. Anne already boasted an eclectic blend of transportation. Various four-wheel drive vehicles, convertibles of every shape and color, mopeds and motorcycles and even good old-fashioned bicycles, made driving seem more like negotiating an obstacle course. Something that Francey Neeley could do with effortless grace.

If Cecil *had* chosen a dark, anonymous sedan, it would have stuck out like a sore thumb. And it probably wouldn't have had the pickup this little baby had, despite Francey's initial hesitation.

"Where would you like to go?" she asked, glancing over at him. With her oversize sunglasses shielding half her face and her sun-streaked brown hair whipping around in the wind, she looked exactly what he'd imagined her to be. A spoiled, thoughtless American, someone with too much money and too little morals. A playgirl, and the wrong sort of female to interest a man who no longer knew how to play.

But he'd seen behind the dark glasses to the huge, shadowed eyes that reflected a pain most people hid. The brave red lipstick couldn't disguise the vulnerability in her mouth, and her slender, delicate hands gripped the leather-covered steering wheel with something close to desperation. A desperation that didn't interfere with her obvious skill.

"You know the island," he answered her question. "You choose." He sank a little more into the seat, his eyes alert behind his mirrored sunglasses.

"We could go north, to the cliffs," she suggested. "On a clear day you can see all the way to the Baby Saints."

"The Baby Saints?"

"A group of tiny, uninhabited islands. They're off limits—part of some secret government program, I gather."

"Probably testing germ warfare," Michael said.

"You're not serious!"

"Of course not," he said easily. Most governments he knew wouldn't hesitate to test anything lethal if they thought it would be to their military benefit. His own government, which happened to own the Baby Saints, was no different from Middle Eastern fanatics or right-wing extremists when it came to protecting their own interests. Who knew that better than he did? At least he also happened to know the Baby Saints were safe.

"Or there's the town," she continued. "Wonderful shopping, charming restaurants, not too many tourists. That's why Daniel picked this place. It's off the beaten track."

"I'd say so. I was lucky your cousin offered to fly me here in his private plane. I would have had trouble finding a commercial flight."

"Daniel's a very generous man," Francey murmured. "How did you happen to meet him?"

"Mutual friends," he said blandly.

She was too sharp. He had a long, involved, totally believable scenario he was prepared to spin for her, and he chose not to bother. She wasn't really expecting explanations, and one of the first mistakes people usually made in his line of work was to lie too elaborately when they wanted to cover up.

"So there're the cliffs and the town," he said instead. "I'm not sure I'm ready for souvenir shopping. What are our other options?"

"I think we've already had enough of the bay," she said, a small, wistful smile curving her mouth. "But we could drive to the dunes on the west end of the island. Or we could do all of the above, ending with lunch in town."

Where there was a town, there would be public telephones. He needed to check in with Cardiff, much as he disliked the notion, and he certainly wasn't going to trust either the phones at Belle Reste or anything as easily compromised as Cecil's cellular phone. "Sounds perfect," he said, flashing his practiced smile.

He was unprepared for her reaction. She stared at him, her mouth open slightly in amazement, then swerved just as she was about to go sailing into a ditch.

"Stupid," she muttered under her breath.

He was inclined to agree, not in the mood for another car accident, but he didn't say so. "What's wrong?"

She kept her face averted, eyes staring at the cement roadway in front of them. "You look different when you smile," she said flatly, surprising him.

He knew he did. It was one of his stocks in trade, a boyish, engaging grin that could seduce the most hard-hearted of females. And despite his initial, logical suspicions, he was coming to realize that Frances Neeley was one of the most softhearted creatures he'd seen in a long time. Did that mean he wanted to seduce her?

"Yes, well, I'm not always so grumpy," he said easily, brushing past the awkward moment. "I can really be quite charming when I set my mind to it."

"I'll just bet you can," she murmured, mostly to herself.

He glanced at her again, at the slender wrists, the narrow ankles, the clean, smooth lines of her beneath the sundress. She even had nice breasts, fuller than her slender body would suggest. He could spend a pleasant time between those long, shapely legs and have ample justification for it. Women liked to talk after they made love, and they babbled on without paying any attention to discretion or common sense.

He might, he thought, feeling his body react as he went with the fantasy. There was only one problem. What if he was wrong? What if she were everything he'd first suspected? What if he had sex with her. And then had to kill her?

He didn't have much of a soul left, after some fifteen years in the business. But no matter who and what she was, no matter how evil she turned out to be, he didn't think what little kernel of decency still resided inside his burned-out hull of a body would survive. And then he might as well be dead himself.

Very deliberately he toned down the wattage of his smile, keeping it distant, friendly, deliberately asexual. She wasn't looking at him now; her attention on the roadway, and he had the notion that she was almost afraid of him. Wiser than she realized, he thought. She *should* be afraid of him.

He pushed his sunglasses up on his forehead, surveying the lush countryside around them as she sped forward. "Give me a tour of the island," he said, "and I promise to be the perfect tourist."

She did glance at him then. At his innocent smile, guileless blue eyes. And it was with chill despair that he realized she didn't believe him. But did that distrust come from a fanatic's belief in evil? Or an innocent victim's fear?

But she covered up her doubt as easily as he covered up his duplicity, and if her smile wasn't as unguarded as it should have been, most people wouldn't notice.

But he wasn't most people.

"You botched it." The voice on the other end of the line was flat, cold, the Irish lilt a chilling counterpoint.

"We could have taken her out anytime during the past month or so and been gone before anyone realized it," the man protested, clutching the telephone in one meaty fist. "When you do two at once you run greater risks."

"Don't second-guess me, Seamus. I'd be there myself if I could, and you know it. I send my most trusted men, and what happens?"

"We'll get them. Both of them. It'll just take time...."

"It's taken too much time already!"

"You didn't give the word until two days ago. The accident caused too much suspicion. We'd best wait a week or so before we try again."

"Are you a coward, Seamus? Afraid you boys will be caught?"

His fist tightened on the black telephone. "No one calls me a coward. They'll be dead in a week. You have my word on it."

"I hope that's good enough, Seamus. For your sake." And the connection was severed.

Seamus stared at the phone for a moment, then began to curse. There weren't many people he was afraid of, in this life or the next. But the chill, disembodied voice half a world away terrified him as no one else's could. Francey Neeley was going to go up in a blaze so huge they'd see it over in Ireland.

And her buddy, the Cougar, was going with her. Or his own life wouldn't be worth living.

Seven days later, Francey could feel Michael's eyes on her from behind his mirrored sunglasses as she sipped from her second glass of wine. She didn't know whether he was passing judgment or not. She didn't care. She'd tried tran-

quilizers the first few weeks after Patrick's bloody death,
then given them up when they made her too sleepy. An occasional extra glass of wine tended to take the edge off
when she was feeling nervous, paranoid, worried.

There was a gentle trade wind blowing off the Caribbean as she sat outside Marky's Cafe, and she lifted her
face slightly, reveling in the breeze. She ought to be getting
used to him by now. He'd been on St. Anne's for more than
a week, and this was the fourth time they'd come to
Marky's for lunch. But instead of getting more comfortable with him, she found her uneasiness growing.

Maybe it was as simple as the fact that she was attracted
to him. Overwhelmingly so, when she'd thought she would
never be interested in men or sex again. She'd realized it
early on, with the feel of his surprisingly muscular arm beneath the loose white suit, with his dazzling smile that had
an almost nuclear meltdown capacity. She'd realized it even
more during the quiet moments, during their long drives in
the absurd red sports car, with their companionable si-
lences and easy talk about nothing whatsoever.

She didn't want to be attracted to him. She preferred safe
friendship to the hot spice of desire that trickled through
her when she least expected it. She tried to concentrate on
her paranoia. Every time they went out driving she had the
absolute certainty they were being followed. There was
nothing to base that fear on. It was never the same car, nor
the same driver, they were never bothered, never tailed too
closely. When she was being reasonable she told herself it
was simply that the tourist season was heating up. More
strangers on the road. She wasn't often reasonable.

When she didn't think about who was watching them,
she tried to think about whether or not she should trust
him. She had absolutely no reason not to. But something
kept her holding back, even as she smiled and laughed with
him.

For instance, the photograph. Marky hired a down-on-
his-luck artist to take photos of the tourists. It was a lucra-

tive sideline, and Andre was very subtle about it. So subtle, in fact, that Michael never even noticed his picture was being taken, and Michael was the sort of man who noticed things.

She'd stopped Andre from offering it to him. On a deceptive trip to the ladies' room she'd taken him aside and asked for the photo herself. Andre was French and worldly-wise. He'd simply nodded, and Michael never knew of the photo's existence.

There was no reason why he should mind. Why he wouldn't want his picture taken. He was exactly who he seemed to be, a weary, wounded man, recovering slowly in the bright Caribbean sunlight, a man with charm and sensitivity, a harmless, gentle man who probably didn't view her in a sexual light at all. Who probably never lay awake at night listening to the sound of the waves outside, to the wind through the trees, to the heat and longing that swept through the house like a mistral, making her dream of skin and sweat and muscle and...

"Penny for your thoughts," he said, watching her. "I do believe you're blushing, Francey. They must be highly erotic thoughts. Is there someone here...?" He glanced around them, at the locals clustered inside at the bar, at the middle-aged couples near the door.

"Not erotic," she said firmly, looking at his hands on the green bottle of Dutch beer. Long-fingered, deft hands. Narrow palms. With scars. "I was thinking about what's on our agenda for this afternoon."

He raised a questioning eyebrow behind the mirrored sunglasses. "Don't you want to go swimming? You've promised me the water is absolutely tepid. If you'd rather not..."

"It's not the water, it's my bathing suit," she said flatly.

He waited patiently for an explanation, his hand still on the beer. That was one of the things she liked most about him. And found the most irritating. His seemingly inexhaustible patience. It always ended up with her saying more than she needed or wanted to.

"I didn't expect to enjoy myself when I came down here," she continued. "So I didn't pack a bathing suit. I bought one once I realized...well, once I realized how nice the water was." She was going to say once she realized she wanted to live after all, but she'd stopped herself in time. After all, Michael Dowd was a virtual stranger. A sympathetic, kindly, attractive stranger, but not one who needed to be privy to the darkest days of her life.

"Then what's the problem?" It was a reasonable enough question, one that required a reasonable answer.

"The only bathing suits they sell on St. Anne are French," she said flatly.

He was sharp; she had to admit it. He didn't ask for an explanation. He simply said, "Oh."

"Oh," she echoed.

He leaned back, taking off his sunglasses and letting them swing lazily in one hand. The sickly pallor of his skin had faded somewhat during his days under the bright sun, and she'd even noticed a dusting of freckles across his strong nose. "I tell you what," he said. "You don't look at my skinny, white, scarred body in baggy drawers, and I won't look at you in your skimpy bikini."

"You've got yourself a deal." She believed him, of course. He'd never done anything to give her the impression that he was as aware of her as she was of him. He probably had a wife and five kids tucked away back in Somerset.

Except that she knew he didn't. He hadn't told her much about his personal life, except to say he'd never been married, though he'd come close a number of times. He figured he was married to his job. And he certainly had enough fathering to do, with the hordes of schoolboys who passed through his care at Willingborough. Everything normal, upper middle class Brit, including his two years in

military service when he was younger. He hadn't been stationed in Ireland—she'd made sure of that.

She knew he was thirty-seven, that the car accident
hadn't been his fault, that he was expected back in England sometime soon to pick up the pieces of his safe, comfortable life. If he knew what she'd gone through, he would
draw back in well-bred horror.

But he didn't know, and there was no reason why he
should. As far as he was concerned, she was a motherly,
friendly American with few responsibilities and ties,
someone spending a few idle months in the Caribbean. And
she preferred to leave it that way. Her attraction to him was
an aberration, a brief moment of madness in reaction to her
earlier foolishness in believing in Patrick Dugan. Michael
Dowd was the antithesis of Patrick, safe and sane and
harmless. It was no wonder she was drawn to him.

And that attraction would safely wither and disappear
the moment he left for home. In the meantime, it did her
no harm to let her mind drift into vague, erotic fantasies.
Knowing she had absolutely no intention of following up
on them.

She smiled at Michael, reaching out and putting her hand
over his in a friendly gesture. His skin was cool, smooth
beneath her innocent touch, and if she felt prickles of
awareness between their flesh, his expression was completely bland and unmoved.

Harmless, sweet and definitely undersexed, she thought
with dismay and relief. She couldn't be safer.

"You slept with her yet?" Ross Cardiff demanded. He
had a high-pitched, nasally whine of a voice, with a trace
of Northern England thrown in. Michael was originally
from the North himself, and he'd always liked the sound of
Yorkshire in a man's voice. But not since he'd been working with Ross Cardiff.

"None of your bloody business."

"The hell it's not. You talked me into this, against my better judgment. We need to keep on Daniel Travers's good side, and we need to move very carefully in this issue. Patrick Dugan wasn't the only one involved in the attack on the Queen. There's no guarantee that he was the head of the Cadre...."

"I thought we'd already agreed that he wasn't," Michael said sharply, glancing through the smoked glass of the phone booth to Francey. She was sitting back in the white mesh chair, staring out at the sea, waiting while he put in a call to his dear old Mum. His mother had been dead in a drunken car accident since the early sixties, and no great shakes as a mother anyway. He smiled sourly, turning away from her.

"You decided," Ross corrected. "I'm not convinced. However, there's no denying that the Cadre's been active recently. Gearing up for something. Any more attempts?"

"Not as far as we can tell. Cecil's been clinging like a burr, and I upgraded the security system while she was sleeping. James Bond couldn't get through it."

"I rather thought you fancied *you* were James Bond," Ross said nastily.

"Hell, no, Ross," he said pleasantly. "You're the one with fantasies."

The dead silence that greeted that remark reminded Michael that there was a limit as to how far he could push Ross. Cardiff's sexual proclivities were not a topic of conversation, even if Michael's were.

"How long are you going to be there?" Cardiff demanded finally. "Why don't you just boff her, find out what she knows and get the hell out of there?"

"Not that simple. She seems fairly traumatized by her run-in with Dugan."

"And you believe that? You're getting soft."

Not likely, Michael thought absently, remembering his intermittent discomfort when Francey brushed by him in that huge, empty house that was too small for both of them. "I never believe anything until I'm ready to, Ross," he said. "I need more time."

"Two more days. If you can't get her in bed and find out her secrets by then, then you shouldn't be back in action. I told you that you should take some time off, spend a few months at your cottage in the Lake District...."

He was tired of this, Michael thought. Mortally tired of taking orders from shortsighted bureaucrats and weaselly, narrow-minded idiots like Cardiff. He'd done everything he could to get transferred from Ross's jurisdiction once he realized what a venal bungler the man was, but the bureaucracy had been adamant. Besides, he had a reputation for being a lone wolf. The powers-that-be figured at least Cardiff would irritate him enough to check in.

"I'll take as long as I bloody well need," he said flatly. "I'll check in tomorrow."

"Cougar..." That nasally whine was cut off as Michael slammed down the phone, keeping his back to Francey. He hated that name. There'd been a time in his life when he'd taken a romantic pleasure in it. That time was long past.

The damnable thing about it was that Ross was right this time. He was just wasting time. Francey Neeley was vulnerable, ready to fall, and all he had to do was reach out a hand. She would go—into his arms, into his bed—and she would tell him absolutely anything he wanted to know once he'd spent a few hours reminding her what bodies were made for. He was mad to hesitate.

He turned to look at her. The wind was tossing her sun-streaked hair back from her profile, and she looked both strong and vulnerable. Her mental health once he was finished with her wasn't his problem, his consideration. All he needed to think about was the Cadre, who and what and where they were. And how to stop them. In comparison to their vicious destructiveness, the well-being of one rich American female wasn't of great consequence.

He'd been sidelined too long. But he was no longer completely sure of that fact, even as he told himself he was.

Maybe, much as he hated to admit it, for once in his life Ross Cardiff was right. He'd grown soft, emotionally and mentally, as his body had hardened.

No, he couldn't ever admit that a bug like Cardiff was right. Francey wanted him, whether she was completely sure of that fact or not. Tonight he was going to take her. He was going to spend a long, energetic night with her, working off the longest stretch of celibacy he'd known since he'd reached puberty. And by midday tomorrow, in a postcoital haze, she would tell him absolutely everything he needed to know.

"You look grim," she said when he reached the table, her eyes as sharp as usual. "Is your mother all right?"

"Mum's in fine shape. Just crabbing about the change of life." It was his only small measure of revenge against Cardiff's nit-picking. Referring to the man as his menopausal mother had the capacity to amuse him as few things did.

"Isn't she a little old for that?" Francey asked.

Michael's smile didn't waver, even as he mentally cursed. Maybe Cardiff was right after all. "She had me when she was a teenager," he said easily. "Are we going swimming?"

She made a face. "We're going swimming."

He was smiling at her again. Francey wondered absently whether he knew what it did to her when he smiled like that. She doubted it. If he knew his smile could be that powerful, he wouldn't be the gentle, unassuming man that he was.

But that smile made her nervous. It started her thinking that maybe he was just as attracted to her as she was to him. He seemed to have gotten a lot stronger in the time he'd been on St. Anne, and every now and then she thought she'd surprised a heated expression in his usually bland blue eyes. But it would be gone as quickly as she noticed it, and she'd told herself it was her imagination.

But ever since his troubling conversation with his mother, during the long drive back to Belle Reste, he'd been sending forth waves of charm that disturbed her as much as they drew her. She had the uneasy sense of being manipulated. Absurd. Patrick had managed to twist her mind around past common sense. Things had gotten out of hand when she couldn't even trust a straightforward schoolteacher.

"Funny," she said, fiddling with the front door key while Michael blocked the light behind her.

"What's funny?"

"The lock's not working properly. I'm certain I locked it when I left. Not that it's necessary, but you're so paranoid..."

"You locked it," he said easily, reaching out and taking the key from her. A second later the door swung open, and she started into the shadowy coolness.

His hand on her bare arm stopped her. "Wait a minute."

"But..."

"Hold still," he said, no longer gentle and polite. There was a wariness about him, and all gentleness, all sweetness, seemed to have vanished. "Someone's been here."

"Don't be absurd. Why should someone...?"

"Move back." It was a ridiculous statement. His hand was clamped around her upper arm so tightly it would likely leave bruises, and he was already moving her back, slowly, steadily.

"What's wrong, Michael?"

"Can't you smell the gas?"

She could. She hadn't noticed—indeed, she'd been so caught up in her confused feelings about Daniel's guest that she hadn't been paying much attention to anything. "The gas heater must have malfunctioned...."

They were back at the car. He practically shoved her into the passenger seat, and there was no hesitation in his movements, barely a trace of his troubling limp. "It was tampered with," he said flatly.

"Don't be ridiculous. Who...?"

"The same person who cut your brake lines. Face it, Francey, someone wants to kill you." He started the car, spun it around and took off.

"Where are we going? We can't just leave it like that," she protested, dazed by his sudden forcefulness.

"We're getting the hell out of here. I only know one person I can trust on this island. Your friend Cecil."

"He's not my friend," she said. "I never saw him before last week."

He stopped the car in the middle of the narrow, deserted roadway. "Take your choice. Is there anyone else you want to turn to?"

She couldn't think of a soul. She didn't trust anyone. Except maybe this suddenly enigmatic stranger beside her. "Cecil," she said.

He didn't smile or look triumphant. He simply nodded, putting the car into gear once more. She glanced back at the house that had been her haven, her safety, her place of healing, just before the road twisted, putting it out of sight. And she wondered if she would ever see it again.

Chapter 5

"Stay in the car," Michael ordered, vaulting out with a lithe strength that was entirely at odds with his previously fragile air. They'd pulled up at a tumbledown shack near the harbor, one she hadn't realized was even inhabited. The windows were darkened, the door tightly shut, strange occurrences for a climate like theirs. But for the moment she was numb, too bewildered by the swift turn of events to even consider moving.

He was back in a moment, his face as shuttered as the ramshackle little cottage. "You know where Shaman's Cove is?"

She nodded. "It's a small, rocky inlet on the northern side of the island."

"Directions." The word was a command, brief, to the point, one she obeyed without question.

A car passed them as they drove up the long, winding road away from the deserted cottage, a new Land Rover with smoked windows, going so fast it nearly ran them off the road. "Was that Cecil?" she asked.

"Land Rovers cost more than that entire village makes in a year," he said flatly.

He hadn't answered her question, she noticed. "Was that Cecil?" she asked again.

He glanced at her. The sunglasses were covering half his face, and his mouth was thin, grim. "Your guess is as good as mine."

He wasn't going to tell her anything more specific,. To ask again would be a waste of breath. "What's in Shaman's Cove?"

"Cecil will have a boat waiting. We're getting the hell out of here."

"But..."

"I've told him how to get in touch with your cousin. We'll have to leave it up to Travers to rescue us."

"The house. It'll blow..."

"Maybe. Cecil's going to see what he can do about it."

"Are you certain we're not overreacting? I mean, brakes do fail. Gas heaters do malfunction."

"You want to wait for the third attempt to be convinced? Chances are, that time they'll be successful."

Francey was suddenly very, very cold. She rubbed her bare arms, wishing she could ask him to put the top up on the convertible, wishing she'd brought a sweater, a bulletproof vest, a quart of Scotch. Anything for protection from the ice that was slicing down into her heart.

She'd been ready to put it all behind her. Even the near miss last week had been easy to explain away. Her involvement with Patrick Dugan had been a brief sojourn of misery, but it didn't need to wreck her life.

But now it seemed as if it was coming close to ending her life. She couldn't imagine how they'd managed to find her, or why they even wanted to kill her. For revenge, perhaps, for Patrick's and maybe Caitlin's deaths. She hadn't been responsible for Patrick, and she hadn't meant to push Caitlin in front of the car. She'd been fighting for her life.

But obviously someone didn't see it that way. Someone had come to her peaceful haven of St. Anne to make her pay. And the innocent, harried man beside her was going to pay the price, too, for something he'd had no involvement in.

"Stop the car," she said suddenly.

He glanced over at her, not slowing their hurtling pace in the slightest. "Why?"

"I want to get out."

"Don't be a fool." The words were calm, without rancor. He drove well, she noticed. Better even than she did. "I suppose there's a chance in hell that this was simply a coincidence, but I don't plan on taking that chance."

"It's not your chance to take. It's not you who's in danger. It's me. Stop the car and let me out."

"Virgin sacrifice?" he said pleasantly. "You want me to find a live volcano so you can throw yourself in?"

"Don't be a fool."

"Don't you be a fool!" he said. "You seem to forget, I'm a perfect British gentleman. I was brought up to bring aid and comfort to damsels in distress."

"Not at the cost of your own life."

"Nobility makes me want to puke."

"Michael..."

"Which way?" They'd come to a crossroads. The narrow little-used dirt roadway led down to Shaman's Cove.

"I'm not telling you," she said.

He slammed on the brakes, hurling them both toward the padded dashboard. He took her wrist in his large hand, and the pain was sudden, numbing, unbelievable. "Which way?" he repeated in a calm, emotionless voice.

"The dirt road."

He released her, putting the car in gear again, and she glanced down at her wrist as she hugged herself. There was no mark. The sudden, shocking pain must have been in her imagination, part of this entire, unbelievable nightmare. Michael Dowd wouldn't hurt her. Wouldn't know how.

She didn't know whether Michael was fearless or simply terrified as he plowed the sports car down the narrow, overgrown roadway. At one point she closed her eyes, too frightened to watch as they hurtled toward certain doom. He was going fast, too fast, and he didn't know the area. They were going to die, no thanks to whoever had rigged the gas heater. She told herself she should regret dying, and, indeed, she did. She thought of the man beside her, driving with consummate skill and recklessness, and thought she might really want to live after all.

The car slammed to a stop, and her eyes flew open. By some miracle they'd made it to the bottom of the narrow roadway, out onto the tiny spit of pink sand. He killed the engine, glancing around them, and she told herself it was only her imagination that he seemed wary, dangerous, like the hunter instead of the hunted.

"Are you all right?" He had to ask twice before she pulled her scattered thoughts together enough to respond.

"I guess so."

He reached out, and it said a lot for her disordered frame of mind that she didn't flinch from hands that had hurt her. He touched her face with consummate gentleness, and she knew then that she'd imagined the moment in the car, the icy pain in her wrist. She smiled at him shakily, and for a moment his face darkened, shadowed by some distant emotion she could only guess at.

And then he was tugging her out of the car. "We've got to get out of sight. Cecil said he'd come by with a boat, but in the meantime, we don't want anyone seeing us."

"No one comes here," she said, following him as he headed for the underbrush. "They think it's haunted."

He glanced around him. Funny, she hadn't realized how tall he was. He was usually hunched over the cane that had somehow gotten left behind, and she wondered for one absurd moment whether he really needed it. Whether he was the innocent schoolmaster he pretended to be.

"Haunted, is it? I think we'll need more than ghosts on our side to keep us safe." He sank behind a hummock that gave them a decent view of the dazzling blue sea, pulling her with him. "So tell me who haunts it while we wait."

His body was warm beside her, warm while she was cold, so very cold. Ghost stories were a good enough way to pass the time, and part and parcel with the unreality of the situation. "There are rocks out there," she said, rubbing her bare arms absently as she hunched closer to him. "I presume Cecil knows that, since he must have grown up here. Back in the seventeen hundreds there used to be wreckers here, pirates who never bothered to set out to sea. They'd wait for people to go off course, blown by the storms, and they'd use lanterns to lead them to a safe harbor. Except that the harbor was protected by a coral reef, the boats would founder, and the people of the island drowned anyone who happened to make it to shore."

"Nasty business," he said absently. "I thought they only had wreckers in England."

"These were English convicts, sent out as slave labor for the sugar plantations," she said, clenching her muscles to keep from shivering. "Nice bunch of people you're descended from."

He smiled then, a brief upturning of his mouth. Not the devastating charm he'd sent in her direction on several occasions, not the sexless, friendly smile of a housemate. It was a smile of real amusement, devoid of any particular role he was playing. She didn't even stop to consider why she thought he would be playing roles for her.

"You're from the same stock," he said. "Anglo-Saxon Protestant to the core."

"Actually, my father was Irish Catholic."

"Same difference," he said, shrugging. A man who'd grown up in Great Britain during some of the bloodiest Irish Catholic struggles, and he dismissed the differences. Before she could even think further about that, he reached out, putting his hands on her, pulling her into his arms.

"You're freezing to death," he said, tucking her close against his heated body. "Shock will do that to you."

She wanted to resist his comfort. She didn't trust him. She was back to the way she'd been months ago, after Patrick had been killed. She didn't trust a soul, friend or stranger, relative or enemy. She didn't want to trust him.

But his heat was insidious, working through the block of ice around her body, melting it, melting the fierce tension within her. She tried to hold herself stiffly in his arms, but she couldn't, not with his long fingers kneading the cords of tension at the back of her neck, exposed by the skimpy cotton sundress.

She sighed, letting the fear drain out of her body, and leaned against him. "That's better," he murmured approvingly, and his accent was oddly more pronounced, and yet softer. "I'm not your enemy, Francey."

"I know you're not," she said wearily. "Honestly I do. I just get so frightened, so confused, not knowing whom I can trust...."

"You can trust me," he said. "You *need* to trust me. I'll do my best to help you, but you have to tell me what the hell is going on. Who would want to kill you?"

She sighed again, closing her eyes to the endless blue sea, afraid to look for the boat that would bring them salvation, afraid it would be the wrong boat, one that would bring them both death.

"It's too complicated," she murmured.

There was no answering tension in his body. His hand continued, warm, at her nape, stroking her beneath her heavy fall of hair, spreading heat and security through her chilled body. "Since it seems likely that they'd just as soon kill me along with you, I think I deserve to know. No matter how complicated it might be."

"You're right. It's just..." Her voice trailed off in the stillness. "Is that a boat?"

He was motionless, so utterly still that he might have been turned to stone. She didn't know a human being could be so still. "Yes," he said finally. "Either Cecil is unbelievably efficient, or we may be in real trouble."

She should have been frightened. But once more his hand moved, that sinuous, stroking motion on the back of her neck, and the panic couldn't spread over her as it wanted to. "I thought we were already in real trouble."

"Trouble's relative," he said. "I want you to do exactly as I tell you."

"Why? Because you're a man? Why should a math teacher from England be better able to get us out of this mess?"

For some reason he looked amused. "Don't go all feminist on me, Francey. You're on the border edge of hysteria, and it's taking all your considerable strength of purpose not to crack. I'm too unimaginative to be that frightened, particularly since you haven't told me what we're up against. And I have the advantage of having spent two years in the military, even if it seems like a century ago." His fingers tightened, just marginally, on the back of her neck. "Will you do what I tell you to do? No noble gestures, no flinging yourself on the sand to save me?"

She flushed, not even surprised that he'd managed to read her mind. "This isn't your fight, Michael. There's no reason why you should die because of me."

"No one's going to die, Francey. If you do as I tell you. Will you give me your word?" The amusement was gone from his voice. She wished he weren't wearing the dark glasses—maybe she could have read something from his eyes, something she couldn't fathom from the set of his mouth, the alert tension in his body.

"I'll do my best," she whispered as a boat rounded the point.

"Not good enough, love," Michael said in a gentle, almost loving voice. And then everything went black.

He laid her down gently in the thick undergrowth. It was a neat little trick he'd learned during a stint in Southeast

Asia. Painless, swift, foolproof, if you knew just where to apply pressure, it brought instant unconsciousness to the victim. The drawback was they had to trust you enough to let you that close in the first place, so it was a tool used to betray people who cared about you, but it was a talent that had saved his life on numerous occasions. Today it just might save Frances Neeley.

"Hey, mon," Cecil called out from the disreputable-looking fishing boat. "You in trouble, mon?"

Michael rose from his spot in the bushes. "You can cut the accent, Cecil. She's out for the count."

Cecil dropped his huge bulk over the side, into a small, battered looking dinghy. "She faint?"

"With a little help," Michael said. "Did someone take care of the house?"

"I sent someone to work on it." He started the motor. It was a small, rusty looking machine that started with a well-oiled purr, and in moments he was up on the crushed coral beach. "Since we haven't heard an explosion, I expect he managed to take care of the problem." He waded toward Michael. "What happened?"

"How the hell do I know? You were supposed to be watching," he snapped, letting his temper out.

"We were watching, mon," Cecil protested, mocking him with his accent. "We were watching the two of you at the café, someone else was watching the house, and we had men stationed down at the beach where you two were supposed to go swimming. They were placing bets as to whether you were going to séduce her on the sand or wait until you were back in the house."

"Voyeurs," Michael muttered, more as a token protest. "She's not my type."

Cecil peered through the heavy foliage at the body lying in the brush. "You must be crazy, mon. Then again, you work for Cardiff...."

Michael glanced up at him. Cecil was a good deal taller than his own six foot two and outweighed him by several stone. On top of that, he hadn't spent the past few weeks in hospital. "You want to elaborate on that, Cecil?" he inquired gently.

Cecil took an involuntary step backward, a fact that amused Michael. Cecil's reputation had preceded him—he was a man who wasn't intimidated by much of anything, and his physical courage was enormous. Apparently the Cougar's reputation had preceded him, also. Enough to make Cecil wary. "No offense, mon. The lady's mighty fine looking, that's all."

"What I do or don't do with the lady is my business," he said. "Your only concern is to ensure our safety."

"My concern is the success of your mission."

Michael nodded, granting him that. "I'll find out what I need to know. It's up to me how I go about doing that."

Cecil didn't move as the two men measured each other. And then Cecil shrugged. "I'm glad we're on the same side, Cougar," he said. "I don't imagine you lose very often."

"Battles, sometimes. Never the war."

"You want me to get her?" Cecil started toward Francey's unconscious body, but Michael forestalled him.

"I'll take her."

"I'm stronger than you are right now," Cecil said, and Michael knew perfectly well he was goading him, testing him. This time he didn't mind.

"I'm sure you are," he said with a crooked smile. "But whether I want her or not, she's mine." In fact, she was lighter than he would have guessed, even as a dead weight. His bad leg gave way as he stood upright, and he staggered for a moment. Cecil wisely looked away.

The waters of the Caribbean were warm as he waded out to the dinghy. "She said there were coral reefs out here," he said over his shoulder.

Cecil was busy under the hood of the sports car. "She was right. If I hadn't had a local man with me, you would have been a sitting duck." He slammed down the hood, cursing. "Get the hell in the boat."

He dumped her body on the floor of the boat, vaulting in after her. "Why?"

"They're thorough bastards. They've got a bomb set in the car for good measure. Just in case you caught on to the gas. You're just damned lucky you didn't jar it into going off when you came down that old road."

Michael didn't even feel a trickle of fear. Might-have-beens wasted time. He glanced down at the woman lying at his feet, and he flipped her cotton skirt over her long, tanned legs. "Let's get the hell out of here."

"You got it, man," Cecil said, forgetting his accent as he raced through the shallow water. "She's about to blow."

He'd just managed to reach the boat when the explosion rocked the landscape, sending the dinghy hurtling backward through the suddenly stormy sea. Michael reached down and hauled Cecil's impressive bulk into the dinghy, then stared back at the cove.

Flames were shooting up from the skeletal remains of the car. Trees had been uprooted by the force of the explosion, and the underbrush was burning sullenly.

"They were pretty thorough," he remarked as Cecil settled himself by the engine. He had a gash over his cheekbone, one that was oozing blood, and they were all drenched from the sea spray that had shot up.

"Not a trace left of you, mon," Cecil observed cheerfully. "Maybe that'll keep them off your tail for a while. I considered letting the house blow as a decoy, but I figured your buddy Travers might think that was going a little too far in the way of cooperation."

"Good thinking. They'll be just as likely to be fooled by the car exploding as the house."

"Which means . . . ?"

Michael looked down at Francey, lying huddled on the floor of the dinghy. She was soaked to the skin, her sun-streaked brown hair matted against her face, and he found himself wanting to pick her up and cradle her in his arms.

To strip off his damp shirt and dry her. To warm her chilled flesh, soothe her chilled soul.

He let her be. "Which means they're not likely to be fooled at all. Or not for long. So better to sacrifice a car than a house. I rather liked that house."

"I got through to Cardiff. It's going to be a few days on the island."

Michael lifted his eyes to meet Cecil's. "How many days?"

"You know Cardiff. He wasn't sure how he was going to get you off, or how long it was going to take, but I'd say thirty-six hours, at least."

"I imagine he sent some smarmy message for me."

"Just to be careful. And enjoy yourself."

"Bastard," Michael said carefully. He didn't want to enjoy himself. Not with the vulnerable woman lying at his feet.

"You've got enough supplies, the weather's supposed to be fine, and you've got yourself a pretty lady. If I were you, I wouldn't complain."

"You're not me," Michael said dispassionately as the dinghy pulled up next to the fishing boat. He had no choice but to hand Francey's body up to the waiting men, and he wondered briefly if he'd used too much pressure, or not enough. The ride out to the Baby Saints would take forty minutes. He didn't want her waking up too soon, asking questions before he'd decided on the answers. Or too late. He didn't want to hurt her any more than was completely necessary.

The problem with Francey was that she didn't accept easy answers. Easy lies, automatic excuses. She saw through them, and he wasn't quite sure why. He only knew that she was a lot harder to fool than he'd ever imagined.

It the end, though, it was easy. She didn't begin to come out of it until Cecil and his men had disappeared, leaving them on the tiny, lush island of Baby Jerome, with enough supplies to last them a depressingly long time. He'd laid her out on a blanket, his rolled-up white suit jacket beneath her head, the late-afternoon sun baking her skin, drying the salt-stiffened dress and smoothing away the chill that rippled her skin. He'd turned away to rummage through the packages Cecil had dropped, looking in vain for fresh clothing, and when he turned back her eyes were open, and she was watching him, expressionless, motionless, and he waited for her accusation.

"Did I faint?" Her voice was rusty, strained, her eyes still faintly dazed with shock.

He almost wanted to deny it. To tell her she'd had some help. But he couldn't. Why would a math and soccer master from Somerset know how to render someone unconscious like that?

He gave her a charming, impartial smile. "I'm afraid so. You missed all the excitement."

"Excitement?" She struggled to sit up, glancing around her at the deserted beach. "Where are we?"

"On one of the Baby Saints, I gather. Cecil assures me no one comes here, that we'll be safe for the time being. Until your uncle can mount a rescue."

She shook her head, patently trying to clear the mists that still clung to her. "So they never showed up?"

"Who?"

"The bad guys. Those mythical people who are supposedly trying to kill me," she said with a trace of sharpness, a sharpness that amused him.

She didn't like being passive. She was already fighting back. He wished he were a normal man, with even a trace of a normal life. He would like to see her when her emotions hadn't been battered. "They never showed up," he agreed, sitting back on his heels.

"I told you, this is crazy. No one—"

"They did, however, leave you a present." He interrupted her protests.

She went very still, and he could see a shiver dance over her tanned skin. "A present?"

"A bomb in the sports car. I'm afraid it blew just as we took off out to sea."

She looked ill, and he wondered whether she was about to throw up. The thought didn't disturb him—he'd done worse in his life than hold a lady while she puked her guts out.

She shut her eyes, murmuring weakly, "Oh, my God."

"With luck, they'll assume we died in the car."

She opened her eyes again, and her gaze was remarkably calm and steady in the whiteness of her face. "And if they don't?"

"Then we're likely to have visitors. Sooner or later. We'll just have to hope Travers gets here sooner."

"If he doesn't?"

He wanted to reassure her. To tell her he wouldn't let anyone touch her, hurt her. But he couldn't, even though he knew he was more than capable of protecting her. "Then we've got a gimpy schoolteacher and a broken bird against a bunch of very nasty bad guys," he said flatly. "What do you think will happen?"

She was still dazed and confused by the tumultuous events of the afternoon, by her too-long period of unconsciousness. Otherwise she never would have reached over and plucked the sunglasses from his face, looking into his eyes as if she knew him. "I think we'll be fine," she said in a small, sure voice. And then she lay back again, closing her eyes and breathing deeply. In her hand she held the sunglasses that were his shield against the world.

And his shield against innocent young woman who could see far too much.

Chapter 6

He must have been the British equivalent of a Boy Scout, Francey decided later. His efficiency was almost frightening as he bundled her off into the overgrown island.

"One thing's for sure, we can't sit out on the beach and wait for them," he said. "Might as well send a telegram. Cecil tells me there's a fresh-water lagoon not too far inland. We'll camp there and trust Travers will have better luck finding us than the men who are after you."

Francey struggled to her feet, pushing her hair away from her face. She felt dazed, oddly sleepy, considering the extremity of their situation. "How far inland?"

"Why don't you sit here while I scout out on the situation?"

She didn't want to admit to the fact that she was frightened without him. There was no reason to put such faith in him, no reason at all. Except for the merciless chill she sometimes surprised in his blue eyes, which told her he was quite capable of anything. "I'd rather come with you, if you don't mind," she said.

"Suit yourself. I can't promise that they won't find us eventually, but it'll take them a while."

"How do you know that? Maybe they were watching us. Maybe they're on the other side of the island. . . ."

"The other side of the island is protected by coral reefs. It would take an island man to get through them, and I don't think it's a St. Anne native who's after you. Is it?"

"I don't know."

"Don't know? Or won't tell me?"

She bit her lip, hoping the small amount of pain would help clear her fogged brain. "I'll tell you," she said. "I owe you that much."

"You do indeed. But it can keep until we get off the beach. We're going to be here a while—we'll have plenty of time for bedtime stories."

She looked at him sharply, wondering what he meant by that. But he'd already turned and headed toward a narrow path cut through the underbrush, a box of supplies on his shoulder. He was barefoot, wearing his rumpled white linen trousers and a pale blue shirt, and his gait was completely steady. Obviously his so-called wound was a fake.

Would she be following her executioner into the jungle, away from witnesses? Absurd. If he'd wanted to kill her, he'd had innumerable chances. She was being a hysterical, paranoid ninny.

"Are you coming?" He'd paused at the edge of the thicket, his expression patient.

"I'm coming," she said, reaching down to scoop up the blankets she'd been lying on.

It seemed to take him no time at all to set up a rudimentary camp. Even with the sun dipping low, the air was warm, torpid, the gentle trade winds that abounded around St. Anne cut off by the heavy greenery surrounding the lagoon. It was a small, translucent pool of water, warm from the midday sun, and Francey knelt beside it, sluicing some over her face to help wake her up.

"The weather's supposed to be good for the next few days," Michael said in a diffident voice. "I thought we might not bother with any sort of shelter for the time being. Unless you'd rather I rigged something up."

We, she thought. Was she going to be sleeping with him? It was all part and parcel of this gathering sense of unreality. "I'd like to sleep under the stars," she said.

He nodded, moving back to the boxes of stores that had been left there. "The one thing Cecil didn't manage to provide is a change of clothes," he said, his back to her. "You might want to rinse out your dress in the lagoon. If it's like my clothes, it's probably all stiff and sticky from the salt spray. You needn't worry about the drinking water— Cecil brought plenty of that. We can use the lagoon for bathing."

"That's a good thing," she said. "I'm all stiff and sticky, never mind my clothing." But she made no move to unfasten her dress. She was wearing her French bathing suit underneath, a reminder of the innocent day they'd planned, but some idiotic remnant of modesty kept her from moving.

Michael didn't have any such inhibitions. With one last glance at the makeshift kitchen he'd set up, complete with propane cookstove, he turned and walked to the edge of the lagoon, stripping off his shirt as he went and sending it sailing. She almost looked away as he reached for his belt, wondering for a moment just how immodest he was, and then she realized he must be wearing his bathing suit, too. She couldn't keep from watching as he stripped off the water-stained trousers and dumped them beside the lagoon.

She laughed then, in a kind of nervous relief, and he turned to look at her. "I warned you I was pale and skinny," he said. "I didn't think I was that amusing, however."

"I was afraid you weren't wearing a bathing suit," she confessed. "And I wouldn't have expected you to wear something quite so baggy," The bathing suit was a huge pair of trunks that ballooned around his body. But he was wrong; he wasn't pale and skinny at all. He couldn't match her own darker tan, acquired after several weeks beneath the Caribbean sun, but he was a lovely sort of golden shade. And he wasn't skinny. Lean, possibly leaner than he usually was. But there was no disguising the corded musculature of his chest, his shoulders and arms, even his legs. And, oh, my God, his legs.

The limp hadn't been faked. None of his injuries had been. As she looked more closely, past the momentary distraction of sheer masculine beauty, she saw the vicious red scar on his thigh, the jagged tear in his side, and older, paler scars scattered across his golden skin.

All amusement fled in shocked horror at the pain he must have been through. "Michael," she said in an anguished voice. "What did they do to you?"

A shadow crossed his face, a hint of such strong emotion that she couldn't even begin to decipher it. And then it was gone again, and he'd crossed the clearing to her, his hands warm and hard on her shoulders. "Doctors can be butchers," he said easily. "But they put me back together after the accident, and I have to be grateful to them."

She wanted to say something about the other scars, the older ones. The kind of scars she'd never seen before, not ones that had come from a surgeon's knife, but something rougher, cruder. "Yes," she said vaguely.

"Now take off your dress so I can laugh at your bathing suit," he said gently.

It was an unfortunate fact that when he was so close, touching her, looking at her with unexpected tenderness, she could deny him nothing. She reached for the tiny row of buttons between her breasts, and then jerked back in sudden pain.

His face darkened. "What's wrong?"

"I must have hurt my wrist. Sprained it, perhaps..." And suddenly she remembered those brief, paralyzing moments in the sports car, when he'd taken her wrist.

His face showed no expression at all. The very blankness of it told her more than obvious guilt or regret would have. "You must have hurt it when you fell," he said flatly, his hands leaving her shoulders. Moving to the buttons between her breasts, unfastening them, his strong, clever hands brushing against her.

She held herself very still, afraid to breathe. Not afraid of the pain he'd inflicted on her in a moment of desperation, but afraid of her reaction to the feel of his hands on her breasts, the warmth of his body so close to her.

He had freckles on his shoulders, she saw. A faint tracery of golden hair on his chest. And for a man as deft as he was, it was taking him too long to undo the buttons.

She stepped back, away from him, tearing at the dress with sudden anger. He let her go, watching with faintly hooded eyes as she stripped off the dress and dived into the lagoon, slicing beneath its cool depths in one graceful arc.

By the time she surfaced he was in the water at the opposite end of the pool, and that odd, breathless moment might never have existed. "Well, I'll say one thing," he drawled in the gathering twilight. "You couldn't call your bathing suit baggy."

She wasn't going to blush. The two scraps of black cloth had been the best she could manage in the small, trendy boutiques on St. Anne. She'd tried to get a larger size to cover more of her, but it simply fell off her body. In the end she'd settled for this, knowing that no one else would see it.

But it hadn't worked out that way. Still, she had every intention of staying in the water until it was fully dark, rather than let Michael see her with those unsettling eyes of his.

"There're some soap and shampoo in one of those boxes," Michael added, treading water. "You want me to get them for you?"

It was the one thing he could say that would make her lower her guard. At that point she would have accepted soap from the ghost of Caitlin Dugan herself. "Yes, please," she said.

He levered himself out of the pool, and she watched him, watched with interest as she saw a strip of dark material beneath the flamboyant swim trunks. If he could embarrass her, she could return the favor. "Are you wearing underwear beneath those trunks?" she called out.

He turned back to her, his clothes in his hands, and leaned over to pick up her discarded dress. "I don't wear underwear," he said. "That's my real bathing suit."

Before she could realize his intent he'd tossed all the salt-stiffened clothes into the water, including her only decent piece of clothing. She dived for it, hoping to save it from a watery fate, but it sank beneath the surface before she could make it. then he was in the water with her, swimming towards her with clean, long strokes, unhampered by the soap and shampoo he was carrying.

And suddenly he was close, too close, in the water. "Need some help?" he asked.

Her wrist was feeling better with the cool water surrounding it, and she wondered again whether she'd imagined the pain. It didn't matter. Even if it was broken, she wouldn't ask him for any kind of help that would require him to put his hands on her again. His touch was too overwhelming in her current fragile state. "I can manage," she said, backing away from him.

He let her go, a fact that surprised her, moving away through the water to gather the scattered wet clothing. She turned her back to him, using the shampoo and soap he'd given her to manage a fitful bath, then dived beneath the water to rinse the bubbles from her hair. When she surfaced she saw she was alone in the pool. Michael was standing by the cookstove, and the damp, oversize trunks were low on his hips, clinging to the black strip of material.

She grimaced. At least he had something baggy to cover his modesty. Except that she didn't think he was in the slightest bit modest. If she said anything at all about it, he'd probably strip off the baggy trunks. And she didn't think that would be a good idea at all.

"It's getting dark," he said, his back to her. He had a beautiful back, she noticed now, even through the gathering shadows. She'd never really noticed a man's back before, but his was quite extraordinary. Strong shoulders, narrow hips, golden smooth skin. She sighed, treading water, and a stray chill rippled through her skin.

"I'm not finished," she said, taking a few strokes to warm herself.

"You can't spend the night in the pool, Francey," he said with a great deal of patience. "You'll have to come out sooner or later."

"Later will do me fine," she said, swimming backward, then diving under the water again. Later might not be such a good idea. He was busy right now, managing some sort of dinner with his Boy Scout training. She could probably manage to slip out unnoticed and wrap herself in one of the scratchy wool blankets Cecil had thoughtfully provided in lieu of clothing.

She surfaced by the far edge of the pool, shaking the water from her face, and she realized with sudden horror that he was gone. The camp stove was untended, the clearing vacant, and she was alone. . . .

Strong hands caught her, hauling her out of the lagoon with seeming effortlessness. She struggled for a moment, but he stilled her with the simple expediency of wrapping his body around her chilled, almost nude one. "If you make us both fall back into that lagoon, Francey," he growled in her ear, "I'm going to be very irritated."

She stopped her struggles. Not so much because of his threat, but because her skimpy bikini wasn't made for wrestling matches. And the more she struggled, the more her chilled, damp body rubbed against his warm, dry one. The effect it had on her was disturbing and undeniable.

And she didn't even want to consider whether or not it was having an effect on him.

He released her then, abruptly, only his hand steadying her from tumbling back into the lagoon. If he'd made a smutty remark, tried to touch her in any way, she would never have forgiven him. But he kept his gaze on her face. "Dinner's almost ready," he said. "And I found a T-shirt in the bottom of one of the boxes. Now, I'd much rather wear it. For one thing, it's getting cooler, and I'd just as soon keep you wearing as little as possible. But as we've already ascertained, I'm a perfect gentleman. So the T-shirt's yours."

She didn't know what to say. Except that his blue eyes were looking steadily into hers, and his manner was back to what she was accustomed to. Calm, sexless, friendly. She was the one suffering from an excess of awareness, an excess of imagination. Not Michael.

"That would be very nice," she said politely. "What's for dinner?"

His mouth curved up in a smile. "Now, that's the bad news. Cecil might have left us plenty to eat, but it's all godawful. Tonight we have freeze-dried shepherd's pie. Fresh shepherd's pie is bad enough, but freeze-drying it is a crime against humanity. After that, I suggest we try to get some sleep. It's almost full dark, and there's not much we can do once the sun sets completely. I don't think it would be wise to keep a fire going after dark."

She glanced over at the clearing. He'd managed a make-shift bed. One. Big enough for both of them. She looked back at him, a question in her eyes. "We're sleeping together?"

"Unless you want to freeze. I'm looking forward to your bedtime story. Who'd want to kill you, and why?"

"You wouldn't believe me," she said glumly.

He smiled then, just a faint, amused crinkling at the corners of his eyes. "Try me," he said. "I'm a lot more gullible than you'd think."

The T-shirt was a vast improvement. It was of a heavy cotton jersey and hung halfway to her knees. She wished she dared take off her wet bathing suit, but she didn't. Not because of the effect it might have on him, but what it might do to her.

Dinner was as horrendous as Michael had predicted, but they polished off every scrap of it, including emptying a bag of tasteless *muesli* for dessert. The water carried a designer label, and there was a full case of it, and there were even a couple of bottles of an excellent Chardonnay. When Michael extinguished the camp stove, darkness closed in around them, lit only by the brightness of a thousand stars in the inky sky overhead.

"Sorry there's no moon." His voice was slightly muffled in the darkness. He was over by the lagoon; she could see his body huddled down beside the water.

"Could you have arranged one?" she countered. The makeshift bed was behind her, and she wished she could come up with a reasonable alternative.

"Maybe if I'd had prior warning," he said lightly, rising and moving toward her, his gait smooth and even despite the evidence of his recent injuries.

"Your leg's much better," she observed, hoping to disconcert him, stalling for time.

"Yes, it is." He stopped a short distance away from her, as if he knew she was frightened. "You could probably still outrun me if you had a mind to."

She swallowed. "Is that supposed to set my mind at ease? Because if it is, it's failing."

Even in the inky starlight she could see the smile that creased his face. "I'm not going to chase you, I'm not going to rape you, I'm not even going to seduce you. Right now all I want to do is get some sleep, but I can't until you stop acting like a skittish virgin and lie down."

"I'm not a skittish virgin."

"No, you're not. So stop behaving like one and come to bed."

She couldn't come up with anything else to stall him. And suddenly she was bone-tired herself, the tumultuous events of the day catching up with her. Without a word she went over to the makeshift pallet, climbing in and pulling the light cotton cover over her. It was more comfortable than she'd expected, dangerously so. He'd fashioned some sort of mattress from the abundant greenery, and the smell of the crushed leaves was thick and evocative in the night air. She lay very still, legs together, arms crossed over her chest, and waited.

"You look like a mummy," he said affably, sliding in beside her. He was still wearing the baggy trunks, but he still had far too much skin exposed and was far too close. She could feel the warmth of him, even though they weren't touching. "Or maybe a crusader's wife, lying on her bier."

"I'm comfortable," she said stiffly.

"Well, I'm not." Before she realized his intent, he'd dragged her hands down from their protective position against her chest and pulled her body closer, his long bare legs brushing hers. She remained still, stiff, not bothering to try to move away. She knew without a doubt that he would simply haul her back. Besides, he was making no move to touch her, to caress her, to run his strong, beautiful hands down her arms, up under her loose white T-shirt. He was being as chaste as her posture dictated. "So tell me, Francey? Who's trying to kill you? And me, as well?"

She didn't want to talk about it. Here in the tropical darkness, she wanted to lie back and look at the stars, to feel the warmth of the man beside her and pretend life was still innocent. "It's a long story," she said.

"We've got a long time."

"I thought you were tired."

"I've got my second wind. Distract me."

She didn't want to think about the ramifications of that statement. It had been delivered in a bland enough tone, but she no longer knew her own mind. On the one hand, she wanted him safe, sexless, a boon companion. She didn't need the complications of desire so soon after the disaster of her involvement with Patrick Dugan.

On the other hand, whether she needed it or not, she had it. Desire. For the man lying so close to her. And while she usually had the good sense to be grateful he didn't seem to want her, a part of her was miffed at his immunity.

The few suggestions she'd had that he might not be as immune as he seemed frightened her. She told herself that she was frightened of her own ability to cope. But she had to admit, deep down inside her innermost heart, that she recognized something about Michael Dowd that terrified her.

She looked up at the stars, taking a deep breath, willing herself to relax. "Once upon a time," she said in a low voice, "there was a very stupid girl. She had no excuse for her stupidity—she had a good enough brain, a good enough education. But when it came to people she didn't have much common sense. She believed what they told her. She wasn't hopelessly naive, mind you. She knew there was evil in the world. She just never thought it would touch her."

"But it did." He was touching her, she realized. His hand was on her wrist. The one that still ached. And he was stroking it gently, kneading away the lingering stiffness and pain.

"It did," she agreed. "She met a man."

"Ah," said Michael.

"Indeed. He was a very handsome man. Irish, with all the charm associated with the Irish. He could have had anyone eating out of his hand, including people who were a lot more sophisticated than she was. She was child's play for him. All he had to do was smile at her and she fell in love."

"I think you're too hard on her," he said, his voice a low rumble in the night. "It sounds as if she was up against someone who was completely out of her league."

"That's still no excuse for being so trusting." Her voice was hard. "But she believed everything he told her. Believed in the cause he was working for, believed in the future he had mapped out for both of them. And she would have given him everything, everything...." Her voice failed for a moment at the shameful memory.

"What happened to these happy lovers?" At some point his hand had moved up her arm to her shoulder, and she'd moved closer, either at his volition or hers, she wasn't quite sure.

"He had a jealous sister. No, I keep forgetting, she wasn't his sister at all. She was his lover. And they weren't working together through a peace group, the way they told her. They were part of an organization called the Cadre. A violent, terrorist group that stops at nothing to gain their ends. He was planning on assassinating the Queen of England when she spoke at the United Nations. And then he was going to marry the stupid girl, use her for cover to get back into Great Britain, and then kill her, as well."

"Sounds cold-blooded and practical. What went wrong?"

"Someone betrayed them. Caitlin thought it was the girl. She came to her apartment, where she was waiting for her lover, and told her the truth. She dragged her out to find Patrick, to stop him in time, but it was too late. The girl tried to stop it, to warn someone, she wasn't quite sure. She pushed Caitlin in front of a car. And then she watched as Patrick was gunned down."

"And she's been mourning him ever since? She *is* a stupid girl," he said dispassionately.

"She didn't mourn him. She mourned the loss of her dreams, of what she'd thought he was. She mourned the loss of her innocence, her ability to trust. She mourned the loss of the woman she'd inadvertently killed, even though Caitlin was fully as soulless as Patrick Dugan had been. But most of all she mourned the loss of Francey Neeley. A part of her died, as surely as Patrick died. And there's no way to bring her back.''

"You'd be surprised," Michael said, his voice low and warm, easing beneath her defenses. And then, leaning over her, he blocked out the stars.

Chapter 7

Her lips were soft and cool beneath his. Startled by his actions, she grew stiff and still beneath his hands, his mouth. Michael kissed her gently, just brushing his lips against hers, letting her grow accustomed to the idea, and he kept his hands on her shoulders, no lower, even though the dampness of the T-shirt where it clung to the top of her bikini was having a predictable effect on his body.

She tasted sweet, pure, soft and clean, like a mountain stream. He'd forgotten women could taste like that, feel like that. And he wanted it, wanted her, with a need that could very quickly manage to make him forget all the things he should remember. That there were some very clever people out to kill them. And there was still the remote possibility that the sweet, innocent woman lying there letting him kiss her might be one of them.

He forced himself to lift his head, and her eyes were wide and glittering in the starlight. Glittering with unshed tears.

"Why did you do that?" she whispered, her voice only a thread of sound in the stillness.

He counted on his instincts to keep him alive. They saved his life on innumerable occasions, managed to make the difference between success and failure on others. He'd never bothered to use his instincts when it came to other people, to women, to potential lovers. Only with the basic question: Would they eventually try to kill him?

Looking down at Francey's defenseless face, her bright, tear-filled eyes and soft mouth, those instincts told him that she'd never in her life known passion. Real gut-wrenching, thrusting, pulsating passion. Oh, doubtless she wasn't a virgin. No one was, nowadays. But whatever sex she'd experienced, it hadn't ever really reached her. She was as truly innocent as she seemed.

And at that moment he knew that she was everything else she'd ever seemed to be. A victim of the Cadre's hit-and-run techniques, one more survivor of the vagaries of life and politics.

"You looked like you needed to be kissed," he said finally, answering her question.

"I don't think so. That's how I got into this mess in the first place."

The thought of being equated with a piece of murdering slime like Patrick Dugan, even for a moment, sent a chill down his spine. His hands tightened on her shoulders, then eased, and he sank back beside her, close enough to feel the heat from her body, smell the scent of her skin, far enough away to make it an even greater torment.

He was used to torment. It was good for his soul. Make a man out of him, his Mum would have said, if she weren't too drunk at the time. Lying beside Francey Neeley's scantily clad body was going to make him an iron man. In more ways than one.

"Tell me about your home."

He glanced over at her in the inky darkness. "I beg your pardon?"

"You said we had plenty of time for bedtime stories. Tell me what it was like for you, growing up."

He thought back to Newcastle. Dirty, gray, poverty hanging in the air with the coal dust. A father he'd never known, a mother who'd seldom been sober enough to know him. The street gang he'd joined at eight, commanded at twelve. The first time he'd seen a man die.

"We lived in Yorkshire," he said. "With everything green and hilly and very beautiful. The manor had been in the family for generations. Whipdale House, it was called, and my mother and father and three sisters lived there."

"Three sisters," she murmured sleepily. "No wonder you're so good with women."

He smiled ruefully in the darkness, knowing she couldn't see him. "I had a couple of much older brothers, but they were up at Oxford by the time I was born, the baby of the family. We always had masses of animals around. I remember I had a pet Newfoundland named Beastie. A huge black shaggy creature, he followed me everywhere." He could see the dog clearly, as clearly as if he'd really lived. He could see his three sisters, smart and pretty and dreadful teases; he could see his parents, devoted to each other, plain, upper-class country people. He could see it all.

"Tell me about your sisters," she murmured, and he knew she would be asleep in a matter of moments.

"There was Fiona," he said. "She was the eldest, with flaming red hair and a temper to match. She always wanted to be an actress, but she ended up marrying a banker and having six children. As far as I know, she's never regretted it. Then came Dinah...."

She was asleep, curled up slightly, one hand tucked beneath her chin. Not the hand he'd hurt—that was still wrapped protectively around her middle.

Most of the time she believed what he told her. He was sure she'd swallowed Whipdale House and the five siblings without even a second thought. But there were times when she looked at him out of those warm brown eyes of hers and he could see the doubt, the wariness. The uneasy expression.

He'd seen that look before. In people who had seen him kill.

Maybe Francey saw too much for her own good. While her mind couldn't quite admit that he'd calmly and brutally inflicted pain on her, in her heart she'd known, and she struggled with that knowledge.

That she was now sound asleep beside him expressed a kind of trust that went beyond conscious decisions. He lay beside her, watching her as she slept, and wondered if she would ever come to regret that trust.

Probably. He'd regretted ever putting that much trust in anyone. People weren't made to rely on other people and survive. You had to rely on yourself, and yourself alone, or you were screwed.

The tiny island of Baby Jerome was still and silent. They were alone there, totally and completely alone, at least for now. He doubted there were even the omnipresent mongeese around. Nothing higher on the food chain than a few insects. At least for now.

Tomorrow would be another matter. He hadn't lived as long as he had by underestimating his opponents, and he fancied Cecil was just as cautious. By tomorrow the Cadre's outrunners would have located them. He would simply have to be prepared.

The cache of weapons was just off to the left, under a thick outcropping of palm fronds. He'd had enough time to hide them before Francey had regained consciousness, and he would rather she didn't even know about them. He would rather she didn't know about *him*. While she might feel safer knowing she was sleeping with one of her majesty's most highly trained agents, she would keep that wary look in her eyes all the time. And he'd gotten rather fond of Whipdale House and the three sisters.

No, she was better off not knowing, taking him at face value. After all, there was always the chance that he might not be able to protect her. That they might kill him and expect her to come up with answers. Answers she would be helpless to withhold, given the advanced state of the Cadre's torture capabilities.

No, she was going to continue to think he was Michael Dowd, junior Boy Scout. She thought she'd lost her illusions permanently. She hadn't. And he was planning on doing his best to give them back to her.

And maybe, just maybe, regain a few of his own.

Francey woke once during the long night. She was lying on her side, curled up close to the blazing furnace that was Michael's body. One of her legs was tucked between his, her head was resting against his shoulder, and his arms were around her loosely, possessively, one hand brushing her breast. The top to her bikini had come loose, so that now it was resting in the vicinity of her waist.

The odd thing was, her body didn't stiffen in instinctive protest. She didn't freeze up or try to draw away from him. Maybe it was simply that she was still half-asleep. Maybe not.

She heard a sigh and knew it was her own. Refusing to think about consequences, ramifications or any of those other unpleasant issues, she closed her eyes and went back to sleep.

When she awoke again she was alone in the rumpled, makeshift bed. She felt no panic, no fear that she might have been abandoned. Only a faint regret.

She smelled the coffee, and then there was no room even for regret. She turned her head to look at him, secure in the knowledge that he thought she was still asleep. She could watch him without his even being aware of it.

He was standing at the edge of the lagoon, drinking a tin mug of coffee, and there was water beaded on his strong body, dazzling in the early-morning sun. He'd dispensed with his baggy trunks, and the skimpy black racing suit had hardly more fabric than her own bikini. It left very little to the imagination, and Francey's imagination was already overwrought.

It constantly amazed her that a race as staid and supposedly uptight as the British would wear so little on the beach. The baggy trunks seemed much more in keeping with a math master from a British public school, but then, Michael probably knew that. Probably wore them whenever he had an audience, to enhance his role.

Now why did she think that? Why did she think he was playing a role? If he weren't who he said he was, wouldn't he have told her by now? And surely cousin Daniel wouldn't have sent her a dangerous stranger.

Except that he *was* a dangerous stranger, whether he was a math teacher or no. Dangerous to her, to her state of mind, to her heart. Perhaps even to her body, she thought, moving her wrist experimentally. And yet she trusted him more than she'd ever trusted anyone in her entire life. And she'd spent a lifetime trusting people, mostly unwisely.

"Looked your fill?" he inquired pleasantly, not turning toward her.

She shouldn't have been surprised. He seemed to have far more intuition than a normal man, sixth and seventh senses, at least. "That bathing suit is indecent," she said.

He turned to her then, and a wry grin curved his mouth. She knew, because she was determined not to look any lower than his face. "Depends on whether you find bodies indecent," he said. "You want some coffee?"

"Please." She crawled out from under the covers, tugging the oversize T-shirt around her, and headed for the bushes.

"Where do you think you're going?"

She didn't hesitate. "The ladies' room."

"Don't go too far."

She looked back over her shoulder. "You want to come along and hold my hand?"

"Feisty, aren't you?" he murmured, draining his coffee. "I wouldn't count on being safe here. If the Cadre tracked you down to St. Anne's, then they can probably find us on Baby Jerome."

She paused. "You think it's the Cadre?"

"Got any other ideas?" He obviously didn't expect an answer as he turned and headed for the pot of coffee. "Don't take too long, or I'll come after you."

By the time she returned to the campsite he was dressed, thank heavens, in his wrinkled white trousers, rolled up at the ankles, and his blue shirt left open to the faint tropical breezes. If he was observant enough to notice her relief he didn't say anything, simply handed her a mug of black coffee that was sinfully delicious.

"This is awfully good for instant coffee," she murmured, for lack of anything better to say.

"And isn't the weather lovely, and do you think it will rain, and how about those Mets?" he responded. "Do we really need to waste time on small talk?"

"All right. Do you have any other suggestions? I'm not really in the mood for Robinson Crusoe meets the Blue Lagoon."

"Whether you're in the mood for it or not, we're stuck here, at least for a while. If we're lucky, your cousin will show up to rescue us by this afternoon. If we're not, your friends will get here sooner. I want to scout out the island, see if there's anyplace to hide."

"And I bet you don't want me with you," she said, taking another sip of coffee. It really was good coffee, and she realized with sudden amusement that it wasn't instant at all. Michael was an even more proficient Boy Scout than she'd imagined.

"I never underestimated your intelligence. The bad guys might get here sooner than we expect. I'd be better off alone."

"So you could take them on single-handedly?" she asked, glancing at him over the rim of the cup.

He laughed. "Are you nuts? I'll have a much easier time running away if I don't have to worry about you."

He was doing it again. All gangling charm and asexual cheer. Just a sweet, ineffectual teacher from England, thrown into a situation miles out of his ordinary experience. And she didn't believe him.

"I'll stay here," she agreed. "How long do you think it'll take you?"

"That depends. If I run into trouble, there's no telling when I'll be back. I want you to keep out of sight."

"Michael..."

"Don't argue with me," he said, softening the order with an endearing smile that didn't reach his intense blue eyes. "We've gone over this before. It's in my upbringing—I have to do my best for the damsel in distress. Not to mention the fact that I seem to have thrown my lot in with you. Your safety and mine go hand in hand at this point."

"You could always cut a deal with them if you happen to run into them."

"From what I've heard of the Cadre, they'd slit my throat first and ask questions later," he said.

She grew very still. "From what you've heard of the Cadre?" she echoed. "I hadn't realized anyone knew much about them at all. When I talked to the FBI, they said they were an ultrasecret organization. I'd certainly never even heard their name."

He didn't even blink. "But you're an American. The Cadre's a branch of the IRA—surely your FBI explained that much. And we in England know far too much about the IRA and their various splinter factions. You're right, the Cadre keeps a low, extremely nasty profile. But one hears things."

She suddenly felt very cold, even as the morning sun beat down overhead. "Be careful, Michael," she said, frightened.

He grinned, boyish, freckled, lighthearted. No match for the ruthless killers she'd come in contact with. "Don't worry, love. Even with a game leg, I can run a hell of a lot faster than they can."

She couldn't keep him from going. She could only watch as he disappeared through the thick greenery, and then the silence settled down around her, as heavy as a tomb.

There wasn't much to keep her busy. She finished the coffee, polished off a cellophane bag of *muesli* and tidied the makeshift kitchen Michael had rigged up. She aired out the blankets and folded them; she swam in the tepid lagoon. Out of desperation she read every single printed word on the food packages, then went for the label on Michael's discarded jacket. That one was a puzzle. The labels had been cut out, leaving no clue to the tailor. And it had definitely been tailor-made—Francey remembered her third stepfather's exquisite taste. Turning the jacket inside out, she searched, finding only the trace of threads where someone had scissored out the telltale mark.

She folded it carefully, leaving it on top of the blankets, her mind preoccupied. She could think of no reason whatsoever for a man to have all the identifying labels cut out of his clothes. She found his baggy, discarded trunks and discovered that they were in the same shape.

"What are you trying to hide, Michael?" she said out loud, her voice echoing eerily in the little clearing. There was no answer.

When the overhead sun grew too hot, she made herself a little shelter, draping one of the blankets over a framework of branches and crawling beneath. She slept, her dreams filled with blood and violence. And sex. She woke, and even the birds were still. And she could smell death in the air.

Michael hadn't really expected it to take the Cadre long to find Baby Jerome. Despite the fact that they'd screwed up three times, he didn't make the mistake of thinking they were any less dangerous. He picked his vantage spot carefully, taking a few choice pieces from Cecil's munitions box with him, including his treasured Beretta. It all depended on how many showed up, and whether they made the choice to separate or stay together. He figured he could handle a maximum of four if they stayed together, six if they split up. But if they split, one of them might find Francey before he took him out.

In the end there were three of them, two older men and a boy of about eighteen. He watched them disembark, feeling no emotion at all, other than a faint regret. The young ones were the worst. Soulless, fearless, merciless. If he had any sense, he would take the young one out first.

There was never any question of capturing them or simply putting them out of commission. The Cadre took no prisoners, and they never allowed themselves to be taken. This was going to be a battle to the death, no mistake about it, and Michael wasn't in the mood to kill three people. But he was even less in the mood to let Francey die, and that was the alternative. He didn't really give a damn about himself. But he wasn't going to let them win.

There were some things you never forget. There were some circumstances when even the most compromised body came through. The three split up. The two older men fought fast, well, with a deadly accuracy that would have meant the end for another man. He let them find him first, but even two against one was only a delay in the inevitable outcome. And then he went after the boy.

He found him training a gun on Francey's back. She was wandering around the campsite dressed only in the skimpy bikini and baggy T-shirt, but Michael didn't feel his automatic spasm of lust. Every nerve, every cell, in his body was frozen in momentary panic.

The boy turned, some sixth sense alerting him to Michael's presence, and the empty blue eyes that looked into his were a mirror image. And then he leaped for Michael.

It was over quickly. A brief, vicious struggle that the boy doubtless thought he'd win. And he was good; Michael had to grant him that. Good enough to inflict a fair amount of damage with repeated, vicious blows to Michael's left side.

Only a knowledgeable person would have concentrated on the most vulnerable part of his body. The internal damage caused by Patrick Dugan's bullets hadn't yet healed, and Michael could feel the tearing deep within him as he fought.

And then it was over, the boy's youth and cunning no match for Michael. He pulled away, looking at his fallen enemy, and he thought about Vikings. About honoring a fallen soldier. And he spat at the boy's feet.

He limped back to the beach, clutching his side. A year ago the boy wouldn't have gotten to him. But then, a year ago he wouldn't just have come through pretty dicey surgery. Once again the spectre of retirement rose before him, and he thought of his cottage in the Lake District. He thought of the fictional Whipdale House, the comfortable Mum, the three doting older sisters. Closing his eyes, he sank onto the sand, letting the blackness wash over him.

It was late afternoon when he finally made his way back to the clearing. She'd dressed in her wrinkled sundress, something he would have regretted if he felt any better. She'd managed to concoct something on the cookstove, and he told himself he ought to eat. But all he wanted to do was collapse on the neat pile of blankets and make the last few hours go away.

She looked up when he stepped into the clearing, her sun-streaked brown hair pulled back from her face, and her brown eyes widened as she rose.

"They're here," she guessed, starting toward him, her face pale with alarm. "My God, Michael, what have they done to you?"

He managed to pull himself together. "Not a thing," he managed with an airy wave. "I haven't seen any sign of them. I was just stupid enough to fall down a cliff. Banged myself up good and proper." He swayed slightly, telling himself it was for effect, for her sympathy and warm, strong arms, and knowing it was because he couldn't help it.

She smelled of sun and flowers and innocence. He managed to keep from collapsing, leaning against her just slightly as she helped him toward the pallet, and he gave her a crooked smile. "Sorry to have made such a botch of things. I guess my leg wasn't as strong as I thought. It twisted underneath me, and the next thing I knew, I was at the bottom of a ledge. I was terrified that you might get into trouble, but it took me this long to get back."

It had taken him that long to rouse himself, go back and dispose of the bodies, to try to patch himself up. There wasn't much he could do for the internal injuries, except hope to God Travers would get there in time. Before the Cadre decided to send in reinforcements.

"You look like hell," she said, staring down at him.

"That's nothing compared to how I feel. There's some whiskey somewhere in one of the boxes. I could do with a drink."

"It's Scotch," she said. "I thought you preferred Irish whiskey."

"For some reason I'm not in the mood for Irish," he said grimly, leaning back.

A moment later she was kneeling beside him, a mug of whiskey in her hand. Nicely full, he noticed, taking a deep, shuddering sip. Bless the woman.

"What can I do?" she asked, sitting back on her heels.

He could think of any number of things, none of which he was in any shape to enjoy at that particular moment. "Don't look at me like that, Francey," he said wryly. "I'm not going to die."

"You look it."

"Don't count on it."

"Don't joke."

"You have to joke or cry," he said, thinking of the sightless blue eyes of the dead boy. He'd seen too many dead boys, too many soulless faces. Including his own. "You *can* do something for me," he said, taking another deep swallow, letting it burn through the pain in his gut.

"Anything."

She thought Patrick Dugan's filth had destroyed her soul. She didn't know how far from the truth she was. There was a basic goodness in her that nothing would ever touch, and right then he needed that, more than he needed the whiskey, more than he needed help for his wounds. "Lie down with me," he said.

No arguments, objections, sassy back talk. Stretching out beside him, she drew him very carefully into her arms. And closing his eyes, he let the darkness take him, the whiskey spilling from his hand and sinking into the dirt beside him.

Chapter 8

When he woke it was dark once more. There was a faint sliver of moon overhead, but clouds had come up during the past few hours, and a stiff wind was blowing them across the sky, obscuring, then revealing, the fitful light. The pain in his side was dull, aching, and he knew his body well enough to make a reasonable estimation of the damage. He was bleeding internally, at a slow rate. If Travers made it by tomorrow afternoon, so would he. If not...

He shifted, looking at the woman lying next to him. She was asleep, her tawny hair tangled behind her, and he could see the dried rivulets of tears on her cheeks. Why had she been crying? Was she frightened? Afraid of the future? Feeling sorry for herself?

Or had she been crying for him?

He was a man who'd always attributed the basest, most self-serving motives to the human beings he'd met. And yet he knew without question that her tears, her concern, hadn't been for herself at all. And that knowledge was almost too painful to bear.

Death had never been a despised enemy, just one of the risks of the game. Lately it had been looking more and more like an old friend. But not now. Not this time.

He didn't know whether the Cadre had any other operatives in the islands. If they did, how soon would they come to check up on the first three?

Chances were the three he'd killed had been working alone. There would have been no reason for any one else to remain behind. They would have come here, finished the two of them off, then headed away from St. Anne and embarrassing questions. There were enough islands in the area that they could have made it safely away and been on a jet back to Ireland before the bodies were discovered.

But he couldn't count on his instincts. He needed to wake Francey up, to tell her the truth about who and what he was, to tell her what she needed to do if things moved a little faster with his body, if he were unconscious, or dead, before Travers got there.

Now, while he still felt halfway human, he needed to get her deeper undercover. He needed . . .

He put his hand on her arm, and her skin was soft, warm beneath his cool hand. She opened her eyes, looking up at him sleepily, and before she had time to think about it she smiled. A sweet, sleepy smile that curved her mouth and warmed her eyes. The eyes that had shed tears for him.

"Are you feeling better?" she whispered, her mouth close to his.

Tell her, his training demanded. But his brain refused to obey. In approximately eighteen hours they would separate forever. He would either be dead or on his way to a secured hospital, and she would never see the invalided Brit schoolteacher again. Michael Dowd would cease to exist. It would be up to someone else to teach her passion. To show her that the real Francey hadn't shriveled up and died inside.

"No," he said, to himself, to her. He took nothing for himself. He did what he had to do, whatever filthy job the

well-being of the world demanded, and he came away with
nothing. If these might be his last few hours on earth, he
was going to take something this time. He was going to take
Francey Neeley.

He moved his hand up her arm, sliding it behind her
neck, beneath her thick curtain of sun-streaked hair. "Michael," she said, her voice a soft question, her eyes dark
with worry. He wanted to wipe the questions, the worry,
from her mind.

"Hush," he said, pulling her toward him. "Just hush."
Her mouth was soft beneath his, and not unwilling. He
kissed her slowly at first, dampening her lips with his. Then
he increased the pressure, opening her mouth with his, using his tongue. She jerked beneath him, but he held her still,
ignoring her shyness. He felt her hands come up to twine
around his neck, and at that little gesture of acceptance a
bolt of desire shot through his battered body.

He knew she wasn't wearing anything under the sundress—he'd seen her black bikini drying on the makeshift
clothesline. And she was kissing him back, shyly, her
tongue touching his, her arms tight around his neck.

He moved his hand down the front of the cotton dress to
the tiny row of buttons, unfastening them with unaccustomed clumsiness, needing to feel her skin against his, her
warmth.

She jerked again when his hand closed over her breast,
then grew still as he stroked her, pushing the dress down to
her waist. He broke the kiss, staring down at her in the
darkness, watching her face as he touched her breast, his
long fingers stroking the pebbled hardness of her nipple.

"Michael," she said, her voice rough and sweet. She said
it again, "Michael," but this time it was a strangled cry, as
he put his mouth on her breast, suckling it deeply into his
mouth.

Her hips rose off the blanket in reaction, and her hands
dug into his shoulders. He welcomed the pain. It was a

small distraction from the other pain trying to control his body, warring with the desire and determination he felt.

He slid the sundress down over her narrow hips and flung it away, leaving her warm and naked beside him. She trembled, suddenly aware of her own vulnerability, and he covered her with his own clothed body, ignoring the pain that seared through him. He wanted her, wanted her so badly that he didn't care if it killed him. He pressed his hardness against her, felt her lift her hips in response, and he cursed, slowly, fluidly, savagely beneath his breath.

She put her hands to his face. They were hot, trembling, and her eyes were slightly glazed with desire. The way he'd wanted to see her. "Michael, what's wrong?" she whispered against his mouth, and he could feel the hard peaks of her breasts against his bare chest, feel the soft yielding of her thighs. He rocked against her, slowly, tantalizingly, and she responded, arching up against him, even as he cursed himself.

He couldn't do it to her. Oh, he could perform, all right. His body was raging out of control, and it would take more than a life-threatening injury to keep him from having her. It would take something far more devastating. His own long-absent sense of honor.

He covered her hands with his, pressing them against his face, and he pressed down on her body, trying to still the restless trembling in her long limbs. "Michael," she said again, her voice a strangled cry, and he saw suddenly that he'd pushed her too far. The body beneath his was on fire, raging with a need as great as his. Her eyes were wide and shocked, her mouth pale, and he knew she was aroused to the point of pain, with little knowledge of how to deal with that arousal, how to slow it down, turn it down.

He rolled off her, taking her with him, wrapping his arms around her and stroking her, long, slow, calming strokes, down her arms, her body. But it didn't do any good. She whimpered, a pained little sound in the back of her throat, and each calming stroke of his hand only made her skin jump beneath his touch.

"Calm down," he whispered against her hair. "I shouldn't have done this. You don't need this right now, and not from me. Just take deep breaths, relax...."

She caught his wrists, pulling them away from her, and her expression was dark and hunted. "What do you mean?" Her voice was soft and raw. "I need this. I need *you.*"

He couldn't stand to hear it, not and keep his last ounce of decency. Tell her, his better self ordered. Tell her, so she'll know she could do so much better. But he couldn't. "You're frightened, confused, looking for comfort," he said instead. "That's not a good enough reason."

"Damn you," she said, yanking away. Except that he wouldn't let her go. He was much, much stronger than she was, and his hand was a manacle around her wrist, jerking her back against him.

She fought for a minute, but he stilled her with no effort at all, simply by wrapping himself around her again. He couldn't let her storm off into the night. Damn it, he couldn't let her go at all.

She smelled of heat and flowers and aroused female flesh, and he knew what he was going to do. For her, not for him.

Pushing her back against the blankets, he silenced her mouth with his. Her hips jerked as he moved his hand down her smooth-skinned stomach, sliding between her thighs, and she tried to clamp them closed against him. But she had to fight both his strength and her own need, and it was a battle she was destined to lose. She was wet and soft and sleek, arching up against him, and she was his.

The hands that had been pushing him away now clung to his shoulders, her fingers digging into the loose cotton shirt that billowed around them. She tore her mouth away, burying her face against the side of his neck, and he could feel the wetness of her tears, the heat from her strangled breathing. He talked to her then, a jumble of words, telling her how brave, how beautiful, how sweet, she was, telling her all the things he wanted to do to her when they had the time and place. She was fighting it, fighting her own body, even as she reached for it.

He knew women's bodies, better than she did. She was no match for his knowledge, his experience, his determination. He knew how to balance her on the edge of desire, stringing it out for a breathless eternity, and he knew how to plunge her over, prolonging it until she was sobbing against him, beating against him, as her body convulsed, his hand clamped between her thighs.

He gave her time to calm down. He brushed her hair away from her tear-damp face, whispering to her, words of praise, of love, of sex. He could tell her he loved her. He was Michael Dowd, a math master at Willingborough. He was the kind of person who could love, who could give.

She shivered in the warm night air, and he pulled the blanket up around her body, pulling her tight against him. She looked up at him, but the clouds had thickened, and he couldn't see her face, her expression. It didn't matter. He knew it in his heart.

"Michael..." she said, her whispered voice a question.

He stroked her shoulder, realizing absently that his own hands were trembling. "Go to sleep, love," he said, and meant it. Love.

"But..."

"That was for you, love. We'll worry about me next time."

That phrase, next time, calmed her. It calmed him, even though he knew it was a lie. A moment later she was asleep, her arms tight around him, as if she was afraid he might drift away from her. She knew him better than she realized.

There would be no next time. Tomorrow Michael Dowd would be gone from the face of this earth, either by the grace of the intelligence bureaucracy or a vengeful God. He would never see her again, and for that he was grateful. In barely more than a week she had become the worst weakness he'd ever known, and he couldn't afford weakness.

He wondered with a trace of amusement which part of his body was more uncomfortable: the pooled heat and hardness between his legs, or the damage in his side. A man wouldn't die of frustration, but it felt a hell of a lot more terminal than the slow seeping pain beneath his ribs.

Moving his head, he placed his lips against her forehead. The night was still all around them, dark and silent. There was no danger, not from the three men whose bodies he'd hidden on the far side of the little island. Not from the woman asleep in his arms.

Only from himself, and his own lost soul.

Francey let him sleep when she rose from the tumble of blankets. He looked pale in the early light beneath the golden layer of his tan, and there was a faint film of sweat on his forehead. Even in his deep sleep he'd clung to her for a second as she slid out of the makeshift bed, then released her with a sigh. She'd sat back on her heels, nude in the early-morning sunlight, and watched him for long minutes, wondering if he were going to wake, wondering if they were going to continue what they'd started last night.

She wasn't ready to. Not yet. If she crawled back under the blanket and woke him, then there would be no going back. She couldn't give herself heart and soul to a man again and risk having that gift thrown back in her face.

Not that she'd actually given herself to Patrick, she reminded herself pragmatically, pulling her sundress over her head and fastening the first few of the tiny buttons. Not her heart, not her soul, not even as much of her body as she'd shared with Michael last night.

She could feel the color rise in her cheeks, and she glanced back at the sleeping man. It was a lucky thing for her that he was so exhausted, his breathing deep, noisy, his color pale in the shadowy light. It gave her time to pull her defenses back around her, to decide how she was going to handle things when he finally awoke.

She could admit it now—she'd never loved Patrick. If she had, she wouldn't have waited so long to go to bed with him. Patrick had been wooing her, charming her, for five months before she'd finally decided she trusted him enough to make love with him.

She'd known Michael Dowd for eight days. She didn't believe half of what he told her, but if he asked, she would strip off her sundress and lie down with him again. She didn't trust him to tell her the truth, but she would trust him with her life. In fact, she already had.

The smell of coffee didn't move him. The crash of pans as she cleaned up lacked the power to reach him. She swam in the lagoon, washing her hair and rinsing it with the imported water, and still he slept, his noisy, stertorous breathing the only sound in the stillness.

She was floating lazily on her back, listening to him, when the first trickles of uneasiness hit her. She'd slept with him two nights ago, and before that she'd been sleeping within hearing distance for almost a week. She knew without question that he wasn't a man who snored.

And he wasn't snoring now. He was struggling for breath.

She vaulted out of the lagoon, scrambling to his still body in the bedroll. He didn't flinch as she dripped water over him, and his skin was cool, clammy beneath her damp hands.

"Wake up, Michael," she said urgently, tugging at his shoulders.

His eyes fluttered open for a moment, and they were dazed, blank. They they focused on her, and for a moment she thought she was looking down at a stranger. Some demon who'd stolen into Michael's body and was staring at her out of dark, dangerous eyes.

"Francey," he said, his voice a thread of sound. "Got to tell you…hurt…Travers…watch…" His eyes shut again, as if the effort were too much for him.

"You're hurt," she said, trying to make sense of his ramblings. "You want me to watch for Travers. I will, Michael. I'll go out to the beach and keep watch for him." She started to rise, but his hand shot out and caught her wrist with unexpected strength.

"Don't go," he said, his eyes shut. "Don't…leave…." And then he released her, his hand dropping limply beside his body.

"I have no choice, Michael," she said, but he could no longer hear her. He'd lapsed back into unconsciousness, not sleep. "I have to get help."

He didn't move; he simply lay there, cold and still, and she knew he would die. For a moment she gathered him into her arms, holding him against her. "Hang on, Michael," she whispered. "I won't let you die, damn it. I couldn't bear it."

It never occurred to her in her panic that the path to the beach would be obscured. She'd been tired, dazed, when she'd first followed Michael to the lagoon, and she hadn't left since. She'd assumed the path to the beach was wide and well-marked, but she couldn't find it.

"Don't panic, Francey," she muttered beneath her breath as she took one wrong turn after another. "If you don't find them, they'll find you. And they'll find Michael, and get help for him. Just be calm, and you'll make it." But her voice sounded frantic, even to her own ears, and her heart was racing beneath the light cotton dress. Maybe she'd been crazy to leave him alone in the clearing. What if the people who'd been after her found where they'd run to? They'd been lucky so far—except for Michael's tumble down a cliff, no one had managed to hurt them. But their luck hadn't held out. Michael was deathly ill, and the Cadre was bound to track them down sooner or later. What if they found Michael when he was unconscious, unable to defend himself?

She lost track of time as she struggled through the junglelike growth. The sun was blazingly hot overhead, and she knew it must have been hours since she left him. Was it already too late?

She could see a faint shimmer through the tangle of trees, a shimmer that had to be the sea. There was no pathway, just fallen trees and overgrown bushes, but she didn't dare turn around or look for another way around. She would get lost again, and who knows when she would get near the sea again.

She started climbing over the thick fallen trunks, her bare feet bruised and bleeding from her endless trek through the island forest. The closer she got to the light, the more hope filled her heart. It was the sea, and salvation had to be close at hand. It almost looked as if there might be a boat out there, something large and white, bringing safety and salvation, bringing help for Michael. . . .

She broke through onto the sand, sinking to her knees in relief. The brightness of the sun was so intense that she could make out no more than the outline of a large white boat. And then the sun was blocked out, and her eyes narrowed in panic as she saw the men.

Two of them. Soldiers, they looked like, though she didn't recognize the uniform, and armed to the teeth. They were advancing on her kneeling body, and she knew death was staring her in the face.

One man had already drawn his gun, and it was more than sufficient for the job. She bowed her head, waiting. She wasn't quite ready to stare death in the face.

After that, events happened so quickly that it took her days to piece things together. One moment she was expecting death. In the next, something, someone, had dropped down in front of her, shoving her out of the way. There were gunshots, the stink of cordite, and he fell in front of her. Michael.

Francey no longer cared about the death-dealing soldiers. "Michael!" she shrieked, flinging herself on him.

He grimaced, writhing in pain, but his hand was still on the gun, still trained at the advancing soldiers. "Keep the hell back," he said weakly, and she didn't know whether he was talking to her or the soldiers. Or both.

"Good God, man," one of the men said. "What the hell happened to you? I thought you were invincible." His accent was pure Cockney, no trace of deadly Irish lilt whatsoever.

And then Francey saw the others on the beach. A short, impeccably dressed man with dark glasses, picking his way carefully toward them. Followed by the rough-hewn, untidy figure of her cousin Daniel.

Never had safety seemed so dear. She wanted to run to him, fling her arms around his elderly body and weep for joy. But the man in her arms mattered more than her own safety. She looked down at him; his eyes were closing, and she had the sudden, horrible fear that he was dying.

"Get a doctor!" she screamed, clinging tightly.

One of the soldiers had already reached them. "I'm a medic, miss," he said, and the other man pulled her away, gently but inexorably, passing her to Daniel's waiting arms.

She tried to tug herself away. "He's hurt, Daniel. He's dying. He's..."

"There's nothing you can do for him right now, Francey," he said patiently. "Let the medic work on him. We'll get him evacuated to the nearest hospital, and I promise, he'll be right as rain."

"But..."

"Miss Neeley?" The short, dapper figure had a high-pitched, nasally voice, with an accent from somewhere in the north of England. "You've had a rough time of it. Let's get you on the boat while the men deal with Mr. Dowd."

"Daniel!" Francey cried, ignoring the newcomer, turning to her cousin for help.

"He'll be all right," Daniel said firmly, pulling her away. "You're just making things worse. Come on, Francey."

There was nothing she could do. Two men were working on him, shielding him from her view, and she had the sudden, aching certainty that she would never see Michael Dowd again.

"Come along," the shorter man said, his voice filled with concern. A concern Francey didn't believe for a moment.

But the hands on her arms were inexorable, pulling her away from Michael. She could hear the sound of a helicopter overhead, and she looked up.

"They'll get him to the hospital, Francey." Daniel followed her gaze.

"Will it make you feel any better if I go check?" the little man demanded.

"Yes," she said flatly, digging in her heels.

"Wait here, then."

Daniel kept his grip on her arm as they watched the man step carefully over the sand. He knelt down beside the men working on Michael, leaning over and saying something in Michael's ear.

Michael wasn't unconscious after all. The stranger was yanked down by his impeccable silk tie, and it took him a moment to break free. When he came back to Francey his face was flushed beneath his mirrored sunglasses. "Your friend still has some fight in him," he said stiffly.

"What did you say to him?" Daniel asked the question Francey longed to.

The little man straightened his mangled silk tie, and Francey saw there was blood on it. Michael's blood.

"I just told him he didn't have to worry about Miss Neeley any longer."

He was lying; Francey knew that. She also knew there was nothing more she could do. Sooner or later she would find out the truth. From Daniel, or from Michael himself. He was tougher than she dared hope. Even if her heart was terrified that he was disappearing from her life forever, she knew better—for the simple reason that she wasn't about to let that happen. She was taking responsibility for her own life, and happiness. She'd lost too much in the past several months. She wasn't going to lose Michael without a fight.

Half a world away, a battle of wills was raging. A battle to the death.

"You can't do anything about it," the young man said wearily, tired of dealing with a lunatic. "The three of them are dead, the girl's gone off with Travers, and God knows when we'll get a shot at her again. Give over."

"Don't tell me to give over! My brother's been murdered! That bitch has gotten off scot-free. And even Cougar stands a good chance of surviving! I won't have it, do you hear? I'm not going to let go—"

"We have a shipment waiting for us. We can't afford to chase after your quest for vengeance right now—there are larger matters at stake. Put it to one side, at least for now. Your time will come."

He felt the hatred blazing in her, the fanatical, murderous fury that had served the cause so well in the past. The Cadre's leader had always been an obvious choice, because of that single-minded dedication. He was no longer so certain.

"Another month. You can wait that long till we get to Malta," he said. "We get the shipment, we get things settled, and then I promise you, I'll bring you the girl's head on a damned platter if that's what you want."

"Her head. And his."

The man nodded, seriously doubting anyone would get close enough to the infamous Cougar to separate his head from his body. "And his," he promised.

Chapter 9

New York was hot and sticky, the smell of tar and garbage rising from the streets. Francey stepped out of the unair-conditioned taxi and stared around her with a sense of wonder, as if she were seeing the place for the first time.

She'd always loved Greenwich Village. The tiny, little walk-up on Twelfth Street was the first real home she'd ever had. It came equipped with a key to a private park just two blocks away, and even if keeping the cockroaches at bay was a full-time occupation, she always had a sense of peace and belonging.

That had vanished the night Caitlin Dugan came and dragged her on that hair-raising ride to the UN. She'd spent the month afterward in New York, waking up in the morning, going to work, coming home at night, but she'd been numb, in shock. It wasn't until her cousin Daniel had stepped in, rooted her out of her apathy and sent her off to his villa on St. Anne that she'd started to come back to life.

To be honest, it wasn't until Michael Dowd had stepped off that plane into the warm evening air that she'd decided life might be worth living after all. It wasn't until she'd nearly died that night, and later, that she'd considered there might be life after betrayal. It wasn't until he'd kissed her, put his hands on her, that she'd realized . . .

What? What had she realized? That she was in love? That was absurd. You didn't fall in love with someone you'd only known for a week. Someone out of his own milieu. It was like a shipboard romance, spiced with the erotic charge of danger. If she saw him in England, ensconced in his job as soccer coach and math teacher, surrounded by adolescent boys, she would probably regard him in a much less romantic light. That warm, loving matriarch of his was probably a tartar, his sisters spoiled bitches, his brothers lechers. He'd never mentioned what happened to his father. Probably dead on the hunting field, or of apoplexy or too much port.

In retrospect, his life sounded like an English novel. James Herriot crossed with P. G. Wodehouse and a little bit of Jane Austen thrown in. She hadn't known people really lived like that.

She certainly wouldn't fit in. If she were even asked to. As it was, she hadn't been given the choice. Michael had been whisked off to some hospital with that officious little man, and Daniel had taken her on a long, leisurely cruise northward, on a vacation that had felt more like prison.

She couldn't rid herself of the notion that there'd been some message passed, some word given, that she was now allowed to return home. Daniel had stoutly denied all of her direct accusations and skirted more oblique questions, and finally she'd given up asking. Daniel was a man who knew how to keep secrets. She could only take his word for it that Michael was in a hospital in London, on the mend. That the attempts on her life had been the work of a deranged segment of Patrick and Caitlin Dugan's splinter group of the IRA, and that every single member of that group, the Cadre, had been arrested and imprisoned. And that everyone was going to live happily ever after.

She didn't believe him. Oh, she believed she was safe enough. Daniel wouldn't let her return to New York if her life was still in danger. But his facile explanations were just a bit too unlikely coming from someone who'd learned about life the hard way.

The taxi behind her squealed off into the blazing hot day, but still Francey didn't move. She was home, but it didn't feel like home anymore. She remembered an old gospel song, one she'd heard when her mother had been married to the man who consorted with bootleggers in the hills of Tennessee. "I ain't got no home in this world anymore." She would have to scour the old record bins and see if she could find a recording of it. It felt as though it had been written with her in mind.

Her apartment smelled of stale air and dead plants. She opened the windows to let what little breeze there was blow through, opened her refrigerator, then slammed it shut in disgust. Daniel hadn't given her time to close up her apartment; he'd simply swooped down and carted her off, and she'd been too apathetic to do anything more than go along. He'd even paid her bills while she was gone, keeping things as they were. The result was two rooms full of dead plants and a refrigerator with a whole new definition of the word penicillin.

She dumped the moldy food and dead plants, ignoring the noisy scuttling of displaced bugs as their peaceful haven was disturbed. She made herself some iced tea, deciding to risk her ancient ice, and sank onto her overstuffed sofa, the best piece of furniture in the apartment.

She flicked on the television, discovering it was still set on CNN. She'd been obsessive before she'd left, living and breathing the news. The healthiest thing she could do would be to turn to a game show.

She was reaching for the remote control when her hand stopped. Despite the newscaster's words, it didn't look like Northern Ireland on the television, it looked like Beirut. Bombed-out buildings, smoke rising, sirens wailing. None

of the rolling green beauty she'd always associated with
Ireland. But then, she used to believe in leprechauns, too.

Daniel hadn't been lying after all, even if he'd been a bit
premature. The British secret service had managed to fer-
ret out the headquarters of one of Ireland's most fanatical
groups. The Cadre was destroyed, its leaders jailed, with
only a few members escaping. The authorities expected to
catch up with them in a matter of days.

The picture switched to a sunny, tropical island, and the
voice-over continued with a rundown of the recent up-
surge of terrorism around the world, including three men
found dead on a deserted island near the resort island of St.
Anne, and the deaths of a couple on an island off Malta.

Francey didn't move, but her mind switched away from
the still-stuffy room and the endless drone of the television
as the announcer moved on to gloomy financial news.
Three men dead on Baby Jerome. Michael? Cecil?

Or whoever had been trying to kill her?

None of it made sense. No one had told her the truth, not
since she'd first been unlucky enough to meet Patrick Dugan and his phony sister Caitlin. They had lied, the government had lied, Daniel had lied. Only Michael had told
her the truth. Hadn't he?

She leaned back against the overstuffed sofa and shut her
eyes. She could hear the noise from the street, the cars, the
people, the endless sounds of the city. So different from the
peace and quiet of St. Anne. She wanted to be back there.
Away from the noise and bustle of New York, away from
the news and the lies. She wanted to lie on the beach and
listen to the sound of the surf. She wanted to be able to
reach out and touch Michael. She wanted to finish what
they'd started by the lagoon on Baby Jerome.

She wanted peace. But even more than that, she wanted
Michael.

He slid down on his haunches, his back against the rough
surface of the building, and lit a cigarette. He didn't smoke

much nowadays—just often enough to remind himself he could control it. The smoke tasted harsh, acrid in his lungs. But it cleared away the stench of burning buildings, burning flesh.

Geoffrey hunkered down beside him, his dark, narrow face streaked with soot. "You okay, Cougar?"

The man who'd been known as Michael Dowd nodded, taking another drag on the cigarette. "Right as rain."

"Cardiff said it was too early for you to be out in the field."

Michael's reply was short and obscene. "You know Ross," he added. "Always playing mother."

"He told me about the men on the island."

"Did he, now? You two must have had quite a little chat. Has he started fancying you?"

Geoffrey grinned, scratching his grimy face. "He's saving himself for you, love."

"Sod off, Geoffrey."

"Did he tell you who you got?" he continued, imperturbable.

"Two middle-level operatives and a boy," Michael said flatly. He'd had dreams about the boy. Nightmares, during his most recent stay in hospital, filled with hopeless what-ifs.

"It was Connor Dugan. Brother to the boy-o you took out at the UN."

Michael was adept at hiding his reactions. This time there was no need; he'd worked with and trusted Geoffrey Parkhurst for more years than he cared to admit. "It wasn't."

"Word of honor. You just happened to take out one of the most vicious little killers this side of Beirut. You remember the bomb he set that killed thirty-seven school kids? And then he put out the statement that they should be happy to die for the cause of a free Ireland?"

"And the massacre at Heathrow last summer," Michael added as he felt a black cloud begin to lift. "He was there,

I've seen the video tapes. I just didn't connect him with the boy on the island."

"So you've done the world a favor, pally."

Michael grinned sourly. "So who are you, my guardian angel? Come to cheer me when I'm feeling burned-out?"

"We all get burned-out at some point or another. Sometimes we come back, sometimes we don't. Looks to me like you're back, but I'm not sure if your heart's in it. And if it's not, that can be dangerous to all of us."

Michael reached for another cigarette. He seldom smoked more than two a day, but this had been a hell of a day. "The day you can't count on me, then I'll be gone. I don't do things halfway."

"That you don't, mate." Geoffrey looked over his shoulder at the burned out shell of the building. "You really think we got them all?"

"No."

Geoffrey swore. "Why not?"

"You've seen them. Which one do you think was giving the orders?"

"You've got a point. A bunch of dedicated fanatics, but none of them has the vision that some of their recent antics have required. And the ones we've got won't talk, that's for sure. So what's next?"

Michael leaned his head against the building and shut his eyes. He hated the smells, the noise, the stench of death and despair. And yet he'd stepped back into it so easily, breathing in that stench, moving with lethal accuracy. That should have told him, better than anything, that he couldn't turn his back on his way of life. Only death would free him. There was no room for a woman like Francey Neeley in his life. No room at all.

"What's next?" he echoed, staring at his smoke out of half-closed eyes. "Malta?"

"Malta?" Geoffrey said. "I thought they were traced to Gibraltar."

"That's what Ross tells me, but I was never known for being gullible. According to Ross, his operatives have told him the Cadre's planning something in the area of Gibraltar. But I've picked up a hint or two from my own sources, and my money's on Malta."

Geoffrey nodded. "Will he let you go?"

Michael grinned savagely. "Can he stop me?"

His old friend nodded. "I'd like to see his reaction when he finds out you've gone."

"No, you wouldn't. He can be quite nasty when he's in the mood. Watch yourself around him. Get yourself transferred as fast as you can."

Geoffrey laughed. "You're turning into an old maid, Cougar. I've got enough to worry about, with the Cadre's leader still loose. I can't waste time worrying about my boss's temper."

"Your funeral," Michael said absently. And then his gaze focused, sharpened, on Geoffrey's narrow face. "And it just might be," he added.

"I'm invincible," Geoffrey said. "I've been in the business as long as you have, and I still get a kick out of it. Nothing's ever going to get to me."

"There's a difference between Malta and Gibraltar, you realize," Ross Cardiff said, his face screwed up as if he were tasting something nasty.

That was one of the things Michael disliked most about Ross. His sour expression, his whine, and the fact that he never swore. Anyone else might say there was a hell of a difference between the two islands, but not Ross.

"I'm aware of my geography," Michael said blandly. Ever since Ross Cardiff had been put in charge he'd had little recourse against the man's pettiness. His only act of aggression was to never let Ross know just how much he despised the man. For his pettiness, his narrow-mindedness, his bloody stupidity that had cost people their lives.

"Yes, I forgot," Ross murmured. "You went to Willingborough. They teach young gentlemen such things, don't they?"

Michael allowed himself a small, savage smile. He'd gone to the prestigious school on scholarship, a working-class boy who'd had to use his fists to even survive the first year. But Ross persisted in thinking of him as part of the affluent upper classes, and Michael allowed him to do so. Knowing that it drove Ross crazy was one of the small indulgences he allowed himself.

"They do," he said. "I still think Gibraltar's a blind."

"And you think I'm fool enough to fall for it? It doesn't say much for your confidence in my ability to lead."

Michael wisely said nothing. He'd never known anyone possessing fewer leadership abilities than Ross Cardiff, who'd achieved his current status through brownnosing and the general bloody-mindedness of the bureaucracy, and now he and people like Geoffrey Parkhurst paid the price for it.

Instead he shrugged. It had been six days since he'd left Geoffrey in Northern Ireland, six days in London to consider his current theory. He wasn't about to apprise Ross of the details. He didn't trust the man's discretion any more than he trusted his intelligence. "It's just a hunch, Ross," he said, trying to sound ameliorating. "You don't need me in Gib, and you know it. You've got enough people there already, people who know the layout, know the drill. Let me see what I can come up with in Malta."

"And if I refuse?"

Michael kept a rein on his temper. "What possible reason would you have for refusing? I'm at loose ends right now. I wasn't due back for another month. Let me have that time to see what I can stir up. Or tell me why not."

Ross's small-featured face was a picture of frustration, and Michael wondered for a moment if the man was hiding something. He'd never been good at keeping things secret, a serious drawback in intelligence work. Michael never

FREE BOOKS!

FREE GIFTS!

PLAY THE "LUCKY 7" SLOT MACHINE GAME!

AND YOU COULD GET FREE BOOKS, A FREE HEART-SHAPED GLASS BOX AND A SURPRISE GIFT!

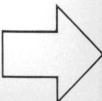

NO COST! NO OBLIGATION TO BUY!
NO PURCHASE NECESSARY!

PLAY "LUCKY 7"
AND GET AS MANY AS SIX FREE GIFTS...

HOW TO PLAY:

1. With a coin, carefully scratch off the silver box at the right. This makes you eligible to receive two or more free books, and possibly other gifts, depending on what is revealed beneath the scratch-off area.

2. You'll receive brand-new Silhouette Intimate Moments® novels. When you return this card, we'll send you the books and gifts you qualify for *absolutely free!*

3. If we don't hear from you, every month, we'll send you 4 additional novels to read and enjoy. You can return them and owe nothing but if you decide to keep them, you'll pay only $2.96* per book, a saving of 43¢ each off the cover price. There is **no** extra charge for postage and handling. There are **no** hidden extras.

4. When you join the Silhouette Reader Service™, you'll get our subscribers'-only newsletter, as well as additional free gifts from time to time just for being a subscriber.

5. You must be completely satisfied. You may cancel at any time simply by sending us a note or a shipping statement marked ''cancel'' or by returning any shipment to us at our cost.

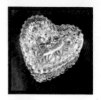

This lovely heart-shaped box is richly detailed with cut-glass decorations, perfect for holding a precious memento or keepsake—and it's yours absolutely free when you accept our no-risk offer.

PLAY "LUCKY 7"

**Just scratch off the silver box with a coin.
Then check below to see which gifts you get.**

YES! I have scratched off the silver box. Please send me all the gifts for which I qualify. I understand I am under no obligation to purchase any books, as explained on the opposite page.

240 CIS AEQW
(U-SIL-IM-06/92)

NAME

ADDRESS   APT

CITY   STATE   ZIP

7	7	7	WORTH FOUR FREE BOOKS, FREE HEART-SHAPED GLASS BOX AND MYSTERY BONUS
🍒	🍒	🍒	WORTH FOUR FREE BOOKS AND MYSTERY BONUS
●	●	●	WORTH THREE FREE BOOKS
🔔	🔔	🍒	WORTH TWO FREE BOOKS

SILHOUETTE ''NO RISK'' GUARANTEE

DETACH AND MAIL CARD TODAY

BUSINESS REPLY MAIL
FIRST CLASS MAIL   PERMIT NO. 717   BUFFALO, NY

POSTAGE WILL BE PAID BY ADDRESSEE

SILHOUETTE READER SERVICE
3010 WALDEN AVE
PO BOX 1867
BUFFALO NY 14240-9952

NO POSTAGE
NECESSARY
IF MAILED
IN THE
UNITED STATES

trusted anyone or anything completely, even his own instincts, but for the moment he put his doubts on hold. He had no reason to doubt Ross, it was just that something didn't quite fit together, and that was probably attributable to his general incompetency.

"Go, then," Ross said, literally throwing up his small, well-manicured hands. "You're right—we don't need you. You're not indispensable, you know, Mr. James Bond-complex. You're an agent, no better, no more important, than a raft of other agents. It would do you well to remember that."

"I'll remember," he said, his voice expressionless, and he had the pleasure of seeing Ross clench his small white teeth.

"Be in touch," he snapped, his voice his characteristic whine. "When you come up empty, you can take your next assignment."

His interview was over. Michael got to his feet, careful not to appear too fit. In fact, he was almost back to full strength; the last bout of surgery had been just a minor inconvenience. But he wasn't ready for Ross to know that. "I'll do that," he said. "Everything all right with the Neeley woman?" He kept his voice diffident. He didn't particularly expect to fool Ross; what the man lacked in political savvy he more than made up for in acuity when it came to people's real interests, real needs.

"Just fine." Ross, too, could be bland. "When will you be taking off?"

"I've got tickets for today."

"And what if I'd said no?"

Michael only smiled.

"Too bad, though," Ross murmured as Michael limped to the door. "You'll miss the funeral."

Michael glanced back at him, his hand on the polished brass doorknob. "Anyone I know?"

Ross smiled, a small, smug little grin, tinged with the appropriate regret. "Didn't I mention it? I believe you

knew him as Geoffrey Parkhurst. Not his real name, of
course. He ran afoul of one of the Cadre's mines. A
shame.''

"Yes," said Michael dully, wishing he could smash
Ross's tiny teeth down his throat. "A real shame."

It was astonishing to Francey how little had changed
during the time she was gone. Within a day her apartment,
including her poor neglected refrigerator, was back to normal. The cockroaches and silverfish stopped their midnight scuttling as the battle waned back into the occasional
skirmish; the neighborhood, always oblivious to her presence, was equally oblivious to her absence and return.

Even work hadn't changed. She'd considered calling in,
saying she was never coming back. After all, that was where
Patrick and Caitlin Dugan had come into her life.

Robin Hood Associates had been created by Francey and
several of her friends from Sarah Lawrence to take from the
rich and give to the poor, the needy, the deserving. Francey had the undeniable ability to cajole large amounts of
money out of very wealthy corporations and individuals for
the benefit of worthy causes, and she'd put that skill to
good use for people who deserved it. And then for the
Cadre. She had nothing else to keep her busy, and a penance to pay. Money diverted into Patrick Dugan's bloody
coffers could have gone somewhere else, and she'd been
part and parcel of that highly successful fund-raising. She
needed to atone.

She'd thought A Peace of Green had sounded like such
a noble organization, dedicated to bringing sanity and calm
back to the strife-torn world of Northern Ireland. It hadn't
been her job to check the bona fides. The very expensive
investigative firm Robin Hood Associates hired was supposed to do that, and A Peace of Green had passed with
flying colors. Patrick and Caitlin had covered their tracks
well.

That was one more thing that had galled her while she lay in the sun on St. Anne. The fact that she'd raised all that money for a sham organization, money that had gone for guns and terrorism instead of peace initiatives. She knew perfectly well that she'd been suspected of collaborating with the Cadre. After all, she was very good at her job, and the money she'd raised had been considerable. She was also half-Irish herself, even though she didn't even remember the Byronic poet her mother had quickly married and just as quickly divorced. He'd drowned when she was three years old, and she'd never even seen a photograph of him. She'd tried to explain that to the investigators, but it had taken her cousin Daniel to convince them. At least, she'd hoped he had.

But there were still organizations in need, people who didn't know how to coax grants and donations from the various fat cats. And at least it was something she could do, something that kept her mind off herself. And her apartment had never felt so empty.

The tempo of the city began to take its toll. She threw herself into fund-raising—an auction for the AIDS Connection, a costume ball for the homeless. She hadn't been too thrilled with that particular idea. The thought of overdressed socialites swilling champagne to benefit the brutally poor bordered on the hypocritical, but she was overruled.

She even accepted her most recent client after some initial revulsion. There could be no connection between the Children of Eire, an organization dedicated to improving the quality of life for the children of Northern Ireland caught in the crossfire, and the murderous Cadre. She had the investigators check twice before she was finally satisfied.

But once she accepted Liam and Siobhan O'Malley, there was no stopping her. She worked nonstop, knowing perfectly well why she was doing it. As some sort of penance to the children and the people who were victims of the

Cadre's fanaticism. She'd believed in what Patrick had wanted, she truly had. She was simply revolted by his means.

She fell into bed at night exhausted, too tired to think about Patrick, about St. Anne. About Michael Dowd. It was only when she slept that the dreams came. Some slow and hot and blatantly erotic, some fast and dark and dangerous. Sex and violence, intertwined. Both stemming from Michael Dowd.

In the daytime she could laugh at what little wisps she could remember, shaking off the lingering emotions. Michael Dowd was an English schoolteacher, a man of middle-class values and, when he chose to use it, world-class charm. A harmless, gentle man.

But that still didn't explain the three dead men on Baby Jerome.

She'd been back in New York for almost a month, but this hot July night was different. She came home alone, as always, but she stopped at the corner and bought herself a chilled split of French champagne. Ignoring the messages on her answering machine, ignoring her mail, she proceeded to drink every last drop, toasting her monumental decision. That very morning she'd gone through with what some people might call rash, ill-informed and downright stupid. She'd liquidated as much of her comfortable trust fund as she could and turned it over to the pathetically grateful representatives of the Children of Eire.

She still had more money than she knew what to do with, but for once in her life she felt free. Gloriously unencumbered by inherited money that she didn't deserve, by guilt that she might have deserved. She drank champagne, kicked off her shoes and danced around her apartment. And when she finally fell into bed, she dreamed once more of Michael Dowd.

Chapter 10

Francey looked up into his eyes. Eyes she knew well, warm, loving blue eyes, open and honest, gentle and caring. And yet they weren't the same eyes. The warm blue was icy now, with tiny pinpoints of rage in the dark center. There was no affable grin on his face. No crinkling smile, no tenderness. She was looking up into the face of a dangerous man. One with a hard mouth, shuttered eyes and a face that was narrow and still. This was no schoolteacher recuperating. This was someone as fully dangerous as Patrick Dugan had ever been.

He was lying stretched out on top of her, and yet she felt only the weight of his eyes staring into hers. And the weight of his mouth settling on hers, draining her soul, taking everything from her until she herself was weightless, floating, lost in some feathery dream world where nothing existed but the warmth of his flesh and hers, touching, heating, igniting, flaming into a flashpoint of brilliant light...

She awoke with a start, a scream of some lost emotion still rattling in her lungs. She was covered with sweat in her air-conditioned apartment, lying sideways across her double bed, and the pillows and covers were strewn around the room. Then she heard it again, the shrill ring of her telephone.

Her digital clock said 3:47. People didn't call at 3:47 a.m. unless it was to announce a disaster. She lay very still, feeling her heart pound against her chest, letting the panic dance over her skin. She didn't want to hear bad news. Her answering machine was still on; it would pick up after the fourth ring. The question was, would the next ring be the fourth?

The phone rang again, and there was no answering click from her machine. Must have been ring number three. If she could just control herself, let it ring one more time, the machine would take care of the problem, and she wouldn't have to deal with it until she was ready.

The wait seemed endless. Francey was fully awake by now, sitting cross-legged on her mattress, her arms wrapped tightly around her chemise-clad body, rocking back and forth, and for a moment she was terrified that whoever had called her had given up, hung up, leaving her forever in limbo.

The apartment was filled with the noisy buzz of silence. She could hear her air conditioner laboring away in the living room, the busy hum of her refrigerator, the ever-present noise from the street below. And then the phone rang again.

She dived for it, knocking it off the nightstand onto the floor and the pillows beside the bed, following it down with a thud, cursing beneath her breath as she first brought the receiver to her face. "Hullo?" Her voice was hoarse, strained, a desperate whisper as she waited for the voice of doom.

"Francey." One word, one voice. It was all she needed.

She started to cry. Tears were pouring down her face, and the more she tried to speak, the faster they flowed, choking her.

From miles, oceans, away, Michael's voice came back to her. "Francey?" he said again, his voice alarmed. "Are you all right?"

By sheer force of will she pulled herself together, wiping the tears from her face as she huddled on the floor in the darkness. "Michael," she said, and her voice was only faintly tremulous. "I'm fine. I just didn't expect to hear from you."

"Lord, what time is it? I woke you up, didn't I? I didn't think. Let me call you back...."

"Don't hang up! Please, Michael..."

"I won't." He sounded so calm, so sure, so safe, on the other end of the line. She closed her eyes, wishing she could touch him.

She shuddered, so alone, and then sat up a little straighter, leaning against the side of the bed. "Tell me about your life," she said, back in control. "You must be out of the hospital—you couldn't sound so healthy otherwise."

"I was in and out in a matter of days. It was a simple matter for them to patch me up. Then I went up to Whipdale House for a stay with my mother and sisters, and I've been back at school for the summer session for the past three weeks. We just won our first soccer match. We were out celebrating at the local pub, and I suddenly needed to hear your voice."

"It sounds as if your life is back to normal."

There was a certain wryness in his words. "As normal as it ever gets, given my life-style. What about yours?"

She remembered the darkness of the night on Baby Jerome, how her bedtime story with its horrors differed from the middle-class English comfort of his, and she wished for a moment that she'd never told him. That she'd kept up with the pretense that she was just a young woman at loose ends, spending time at her cousin's Caribbean estate, not someone running away from pain, from terror, from life.

But she couldn't take it back, and her past had almost killed an innocent man. A man who had come to matter far too much. "Actually, things are going quite well," she said, wondering if she should tell him what she'd done today, then dismissing the notion. "I've gone back to work. Things are hot and busy. I've been doing my best to put things behind me."

"Good for you. Looking back is a waste of time. There's nothing you can do about it at this point. Better to look forward." There was something he wasn't saying. Something in his voice, beneath the light, charming tone, that sent tendrils of alarm through her.

"Michael, are you certain you're all right?" she asked, suddenly anxious.

"Right as rain," he said firmly. "Listen, the boys are raising a fuss, and if I don't get back to them they'll probably spray ginger beer all over the waitress. I just needed to make certain you were all right."

"I'm fine," she said. "Better for hearing your voice. When am I going to see you again?"

The hesitation on the other end of the line answered her better than his evasion. "Sooner or later. It's a busy time for me, after having missed so much. And I don't think I'm in the mood for traveling. I've missed England too much."

"I could come over there."

"I don't think that would be a good idea."

It was said very gently. She hadn't realized pain could be delivered with such a soft touch. She absorbed the blow, shivering slightly.

"You're probably right," she said finally, her voice as artificially cool as the air-conditioned apartment. "It's part of everything that I need to put behind me. Get on with my life and all that. I'm glad to hear you're well, and I wish you the best of luck in the future, Michael. You're a very sweet, gentle man, and I'm sorry if I embarrassed you. I know you'll have a good life. I can't think of anyone who deserves it more, and—"

"Stop it." His words were stripped of all charm and calm, and he sounded bleak, as lost as she felt. "Don't do this to yourself, Francey. Don't do this to me. You don't understand all the ramifications."

"You're right, I don't. Because no one answers my questions, no one is honest with me. I'm trying to be mature about this, Michael. You've made it clear you don't want to be bothered with me again, and I'm accepting that as gracefully as I can. We went through an intense, emotional experience when our lives were at stake and ended up imagining there was more of a connection between us than there really was. Or at least I did. But I'm a big girl now. I know how things work, and I can—"

"Shut up." His voice was savage. She could hear the noise in the background, British schoolboys out on a celebratory lark. She closed her eyes in the darkness, wishing she were there beside him to see his face, to touch him, to try to understand what he wasn't telling her.

"What do you want from me, Michael?" she asked finally, her voice deceptively even.

"Nothing. I want nothing from you, I want a thousand things for you. I want you to have a good life, Francey. Away from death and terror and lies, from people who aren't who they say they are and never will be. Away from me."

"Michael..."

He broke the connection, the transatlantic buzz loud in her ear. She stared at the phone, willing him to be there. She could see him, the cozy English pub around him, uniformed, ruddy-cheeked schoolboys surrounding him, everything as safe and eternal as England herself. And she wondered what in God's name he was talking about.

Michael stared at the phone in mute frustration, rubbing a hand across his face. He'd been crazy to give in to temptation, another sign that his time was running out. He glanced out beyond the beaded curtain to the bar beyond, the babble of a dozen different languages surrounding him. He was suffering from jet lag, a hangover and a need so powerful that it threatened to wipe out his good sense. He needed Francey Neeley; his soul yearned for her. And if he had any spark of decency left within his battered carcass, he would never go near her again.

He'd meant to say goodbye. But it hadn't come out that way. He didn't want to hurt her, but he would rather end up wounding her than killing her. He'd meant to be cool and brisk. But she'd gotten through his front so quickly, so devastatingly, that he knew he didn't dare contact her again. She had too much pride to try to contact him, and even if her pride failed her, she had no idea how to find him. She would be safe, whether she liked it or not. Safe from the Patrick Dugans of this world. Safe from men like him.

He pushed himself away from the counter and, wandered into the bar, squinting through the heavy cigarette smoke. There was a woman waiting for him, someone with information he needed—if he was willing to meet her price. She was very beautiful, very experienced, very deadly. His kind of woman. There was no room in his life for the Francey Neeleys of this world. If he expected to survive for much longer, he'd best remember that. And not waste his time regretting it.

For a long time Francey didn't move. She sat on the floor, hugging a pillow against her, dry eyed, heartsick and confused. "I don't know what's wrong with me," she whispered out loud to the cockroaches. "Nothing seems to make sense anymore."

The cockroaches didn't answer. She had a headache from too much champagne, a stomachache from too much emotion, and all she wanted to do was crawl back into bed and sleep.

But sleep and security and what dubious peace of mind she'd attained had been ripped from her by Michael's voice. She'd thought she could forget about him, forget those ten days on the islands. Forget those moments by the lagoon.

She knew better now. Michael might want that chapter in his life closed—she couldn't. Not without seeing him once more. She wasn't going to be patted on the head and told to get on with her life. She'd *heard* him, beneath the easy charm. She'd heard his need, as raw as her own. And she damned well wasn't going to forget it.

She was going after him. Willingborough was a well-known boys' school in the south of England; she would fly to London and hire a car. If he could look her in the eye and tell her things were better left as they were, maybe she could accept it. If she saw him surrounded by the accoutrements of English country life, maybe her confusion would fade.

First she would need to book the first flight available. There was six hours difference; if she got a plane out by that evening, she would arrive the next morning and be at Willingborough by evening.

She crawled back up onto the bed, shivering slightly in the too cool artificial air, and started making plans, mentally ticking off all the things she would have to accomplish before making a clean getaway. It wasn't until she was almost asleep that the niggling little discrepancy hit her. Michael had told her that he had taken his schoolboy soccer team to a pub to celebrate the victory they'd just won. According to her calculations, it had been nearly ten o'clock in the morning, far too early for a pub to open, much less for a soccer game to have been played.

Keep away from lies, he'd told her. Keep away from men like me. She hadn't known what he meant; she still didn't. She only knew that was the one thing she couldn't do.

"I'm sorry, Miss, but I'm Michael Dowd," the heavy-set, red-faced man informed her. "I've taught here at Willingborough for the past fifteen years, and I've never been in an auto accident. Someone must have been pulling your leg.''

Francey simply stared at the man. He had thinning blond hair combed back over a sunburned scalp, a petulant expression in his slightly protuberant eyes, and bad teeth. She couldn't blame him for his obvious irritation, she thought numbly. She must seem like a madwoman.

She shook her head slightly, hoping the scrambled picture would come into focus. But the wrong man was still in front of her, glaring at her, and the stately environs of Willingborough loomed menacingly behind him.

"I don't suppose you have a mother, three sisters and two brothers, and live in Yorkshire," she said, already knowing the answer.

"One brother, parents both dead, and I come from the Midlands. Someone's played a nasty trick on you, miss. Particularly if you've come all the way from the States to meet this liar."

Francey was feeling no emotion whatsoever. The combination of jet lag and a long drive across England, only to be faced with the semi-irate stranger, was too much for her. Her emotions, even her brain, simply shut down. "I needed a vacation anyway," she said vaguely. "I'm sorry that I bothered you." She began to turn away, but the real Michael Dowd appeared suddenly contrite.

"You look all done in. Why don't you come in for a cup of tea or something? My wife could fix you something to eat."

"No, thank you. I'd better get moving."

"But where are you going?"

If it was an odd question from a stranger she didn't realize that until later. She answered without thinking. "Back to London. To ask some questions, see what I can find out."

"Don't you think you'd be better off just leaving things be? It's none of my business, of course, but I imagine the man who gave you a phony name doesn't want to be found.''

She looked back at him, resolution forming in her heart. "Perhaps he doesn't. But I don't like being lied to. I'm going to keep looking until I find him. And when I do, I'm going to want some answers."

Michael Dowd looked as if he wanted to argue with her further; then he shut his mouth. "I'd advise against it," he said. "But it's your funeral. Best of luck, then."

She nodded absently, heading back to the car she'd barely mastered. "My funeral," she echoed. "It just might be." She drove out along the spacious drive of Willingborough, with its century-old oaks and chestnuts, its stately grandeur, but her eyes could barely see the road. She drove mindlessly, heading back toward London. Until suddenly everything was awash, and she could barely see. She pulled over, wrestling with the unaccustomed right-hand steering wheel, and put the car into Park. And realized it wasn't raining after all. She was crying.

She wiped her face, but the tears kept coming, an unstoppable flow, and finally she couldn't fight them anymore. Leaning forward, she put her head on the steering wheel, clutching it with her hands, and wept.

The real Michael Dowd lumbered down the empty halls of Willingborough. The little swine were off reading their girlie magazines, blasting rock and roll through their adolescent eardrums. There was no one around to overhear.

He dialed the number quickly and efficiently. "Cardiff," he said when a familiar voice answered. "You were right. She showed up."

"Unfortunate," Ross Cardiff said at the other end. "But I knew she would, I just knew it. What did she say when you told her who you were?"

"She didn't believe me, of course. But I managed to convince her. She looked as if she'd been hit by a bomb.

Just sort of mumbled something and said she was heading back to London."

"Do you think she'll have the sense to drop it?" Cardiff's voice was its usual nasal whine.

"I doubt it. You know Americans. And she had that 'hell hath no fury like a woman scorned' expression on her face. You know the effect he usually has on women. She'll probably walk barefoot over coals till she tracks him down. She said she was going to ask a lot of questions when she got back to London. She could make a great deal of trouble."

"Curse him," Ross fumed. "And curse her, too. He swore he hadn't boffed her. I should have known better. Even on his death bed he couldn't keep his pants on. He probably went through half the nursing staff while he was in a coma."

The real Michael Dowd grimaced on the other end, knowing full well the real cause of Ross Cardiff's fury. "I couldn't say, sir. All I know is she looked shocked, angry and determined. She said she didn't like being lied to."

"I suppose there's no need to overreact. After all, how much trouble can she cause? It's not as if she has anything to go on."

"She has a photograph, sir."

"Impossible! He couldn't have gotten that soft!" Cardiff exploded. "How did it happen?"

"I couldn't say. Obviously he didn't know it was being taken. From the looks of it, it was done at some restaurant in the islands. But it looks like the Cougar, boss. Anyone who knows him would recognize him."

There was a dead silence on the other end, and he could just imagine the expression on Cardiff's weaselly little face. "Then I suppose we're just going to have to do something about this little problem, aren't we, Dowd?"

"Not me, sir. I've got twenty-seven young buggers here to keep me busy. I've done what I can."

"For now," Cardiff said, and his voice was chilling. "I'll get back to you later."

Michael Dowd hung up the phone, staring at it for a moment. Ross Cardiff was a bad man to cross, a petty, back-stabbing little bureaucrat who thought nothing of bending the rules to support his own shortsighted agenda. He paid extremely well and asked no questions, and the real Michael Dowd had always appreciated a little tax-free income. But he was glad he was out of the line of fire in this one.

The girl was going to be right sorry she'd ever come across Ross Cardiff. And she was going to regret even more the time she'd spent with the man who'd appropriated Michael Dowd's name.

Still and all, it wasn't his problem. And if an American tourist was found floating in the Thames in the next few days, he would skip over that bit in the newspaper and concentrate on the tits and bum in the centerfold.

Still and all, it was a hell of a life.

Of all his recent persona, the man sometimes known as Cougar thought, Charlie Bisselthwaite was one of the most annoying. He'd been somewhat envious of the Michael Dowd he'd created, with his basic decency, his solid background, his hopes for the future. Charlie Bisselthwaite was nothing more than an irritating fop.

He squinted up into the bright sunlight. He'd been on Malta for more than a week now, cultural attaché to Sir Henry Putnam, the blustery ambassador, a nothing kind of job that required no more than a decent social grace and appearances at various cocktail parties. Occasionally he might have to squire around someone's angular spinster daughter, but the rest of the time was his, as long as he was discreet about it.

The problem with discretion, of course, was that it was hard for information to find you. In the week he'd been in place he'd put out tentative feelers, showing up in out-of-the-way places, asking casual questions, and so far he'd come up with nothing. Far less than had been apparent during his cursory stop on Gibraltar.

Which had only convinced him further. The Cadre wouldn't leave an obvious trail. Ross was going to have his own troop of goons tromping all over Gibraltar, looking for terrorists, and they would most likely come up with nothing more dangerous than a few Barbary apes.

On his end, he'd just begun to come up with a few stray pieces of information. Enough to keep him going. Enough to keep him so busy that he couldn't even think about Francey Neeley.

At least he knew she was getting on with her life. He'd kept tabs on her before his rash, late-night phone call. She'd gone back to work, had even gone to a few parties. In another month or so she would forget about a man named Michael Dowd and settle down into the safe little life she'd been born to. As long as he kept away from her, away from the telephone, she would be fine.

He only hoped he had the self-control to keep his promise to himself. It was in the middle of the night that it hit him—the remembered scent of her skin, the way her eyes lit up, the softness of her mouth. And nothing could wipe it away; he just had to sweat it out and hope the next day he would forget again.

He had a message waiting for him when he let himself into the villa he was renting on the south end of the island. He made himself a drink first, not certain he wanted to talk to Scott. Scott was stationed in New York—he'd had him watch over Francey from a discreet distance, just to make certain she was all right.

On the one hand, she might be in trouble. On the other, Scott might just be checking in with the latest report. Maybe he would tell him that she was seeing someone. Sleeping with someone. Ready to get married.

He drained his whiskey and water in one gulp, glancing at his reflection in the mirror. The brown hair suited him, and so did the tan. He was getting used to the brown contact lenses—he'd used them often enough before, and he had finally begun to put the weight back on his gaunt body. The man Francey had known on the island no longer existed. He needed to remember that.

"Bad news about your little friend, chum," Scott said flatly when he finally reached him.

He was used to controlling his reactions. He ignored the sudden stab of panic. "Is she all right?" he managed in a calm drawl.

"She left for London more than a week ago, and on Saturday she went missing. There are a couple of possibilities."

"I'm waiting."

"One, that she went looking for you. Someone fitting her description was seen outside Willingborough, but Michael Dowd said he hadn't seen her."

"What's the other possibility?" His voice was terse, strained.

"Before she left she liquidated a large portion of her personal fortune. I don't think you're going to want to know what she did with it."

"Don't make me ask."

"The Children of Eire. She signed it all over to them, after working on fund-raising during the bulk of last month. And you know as well as I do what the COE is a front for."

"The Cadre." He wouldn't believe it. Despite strong cause for doubt, he'd believed her, trusted her. He couldn't believe she was part of that nest of vipers. Not after all this time. It just didn't add up.

"It would fit in with her disappearance. She could have gone over to join them."

"Then why was she near Willingborough? And why did Dowd lie about it?"

"You know who you'll have to ask about that, old man. Cardiff himself. I can't do any more for you."

"You've done enough, Scott. I owe you."

There was a momentary hesitation on the other end. "You think she's okay, Cougar? I got sort of fond of her while I was watching her. Seemed like a nice girl."

"I don't know. I damned well mean to find out, if I have to beat it out of Cardiff."

"And if she's gone to join the Cadre?"

It was a possibility too bleak to even consider. "Then I'll find her when I find the others." And God have mercy on her soul.

Chapter 11

The cell was tiny, foul and terrifying. Francey sat on the edge of the narrow pallet, making herself very small. The voices were all around her, speaking in languages she couldn't understand, Spanish, Arabic, German. And she was frightened.

So very, very frightened. How had it happened? Somehow she'd been thrust into a maze of contradictions and lies that had brought her to this place of horrors. Just days before she'd walked into a sunny Spanish bar. And ended up here.

"I'm looking for a man," she had said, trying to cover the faint quaver of uneasiness in her voice.

The man behind the bar ignored her. She tried again, her voice a little louder, a little shakier. "I'm looking for a man, *señor*," she said.

The bartender stared at her out of black, expressionless eyes. She knew he spoke English as well as Spanish—the sign on the bar informed her of as much. In the two days she'd been wandering around Spain, she'd discovered that

most people were multilingual, and if they didn't understand English, she could just manage to communicate in
her schoolgirl French. The tiny port of Mariz was her third
Spanish city in two days, the smallest, after Malaga and
Sevilla, and the least hopeful.

The bartender spread a meaty hand over the crowded
bar. "Take your pick," he said, turning away.

She had the nerve to reach out and catch his arm. "No,
I'm looking for a particular man. My cousin. He has a big
boat. . . ."

"Lots of big boats," the bartender said, nodding toward the shining blue of the Mediterranean beyond the
grimy, fly-specked window.

"His name is Daniel Travers. He's my cousin. . . ."

A man standing too close beside her sniggered. "That's
what they all say. If you can't find this 'cousin' of yours, I
can get you plenty of work. There are lots of very rich
cousins out there, and I won't expect too much of a cut."

She glared at the man, giving him her best patrician stare.
The man simply shrugged. "Or you can make do with one
of us." He ran a filthy hand down her bare arm, and she
shivered. "A tourist would know better than to come into
a place like this. Why should a man with a boat be here?
The rich ones go to better places than this."

She yanked her arm away, stumbling backward into a
table, knocking over several bottles of beer on disgruntled
customers. It happened quickly, too quickly. Someone
grabbed her purse, another swung a punch, and somewhere a woman screamed. Francey dived for her purse,
landing on her knees on the dusty floor, her purse clutched
in her hands. Landed in front of two pairs of uniformed
legs.

She looked up, way up, into the shuttered expressions of
two members of the local police. They didn't move, merely
stared down at her as she struggled to her feet.

"That one," the bartender was suddenly more voluble. "She came in here, causing trouble with my customers. Said she was looking for a rich boat owner."

Francey glared at him in frustration. "Not *a* rich boat owner," she corrected him. "I'm looking for my cousin. I was told he was somewhere off the Costa Blanca, and I thought..."

"Your passport, *señorita*," one policeman said in a clipped voice.

She considered arguing, then thought better of it. She opened her purse, reaching in for her papers, when the man plucked it out of her hands.

"Hey!" she protested, grabbing for it, but the man simply knocked her backward onto the floor.

She was too shocked to move. She simply sat there, staring up, as the policeman pulled out a neatly wrapped white package from her capacious purse. A package she'd never seen before in her life.

"That's not mine," she protested.

This time they didn't leave her on the floor. The other man hauled her upright, hard hands digging into her arms. "That's what they all say," he muttered. "You Americans come here to buy drugs because you think we're fools. You'll discover we don't take kindly to drug smugglers."

"Drugs?" Francey shrieked. "I haven't—"

"Bring her along, Sandoval," the first man ordered. "If she gives you any trouble, silence her."

"I want to speak to a lawyer," she protested as he began dragging her from the bar. "I want to speak to the American ambassador."

"The nearest consulate is in Valencia. Word will get to them eventually. As for a lawyer, one will be appointed for you. Unfortunately most of our lawyers do not speak English."

"This is ridiculous!" Francey cried as she was shoved out into the blinding white sunlight. "I haven't done anything wrong."

"That will be for the courts to decide. Until that time, you will be a guest of the local government."

"For how long?"

Sandoval opened the back door of the patrol car and shoved her inside. "Spanish justice moves slowly, but it moves very surely. If I were you, I wouldn't expect to be going anywhere for a long, long time." He threw her purse in after her, slamming the door.

She yanked at the door handle, but it was securely locked. The car started with a jerk, tearing off into the late-afternoon sunlight, and Francey swiveled around, looking at the bar behind her. Someone was standing out front, someone she hadn't noticed before. A short man, well dressed, his face obscured by dark glasses. Suddenly she remembered the man on the beach on Baby Jerome, the man who'd arrived with Daniel and disappeared with Michael. She was certain it was the same man, and then he disappeared from sight as the police car screeched around a narrow corner.

Francey sat back, trembling. "Calm down," she whispered to herself. "This is all a dreadful mistake. Things will be cleared up in no time." Then she looked down at the ransacked purse in her lap and wasn't so certain.

She pawed through it, looking for some clue as to who would do such a thing to her. Everything was still intact, her wallet, her passport, her aspirin and her makeup. Funny that they hadn't checked the pill bottle to see if she were smuggling contraband that way. She opened her wallet, looking in the secret compartment for the picture of Michael, wanting to touch it for strength, for anger, for some sort of courage.

It was gone.

The enormity of it hit her then. The drugs in her purse weren't some hideous mistake. The man standing outside the bar wasn't an idle tourist. And chances were Daniel Travers was on the other side of the world, and the obscure messages she'd been receiving at her hotels were nothing more than a wild-goose chase, meant to bring her to this current crisis.

She'd heard about foreign prisons and the Spanish attitudes toward drugs. And she had no doubt at all that she was going to be out of reach for a long time.

She sat back, numb with the horror of it. The men in the front seat were solid, implacable. Not the sort to listen to convoluted tales, particularly when she didn't even know what she was talking about. Was this the work of the Cadre? Was Michael part and parcel of them? If so, why had he saved her life? Why had Daniel seemed to know him?

But Daniel also knew the man who'd set her up. Maybe Daniel was nearer than she thought, part of this scheme. Maybe Michael, or whatever his real name was, was part of it, too.

She shivered in the stifling heat, forcing herself to be calm. She needed to be very reasonable, very patient. They couldn't just take an American citizen and lock her away with no lawyer, no trial, no hope of a quick release.

Could they?

It took him three days to track down Daniel Travers, two days longer than normal, because Travers obviously didn't want to be found. The *True Blue* was anchored near Athens, its radio communications conveniently out of commission as it rode the Aegean under the bright sun.

He posed as a United States customs agent, using his best, flattest American accent to get a ride out on an official boat and then talk his way aboard. He left his real counterpart to argue with Travers's captain, while he went in search of the reclusive millionaire himself.

He found him a darkened room, watching an old Michael Caine movie on a big screen TV. He entered the room silently, sneaking up behind the old man and putting the barrel of his Beretta to his temple before Travers even knew he was there.

"Where is she, old man?" he asked softly.

Travers froze, and in the darkened, air-conditioned room sweat broke out on his wrinkled skin. "Who are you?" he gasped. "Who are you talking about?"

Michael decided, quite sensibly, that if he scared the old man into a heart attack he wasn't going to find out anything. Lowering the gun, he moved into the man's line of vision. "Where is she?" he said again. "Don't ask who I'm talking about—you know perfectly well. And don't make me ask again. I'm not in a good mood."

Travers's shoulders relaxed marginally as he recognized the intruder. "Michael," he said. "Or is it Charlie?"

"Take your pick. It can also be Nigel, James, Erik, Lester or Arvin. Anything but Cougar."

"I can't imagine you as an Arvin."

"Old man . . ." His voice held a wealth of warning.

Travers leaned over and flicked off the big screen television, plunging the room into momentary darkness. Michael remained alert, ready to kill the man if he made a wrong move. A moment later he flicked a switch, flooding the paneled room with light. "I don't know where she is," he said wearily. "I only wish I did."

"Is she with the Cadre?"

"Good God, no! Why would you think such a thing?" Travers was aghast.

"She turned over a large sum of her money to a cover organization. Maybe she wasn't the innocent victim she pretended to be," he said evenly.

"You spent more than a week with her," Travers said. "How can you believe that?"

"Old man, I can believe anything of anybody. If she's not with the Cadre, where the hell is she? Don't try to fob me off. You'd be rotten at intelligence work—you can't even begin to fool me."

"I'm telling you the truth, Michael. I don't know. He wouldn't tell me."

Michael lowered his gun carefully, still ready to use it at a second's notice. "Cardiff," he said flatly.

Travers nodded miserably. "She was asking a lot of questions, Michael. She went looking for you at Willingborough, and then at the hospital you'd mentioned. She even had a photograph of you."

"Impossible. There hasn't been a picture taken of me since I was in the army."

"She's got one, apparently. Or she had one. I gather they got it away from her."

"Who are 'they,' Travers?" His voice was alarmingly gentle, and Travers blanched.

"I've tried to get Cardiff to tell me. He just said he's put her someplace where she can't cause any trouble. As soon as things are settled with the Cadre, he'll see that she's released. He promised me."

"I see." Michael dropped down on one of the leather-covered banquettes, his gun held loosely in his hand. "And where is Cardiff right now, Daniel?"

The old man was no fool. He kept an uneasy eye on Michael's hands. "I believe he's in Gibraltar."

"Then we're just going to have to go see him, aren't we? If he won't answer your questions, I'm willing to bet he'll answer mine. How fast does this tub go?"

"She's surprisingly speedy, as a matter of fact."

Michael smiled thinly. "Fortunate for you. We'll get under way in two hours."

"But, Michael . . ."

"You don't know Cardiff the way I do," he said. "He's not a man who's overly troubled with the niceties of decent behavior. Francey's been at his mercy for far too long already. I'm not willing to wait a moment longer than we have to."

For a moment Travers didn't move. And then he nodded, his face gray. "I was hoping it was simple paranoia on my part," he said heavily, reaching for the phone. "I'll tell the captain to make it one hour."

* * *

One thing about the Spanish, Ross Cardiff thought with the usual disdain he felt for all foreigners, at least they knew when to eat. He could get a respectable meal at ten o'clock at night in Gibraltar, even if he couldn't bring his personal chef with him. It had been a long day, a long week, a devilishly long year, and it was all coming to fruition. If he could just hold all the pieces together long enough, he was going to emerge triumphant.

He didn't mind the juggling of people's lives. In fact, he preferred it. He liked the sense of omnipotence, knowing he could maneuver things to his satisfaction with just a simple order. He also liked the sense of danger, the knowledge that everything could all come crashing down with just the wrong move. Otherwise life would get deadly boring.

He'd even managed to find a decent Spanish winery, though he usually despised anything but French wine. He settled himself into the carved chair, placed the damask napkin over his lap and reached for the Waterford crystal his aide had packed for him.

He dropped the glass. The red wine spilled out over the white linen tablecloth, like a pool of blood. The lead crystal shattered, and the candlelight glittered on the shards like diamonds.

"There must have been a flaw in the glass," the man sometimes known as Michael Dowd said. He sat down in the chair opposite Cardiff. "Interesting, isn't it, how a piece of such beauty, such strength, can dissolve if you simply find the hidden weakness? But then, you know a great deal about hidden weaknesses, don't you, Ross? They're your stock in trade."

"What the hell are you doing here?" Cardiff managed to demand, controlling the urge to look back over his shoulder to see if another, even more dangerous, nemesis was lurking behind his back. "You're supposed to be chasing down wild geese in Malta. Or have you finally come to your senses and realized there's nothing going on there?

If the Cadre are active in this part of the world it will be here, on Gib.''

Michael smiled faintly, and Ross could feel his ulcer kick in. He didn't need to look behind him. There was no danger worse than the man confronting him. It was part of the man's charm.

"You're wrong, Ross. But then, you've been wrong before, haven't you? Isn't that why you were passed over last year when you were so bloody certain you were going to get that undeserved promotion? I was rooting for you, Ross. I wanted you gone, out of my hair, immured in the hallowed halls of bureaucracy so that I never had to see you again in whatever time I have left to me. But it didn't work out that way, did it?''

"I don't like your tone," Ross said stiffly.

"Too bad," Michael said. "I left things hanging in Malta when I couldn't afford to leave."

Ross's panic left him. "You've found something?" he demanded, leaning forward over the stained tablecloth. "You mean you were right after all?"

"I want the girl, Ross. I want her right now, safe and sound. I'll pass her on to her cousin, and then I'll get back to work. But not a moment before."

Ross didn't bother to lie. "You can't just walk out in the middle of an operation, especially if something is happening. This is too important."

"I can do what I damned well please. Up to and including inflicting a great deal of damage on you, Ross, my boy. No one knows I'm here but Travers, and he's not too fond of you right now, either. No one will believe I came over here just to beat the bloody hell out of you. Now, where is she?''

Ross licked his lips. "In Mariz."

"Where's Mariz?"

"It's a small town on the Costa Blanca. She's entirely safe, Michael. The Cadre can't find her. Just let her be for the time being and get on with—"

"Where in Mariz? And how did she get there in the first place?" He was implacable.

Cardiff shrugged, dreading the inevitable. "These things are easy enough to manage. A paper trail leading to Travers. She thought her cousin would have the answers."

"And instead she found you."

"Not exactly."

Michael smiled, and a small frisson of panic scampered down Ross's spine. "Why don't you tell me exactly?" he suggested.

"I had her arrested. I paid someone to plant drugs in her purse, inform the locals and let them do the rest."

"She's in a Spanish prison? For drugs?" His voice was cool and emotionless, and Ross wondered absently whether Michael was going to kill him.

"Yes." His voice came out nervous and high-pitched, but Michael didn't notice.

"For how long?"

"Two weeks."

"Get up."

Panic bubbled over. "Don't kill me, Michael."

"I wouldn't waste my energy. You're going for a boat ride, Ross."

"Michael..."

"Daniel Travers is waiting for us on his yacht. We'll sail up the coast to Mariz, and you will wade in with your full diplomatic regalia and get her out. Immediately."

"I can't. These things take time, Michael. You know how these foreigners work. Everything at its own pace..."

Michael leaned across the table and hauled him out of the chair, and it was all Ross could do to keep from babbling in sheer panic.

"Immediately, Ross. If you don't want to end up feeding the fish."

"I'll do my best. But it's going to have to be tomorrow. We won't even make Mariz until midday, and then everyone will be having their blasted siesta, and—"

"And you'll wake them up," Michael said with deceptive softness.

Ross looked up into the bleak darkness of his eyes. "And I'll wake them up," he said, trying to pull together some of his dignity. "Honestly, Michael, I had no idea you were so fixated on the girl. I expected you to be more professional about the entire thing. You know we have to make unpleasant choices for the good of the nation. She must have been some lay."

For a moment neither of them moved, and Ross knew with complete certainty that he was closer to death then than he had ever been in his life.

"We're going to Mariz," Michael said, his eyes narrow pinpoints of rage. "We are getting Francey released from prison, and then, if you're very lucky, I won't feed you to the bloody sharks. In the meantime, keep your mouth shut unless you've got something useful to say."

"Might I remind you that I'm your superior officer and I..." His voice trailed off as he got a good look at Michael's expression. "And I have nothing more to say," he finished lamely.

"Good," Michael murmured, suddenly affable. "Then I won't have to cut out your tongue."

It was dark and cold in the cell, but Francey had grown used to it. Used to almost anything. The company of rats. The taunts of the other prisoners. The touches of the guards' filthy hands pawing her, mostly for the amusement of their fellow workers. She'd been able to bear it without screaming, knowing the touches weren't going to go further.

But now she was no longer so certain. There was a new guard, one who didn't speak much, who'd already garnered a certain reputation. One who didn't seem to possess mercy, or sympathy, or even reason.

In the countless days since she'd been thrown into jail Francey had carefully hoarded bits of comfort. Whoever was behind her incarceration hadn't abandoned her completely. She knew the guards were being paid, knew that the intimidation and harassment would go so far and no farther. She was alone in the cell, while there were three and four prisoners in those nearby.

It was small comfort. The food, what there was of it, was inedible. The showers were cold and infrequent, and they made her beg for them. Keeping clean was the only thing that kept her calm. If they'd taken away the showers, the change of laundry, she would have collapsed.

Tonight, though, most of her hope had faded. The new guard, Juan, wasn't being paid off as the others were. Or maybe her mysterious benefactor-imprisoner had simply shut off funds. Juan's touches were brutal, direct and quite clear. Sooner or later she wasn't going to be able to keep away from him.

It had happened once already. She'd hidden in her cell, holding her ears, keeping her eyes tightly shut, while one of the female prisoners had been raped, with the other inmates cheering the action. The thought that sooner or later it would be her turn was the worst terror of her life.

She leaned against the hard wall for a moment, ignoring the danger of bugs. And then she hunched forward, huddling in on herself. Looking for Michael Dowd had gotten her into this mess, one she seemed incapable of extricating herself from. She needed rescuing, and there was only one man, unlikely as it seemed, who could do it.

"Save me, Michael," she whispered to the damp, cold cell. "For God's sake, get me out of here."

"I couldn't think of a better place to put her. She's out of reach of anyone who speaks more than a smattering of English, she's wretchedly uncomfortable, and she can't cause any trouble," the man whined. "What more could you possibly want?"

"I want her dead."

The disembodied voice on the other end of the line always gave Cardiff the creeps. Not that he didn't know perfectly well exactly who and what the leader of the Cadre was. But if they wanted to play their little games it made no difference to him. His contempt for them equalled his contempt for almost all forms of life, but still, there was something about that husky, sexless voice that made his skin crawl.

"I'm stalling as best I can. You'll have to hurry on your end of the bargain. I don't know how long I can keep them here. I'm not even sure she's still alive. You know how zealous soldiers can be, and the Spanish government has expressed its disapproval of drugs quite forcefully. You may never have to consider her again."

"You don't understand. I want to be there. I don't want her tidily removed. I want to watch."

Cardiff flicked an invisible crumb off his impeccable jacket. "You are sick. That's one of the things I like most about you."

"I don't give bugger-all what you like about me. I want the girl and I want Cougar."

"Shouldn't your political aspirations come first?" he inquired gently.

There was a long, frustrated pause at the other end of the line. "Sod off, Cardiff."

"Have a nice day," he murmured in reply, replacing the receiver gently in its cradle.

Chapter 12

The day had been endless, one day too many in the small, dark cell. Francey hadn't eaten, hadn't moved, had simply sat cross-legged on the sagging cot and listened to the obscenities fill the air from the cells around her. She'd become adept at shutting her mind off. When things were unbearable, she would send her mind back to Baby Jerome, to the cool, clear blue of the lagoon, water like silk sliding over her body. Michael was there, protection, comfort, shelter from the storm. As long as she floated in the lagoon, nothing could harm her.

There were times when she didn't even need the lagoon. When she could simply fill her mind with a bright blue light, shutting out the squalid surroundings, the noise, the smell. Those times were coming more often, when reality overwhelmed her. And she wondered, quite calmly, if sometime she would go to that place and never return.

There was a new inmate in the prison, another lone inhabitant, this time in the cell across from hers. A huge Arab, dressed in enveloping robes that covered him from head to toe. She tried to distract herself by considering whether he was wearing a djellaba, or was it a burnoose? If the clothes were for religious reasons he was obviously a major hypocrite. Because the huge man was dead drunk, sleeping noisily on the narrow cot, impervious to his surroundings.

Would they let him go in the morning, once he sobered up? Could she get him to take a message for her, a plea for help? No one had come to see her since she'd been incarcerated, not even the Spanish-speaking court-appointed lawyer. She'd had to accept the possibility that no one even knew where she was, except for the people who'd put her there.

She spent hours watching him as he slept, but he didn't move, just snored noisily, his robes wrapped around him. He probably didn't speak English. If he did, he wouldn't talk to her. By the time dinner came and he still slept on, she gave up hope. No one was going to rescue her.

She heard the key turn in the lock, but she didn't bother to look up. If she did, she knew she would see Juan, he of the broad, cruel hands and the dark, piglike eyes.

He said something in Spanish, and the eavesdropping prisoners laughed coarsely. She considered ignoring him, then thought better of it. It would just give him an excuse to put those filthy hands on her.

She turned, keeping her face devoid of emotion. It was full dark again, a moonless night, and the shadows in the jail were deep and ominous. Beyond the guard's back she could see the cell where the Arab slept on. Chances were he would never even know she'd been there. She would simply disappear. "Shower," Juan said, having mastered the word.

For the first time Francey shook her head, rejecting her salvation. She could see from the nervy eagerness in Juan's wiry body that her time had come, and she would be damned if she was going willingly. "No, thank you," she said clearly. "Not tonight."

It was a waste of time. He put his hands on her, dragging her from the cell, and she fought him, suddenly ready to fight for her life. She kicked and scratched in furious silence as he dragged her down the row of cells and the other inmates called out jeers and encouragement, and she wondered numbly if he was going to kill her. If he was going to rape her on the cement floor where the men urinated daily, then cut her throat.

None of the other guards was in sight. Not that they would save her, but they might consider it worth their while to keep their meal ticket going. But then, maybe their payments had stopped. And that was why Juan was being given his turn.

He spun her around and shoved her hard against the wall. Her head smacked against the stone, and she blacked out for a moment, sliding to the ground. When her vision cleared he was on top of her, ripping at her buttons, his hot, fetid breath washing over her averted face as she fought and fought.

And then the magic place came back. The light was white this time, blinding, and no hands were clawing at her, no one was hurting her. She shut her eyes, blocking out everything, willingly accepting the blankness, when she heard a scream, one that echoed chillingly through the cells and then died in a rattling gurgle.

She opened her eyes. She was in no magic place. The stink and the noise of the prison were still around her, the bright white light no peaceful trance world but the brightness of electricity. Quickly she struggled to her feet, pulling her ripped dress back around her, as she surveyed the silent tableau.

The prisoners in their cells were backed against the walls, not saying a word. The Arab was standing by the light, tall, dressed in enveloping robes that obscured everything about him but the blood on the white material. And Juan was lying in a pool of blood on the floor, his mean eyes wide and staring, a knife in his throat.

Francey felt the scream of horror begin to bubble up in the back of her throat as she stared at him. Before it could erupt a hand clamped over her mouth, a hard, brown hand, and she was pulled back against the Arab's voluminous robes, against the strong body underneath it.

"You want to get out of here?" His voice whispered in her ear, a rasping, accentless voice. "Don't nod—I might break your neck. Just raise your hand."

She didn't even consider the alternatives. She raised her hand, and he caught it in his own large brown one. "Then follow me and keep quiet."

He didn't release her hand. Instead he pulled her after him, out into the stillness of the dark, moonless night. She stumbled as she followed him, and for a moment all she wanted to do was breathe in the clean, free air. But the stranger wasn't allowing her any delay. He yanked her after him, moving down a pitch-dark alley, and she followed, trying to hold her dress together with her other hand, trying to empty her mind of everything but the need to follow the huge stranger.

She didn't care where he was leading her. Whether it was to death, to white slavery, to degradation or to freedom. She'd lost the capacity to care, or to choose. She was like a leaf on the wind, swirling with the forces of nature. The last of her fight had been squandered on that fruitless struggle with Juan. If the man taking her away held a knife to her throat, she would accept it without flinching. She had had enough.

He seemed to have no interest in her, other than to lead her through the maze of back alleys of the small town of Mariz. She could smell the sea, growing stronger, and she wondered if he was going to drown her. Or simply sail away with her. It didn't matter.

Except that she wasn't sure she could make it. During those interminable weeks in the prison cell she'd barely been able to make herself eat. Her clothes had grown loose and baggy, and her strength and energy had vanished. She hadn't walked more than a few feet at a time during her stay, and this headlong march to the sea was fast draining her remaining resources.

The hand that gripped hers was hard and strong, callused and deadly. For a moment she wondered who her savior was. And then she decided it didn't matter. All that mattered was that she stayed on her feet until they reached whatever destination he'd decided on.

She wished he were Michael. But Michael was small, frail, Michael wouldn't kill a man that swiftly, mercilessly, efficiently. He wouldn't drag her through the twisty streets of a small Spanish town without a word.

Michael didn't even exist. He was a dream, from a dream world, not belonging to blood and death. She no longer wanted to find him. Searching for him had brought her to this devastating point. She had nothing more she could risk.

They were near the sea, and for a moment she could pretend they were a continent away, with clean white sand and palm trees. They were near the quay, and she could see boats at anchor. Fishing boats, yachts, one that even looked like Daniel's boat, the *True Blue*. But that was impossible.

She stumbled again, too weary to take another step, and she half expected the man leading her to abandon her, or haul her to her feet with unceremonious force.

He did neither. She felt him loom over her, all strength and size and enveloping robes, and a moment later she was lifted effortlessly in his arms. Her dizziness increased with the weightlessness, and she whimpered faintly, clinging to the soft cotton robes. Odd, the drunken man didn't smell like alcohol. He smelled of sunlight and warm male flesh. He smelled like blood.

She shuddered as the vision of Juan's dark, sightless eyes filled her, and for a moment she struggled in the man's arms. She'd forgotten how strong he was. He subdued her effortlessly as he swung up some angled walkway. And then he was setting her down carefully on her unsteady feet, and she blinked in the darkness, at the man waiting for her, the man he'd brought her to.

"Francey," the man said, his voice raw with concern as he held out welcoming arms.

Why had she thought the Arab would bring her to Michael, who would make everything better? Michael didn't exist. "Daniel," she said, her voice a breath of a sigh that covered her crushing disappointment and relief. She reached out for him, falling into darkness, warm and safe at last.

Michael caught her, her slight, weary form no burden at all as he scooped her up again, holding her against the enveloping robes. "Where are you putting her?" he demanded, his voice terse with the tightly suppressed rage that had been riding him for the past few days.

"The gray cabin. It's the quietest, most out of the way spot. What in hell did they do to her?"

Michael didn't bother to answer, shouldering the older man aside as he carried her into the companionway. In fact, he blamed the old man as well as Cardiff. Travers had allowed him into her life in the first place, oblivious to the danger he was putting her into. He must have heard tales of the Cougar—he must have known what she was getting into. If her cousin had made any effort to protect her in the aftermath, that effort had been negligible. Michael was so angry he wanted to kill, and disposing of that sadistic little guard hadn't been nearly enough to slake his murderous rage.

He'd seen the look on her face. The man had been about to rape her. He'd already discovered she'd been put in the care of a man whose reputation for brutality was legion in the town of Mariz, and yet she'd looked at his dead body in horror. Hell, he'd done the world, and her, a favor. Yet her shock and horror had vibrated through her.

At least he hadn't had to force her to come with him. He wasn't sure what he would have done if she'd resisted.

Whether he would have knocked her cold. Or lowered the enveloping hood of his burnoose. Hell, there was even a chance she wouldn't have recognized him. Last time she'd seen him he'd been bleeding to death inside. He'd been twenty pounds lighter, with curly red hair. She might find it hard to reconcile that memory with a man with dark-stained skin and hair, and a hell of a lot more muscle.

But she'd come, compliant in her shock, following him through the streets of Mariz until she'd finally had enough. Her breathing was shallow, shocky against his chest, and he knew a moment's panic. People could die of shock. Or just disappear into their own little worlds and never come out again.

The gray cabin was at the back of the companionway, a relatively large room with a minuscule private bath. He laid her down carefully on the bed, his eyes already accustomed to the dark, and stood over her for a moment. He could hear Travers coming along after him, hear the quiet murmur of conversation, but for the moment he was alone with the woman he'd wounded so grievously.

He touched her pale face, pushing a silky strand of hair back. She didn't move, didn't react to his touch, simply lay there in her own, healing cocoon.

He couldn't help himself. Leaning forward, he brushed her lips with his, clinging for a moment. "Damn you, Francey," he whispered. "And damn me."

He was halfway to the door when Travers entered. "I told the captain to get under way immediately," he said in a hushed tone. "And the doctor's coming down. We'll take care of her."

"You haven't done a bloody good job so far, have you?"

"Look, this wasn't my fault. I didn't know..."

"Didn't you?" Michael interrupted. "Where's Cardiff?"

"Topside."

Michael smiled then, shoving back the hood of his burnoose, and Travers took a wary step backward, coming up against the door. "You're not going to kill him, are you?" he demanded nervously.

"I haven't made up my mind yet."

The *True Blue* was already moving by the time he dumped his robes and found Cardiff. Ross was sitting on a deck chair, an angora lap robe spread across his short legs, a dark amber glass of whiskey in his small hand. He watched Michael approach, and there was no fear in his eyes. More proof for Michael that the man wasn't equipped with much common sense. He should be very, very frightened.

"You look like a terrorist," Ross observed, not bothering to rise from his seat.

"Isn't that what I am?" Michael said flatly. "We have wonderful euphemisms for it, but isn't that really what I do for a living?"

"It's all in how you look at it. I take it you saved the fair damsel? Lovers reunited and all that garbage?" His voice was waspish.

"Ever hear of a man named Juan?" Michael asked casually. The faintest flicker in Ross's eyes told him the answer.

"Half of the male population of Spain is named Juan."

"We're talking about a particular Juan. One who'd been given a free go at the American prisoner. If I'd been a day later she would have been gone."

"Don't be melodramatic," Cardiff snapped. "I know this has been love's young dream, but you don't have to get carried away. As a matter of fact, why aren't you down with her celebrating your happy reunion? Didn't she like you as an Arab? Or didn't she recognize you? Is that what's eating at you? The innocent love of your life didn't even know who you were."

It was amazing how easily Ross could get under his skin. "Maybe I'm more aware of security issues than you are, Cardiff. I thought it would be just as well if she didn't see me."

"You're kidding! How deliciously noble of you, Michael. I didn't know you had it in you. Any other sacrifices you're planning to make for your lady fair?"

Michael smiled then, a thin, feral grin. "Just one," he said, moving forward. A moment later Ross was over the side, floundering in the filthy waters of Mariz harbor, his deck chair floating beside him as the yacht steamed away.

"I'll destroy you!" Cardiff shrieked, treading water. "I'll have you drummed out of the service! I'll have you ruined! For God's sake, don't leave me here, Michael! You wretched, filthy swine."

Even in such an extreme moment Cardiff didn't curse, Michael noticed absently. The angora lap robe had caught on the railing. He tossed it after him, waving a farewell salute. "See you in Malta," he called across the water. And without bothering to see whether Cardiff could even swim, he turned around and went below.

The gray cabin was hushed, still, a sickroom. Francey looked very small in the big bed, lying perfectly still, the dark sheets drawn up under her chin. Even in the darkness he could tell she was pale, and her breathing was heavy, drugged. Travers rose from the chair beside the bed when Michael returned, and his voice was only a whisper.

"She's resting quietly. The doctor gave her something to help her sleep."

"It didn't look to me like she was going to need help," Michael said.

"He thought she'd do better with a deeper, drug-induced sleep. To help her through the transition." Travers fiddled with his tie, the gesture drawing Michael's attention from Francey's still figure. "Er...what happened to Cardiff? Is everything okay?"

"He'll be meeting us in Malta," Michael replied, moving past Travers to the bed.

"Really?"

"Count on it," Michael said grimly. He touched her hand, lying outside the cover. It was cool and limp. "Don't give her any more drugs. She's been through enough as it is—she doesn't need to deal with being out of it. She's tougher than you'd think. Her body will heal itself without any pharmacological help."

"I have to pay attention to my doctor."

"You've been ignoring her welfare for the past month. Another couple of days won't make any difference." He sank into the chair Travers had left. "Leave her alone."

He didn't have to look to know that Travers had puffed up with outrage. Lord, he was so tired of dealing with people and their inflated ideas. All that mattered right now was Francey. In two days they would be back in Malta, and she would be gone from his life forever. He would finish with the Cadre, with no human or emotional distractions to slow him down. But for now nothing much seemed to matter but the woman lying on the bed. The woman who had almost died for him. For his idiot superior's idea of security.

"Listen here, Michael or whatever your name is," Travers fumed, "I don't like your attitude."

"Sod off," Michael said pleasantly. "Get out of here or I'll put you out." He turned to glance at the man, and one look at Michael's impassive face was enough. Travers slammed the door when he went.

Michael slid down in the chair, stretching his long legs out in front of him and tilting his head back. He felt bone weary, and yet curiously more alive than he had in weeks. He refused to worry about Francey... she was far more resilient than most people he'd met in his various lives. Once the drugs wore off she would heal in her own way, her own time. As long as certain people didn't interfere. People with their own twisted agendas. People like her cousin. Like Ross Cardiff. People like him.

He glanced down at his hands. The skin was stained dark on top of the layers of tan, and his short hair was an unnatural black. He should have taken a shower, washed off some of his disguise, but he hadn't wanted to leave her for any longer than he had to to rid himself of Ross Cardiff, at least temporarily. If she awoke in the darkness she would see only his light eyes in his unnaturally dark face, and she wouldn't know him.

But she wouldn't awaken, not if her drugged breathing was any sign. Not for a long, long time. She'd gone someplace safer than the world she'd been thrust into, and she wouldn't be returning for a while.

She wouldn't feel the weight of his body as he sat on the bed next to her. Wouldn't know he'd pulled the sheet down away from her body. Someone had cleaned her up, dressed her in a chaste white nightgown complete with a row of tiny buttons down the front. She hadn't felt it when someone fastened those buttons. She wouldn't feel his long, dark fingers as they undid them.

Her skin was smooth, pale and creamy in the shadowy light. He sank his fingers into her thick, tangled hair, feeling for the lump at the back of her head. She'd hit the wall hard when Juan had shoved her, enough to make her black out for a moment. She might have a concussion, or worse.

The lump was small enough, and the faint moan that broke through her drugged sleep was one of discomfort, not excruciating pain. He moved his hands back, down over her shoulders, pushing her nightgown away from her body.

She had bruises. Cruel marks, some fresh, some older and yellowing, on her shoulders, on her ribs, on her breasts, and Michael wished he'd taken longer with Juan. And that he hadn't been so merciful with Cardiff.

There was a row of striped bruises on her wrist. He put his hand on them, and they matched his long, hard fingers perfectly. He cursed then, slowly, savagely, the whispered words filling the cabin. It took him longer to refasten her buttons, and he realized with abstract amusement that his fingers were trembling. He drew the sheet back up over her chastely, and then lay down beside her, full-length, drawing her unresisting body into his arms.

She felt small, slight, almost not there at all, and his grip tightened. Soon she wouldn't be. His act of throwing Ross Cardiff overboard had been one more rash move on his part, one of a series of rash moves. He'd stated his enmity, loud and clear, and Ross would have his revenge. Michael wasn't afraid of being cashiered out of the service. Even Ross wasn't powerful enough to do that if Michael didn't want to go—too many people were in awe of his reputation.

But Cardiff was the kind of creature who could find a man's weak points and then use them, twist them, until you had no choice but to do his bidding.

He knew Michael's weak point. He'd put her in a Spanish prison. He could use her again and again, until something backfired, as it almost had tonight, and Francey would wind up dead.

He would have no choice but kill Cardiff then. It only made sense to do it earlier. Francey wouldn't be safe as long as Cardiff held any power. And keeping Francey safe had become Michael's prime directive, more important than wiping out the Cadre, the security of what was left of the British Empire, or the safety of the entire free world. And he was perfectly ready to do anything, anything, to ensure that safety.

But for now, for the next few hours, she was as safe as she could ever be. Wrapped tightly in his arms, where no one, and nothing, could wound her.

For the next few hours. And then he would be gone, and she would never even know he'd been there. He would vanish into the night like her drunken Arab savior. And before long she would forget he'd ever existed.

He could only hope that fate would be kind enough to grant him a similar amnesia, because he didn't know how long he would be able to take it otherwise.

Chapter 13

Francey dreamed. For a while she was back on the island, not in the lagoon this time, but lying on the bedroll, wrapped in Michael's arms. She could feel his warm, smooth flesh against her face, the strength of his arms around her, and for a time everything was safe. And then things shifted, and the man holding her was a threat, a dark, huge stranger who rescued her and then abandoned her. Sunlight poured into the cabin, and she refused to open her eyes. The back of her head pounded, her muscles felt thick and drugged, and she wanted to crawl back into the warm dark nest and take Michael with her. Her stomach felt empty, queasy, and the bed felt rocky and unstable beneath her.

"How are we feeling today?" The voice was far too cheerful, but it was blessedly familiar. Making the supreme effort, she opened her eyes a fraction, enough to see Daniel's cherubic face hovering far too close.

"Like pig droppings," she said succinctly. Or rather, she tried for a succinct tone. Her voice came out blurred and fuzzy, and her tongue felt thick. It took most of her strength to lift her head from the pillow, to look at the empty mattress beside her. She was lying in the middle of the oversize double bed, the covers wrapped tightly around her. She was alone, as she had been all night long.

"You need some food," Daniel said, his hands fluttering ineffectually. "You need to lie on the deck in the sun and recuperate. You've been through a ghastly time, Francey, and I can't say how sorry I am that you couldn't find me. You need to just empty your mind and let yourself heal...."

"I need answers." Some of the fuzziness faded. She managed to sit up, fighting off the dizziness, the pain in the back of her head. "I need to know what in God's name is going on."

Daniel looked distressed. "I'll tell you what I can, Francey."

"You'll tell me what you *know,* Daniel," she said. "I'm not going to be fobbed off with vague fairy tales this time. I want to know who Michael Dowd is. More important, where he is. I want to know who that little man was. I want to know why I was locked away in a Spanish prison, and how you managed to find me and rescue me. And I want to thank the man who brought me out of there. I want—"

"All in good time," Daniel said soothingly. "First you need a hot shower, something to eat and a vitamin B-12 shot. Then we'll sit down and I'll tell you everything."

The promise of a hot shower distracted her as nothing else could. She almost gave in. "Where are we going?"

"We're on our way to Malta," Daniel said. "We should be there midday tomorrow, and the next day we'll fly back to the States. Both of us. What do you think of that?"

"I don't know. But if we're on a boat in the middle of the Mediterranean, I suppose you can't get too far. You did say a hot shower?" Even she could hear the yearning in her voice.

"Unlimited. Take your time, and then Dr. Brady will bring your vitamin shot."

"No shots," she said flatly.

"But, Francey..."

"No shots. I need a decent meal, a hot shower and some answers."

Daniel's smile was uneasy. "I'll give you everything I can," he murmured.

She locked the door behind him, moving on unsteady feet across the thick carpeting. Leaning against the door, she stared at her quarters, at the first privacy she'd had in weeks.

She'd been in a different cabin the last time she'd been on the *True Blue*. This was one of the larger ones, reserved for movie stars and heads of state. Being locked in a Spanish prison had its advantages, she thought sourly, surveying the bed.

Such strange dreams, she thought. Would they haunt her from now on? Or would she put them behind her, along with Spain and her fruitless search for Michael?

Only when she knew the truth. And she wasn't going to stop asking, stop demanding, until she did. It didn't matter that her ceaseless quest had led to being imprisoned. She couldn't, wouldn't be a good little girl and go home. Even though she knew Daniel was going to do his best to convince her to do just that.

She walked slowly, carefully, across the room. Her feet hurt. Last night was a blur, but she had snatches of memory, of being dragged through the back alleys of Mariz by a dark, robed figure. She'd lost her shoes somewhere along the way and stumbled along barefoot. It was no wonder her feet hurt.

She moved to the side of the bed, looking down at the rumpled gray sheets, reaching out and touching them, her hands brushing the smooth cotton. She sank, stretching out on the bed, burying her face against the sheets, her fingers clutching the material. And she lay there and shook with longing, and the trace of a lost memory.

"She's asking too many questions," Daniel fretted.

Michael looked up at him, squinting into the direct sunlight. The hot shower had taken only one layer of the stain from his skin, his hair was still dark, and he felt reasonably secure in just keeping his distance from Francey. Maybe he'd been too sanguine about the situation. She'd seemed so exhausted, so apathetic, that he'd assumed she'd given up her quest.

"What kind of answers have you been giving her?"

"None, yet. But I don't know how long I can put her off. Cardiff told me I should keep her drugged until we get on the plane back to New York, but I . . ."

"No." He kept his voice flat and even, but Daniel flinched nervously. Michael was accustomed to having that effect on people, and for once he was glad of it. "No more drugs. She's been through enough. Tell her anything you damned well please, as long as it doesn't compromise the current operation."

"I don't even know what the current operation is," Daniel said fretfully.

"And why should you? All that matters is that she doesn't know where I am. Tell her I'm in Northern Ireland. I don't think you can make her believe I'm a schoolteacher, not if she ran into the real Michael Dowd. Use your imagination. Lie to her. You've been on the fringes of the intelligence community long enough to have learned how to do it."

"She's not too easy to lie to."

Michael closed his eyes for a moment, remembering. "No, she's not. But you'll have to rise to the occasion. Tell her I'm part of a witness relocation program. Tell her you don't know, but you think I'm somewhere in Russia. Tell her I'm dead."

"That might be for the best."

Michael considered his demise unemotionally. "Yes," he said. "It might. For everyone. What's she doing now?"

"She's having a shower, then coming up on deck. You'd better make yourself scarce. I can come up with something if I don't have to worry about her seeing you."

"She won't recognize me if she does. Michael Dowd was a tall, frail redhead. She didn't know me last night, and she won't know me today if she sees me from a distance."

"You were in robes last night, and she was under a lot of stress. I wouldn't count on her being that unobservant, particularly if you won't let me drug her. Maybe you want her to recognize you."

Michael considered that possibility, considered what would happen if she did. And he shook his head. "It would probably sign her death warrant. I'll keep out of her way. You keep her out of mine."

Daniel stared at him. "I don't like you, you know. I don't like what you've done to Francey. I don't like the kind of man you are. I just thought I should mention that."

Michael smiled then, and Daniel took an involuntary step backward. "When she was with me, old man, she was safe. You were the one who knew Ross Cardiff was pulling a fast one, and yet you did nothing to protect her. You sacrificed her for your vicarious thrill seeking, and you don't even have the excuse that you were working for the greater good. You're a voyeur, Travers, a ghoul who feasts on other men's violence. At least Cardiff has no illusions that he's one of the good guys." He rose, towering over the older man, and he could see real fear in his eyes. "Don't worry, old man. Your worthless hide's safe. Unless something else happens to Francey."

"Nothing's going to happen to her," Travers said stiffly.

"Old man," Michael said softly, "see that it doesn't."

She was seeing Michael everywhere. When she stepped out of the cabin, not bothering to wait for Daniel to come fetch her, she saw a shadow disappearing around the corner, a shadow that looked like Michael.

On the deck, in the distance, a tall dark man had the same grace, the same back. She shook her head and he was gone, and she felt a little frisson of unease run through her. Was she going to be tormented by ghosts for the rest of her life? How long would it take her to forget him?

"Have some more coffee, Miss Neeley." Daniel's private doctor, a jovial soul named Elmore Brady, pushed her cup toward her. "You've been through quite an experience. Caffeine's the drug of choice, don't you know?"

Francey managed a polite smile. She knew perfectly well why Daniel had invited Elmore to join them for breakfast. He thought she would be too discreet to ask the questions that were plaguing her, to demand the answers she deserved. He was wrong.

She took another sip of her too-sweet coffee, squinting into the bright sunlight. Daniel's yacht was making good time, plowing through the bright blue of the Mediterranean, heading toward Malta and eventually home. She had no intention of stepping on any airplane until she had a few answers.

"So tell me, Daniel," she said sweetly. "Who is the man you sent to stay with me on St. Anne?"

She didn't miss the look that passed between the doctor and Daniel, a look that hinted at more knowledge than anyone felt like giving her. For a moment a black rage swept over her, one that left her weak and shaking.

"You mean Michael Dowd? You know perfectly well who he was. A recuperating schoolteacher from Willingborough. Why should you assume any differently?" Daniel didn't meet her accusing gaze, concentrating instead on his fresh-squeezed orange juice.

"Because I met the real Michael Dowd. The man you sent me was a phony. And it was searching for him that got me locked up in that Spanish prison. So I think I have every right to know who and what he is. And *where*."

"I really don't know, Francey. The little man...Cardiff's his name, by the way. I know him through some of my volunteer work. He asked if I knew of a place for a friend of his. I had no idea that the friend was using an assumed name, or that he was putting you into any danger. I really thought—"

"Bull," she said flatly. "You may be shortsighted, but you're not a fool, Daniel. The man calling himself Michael Dowd came to St. Anne for a reason. I want to know what that reason was."

"Don't you think," Dr. Elmore Brady suggested gently, "that you might be better off not knowing?"

The sun was too damned bright. It was giving her a blinding headache, making her joints ache, her heart thud, her eyes feel leaden, swollen. "How dare you?" she tried to say, but her tongue was thick. For a moment her eyes widened, to look at the two men watching her with such concern. "You...bastards..." she said. "You've drugged..." Her mouth no longer worked.

She heard Daniel's voice. "I'm sorry, Francey, but it's for your own good. I had to—" And then his voice stopped in a strangled, pained squeak.

"I should kill you," Michael's voice came from nowhere, from the blinding brightness of the sun. But Michael wasn't there, and why should he want to kill her? It was all too confusing, and for now she couldn't fight to make sense of it. She needed to use all her energy to fight the insidious effect of whatever filthy drug they'd given her, fight to open her eyes, fight to stay awake, fight...fight....

Michael was getting too damned used to this chair. He hadn't left her since he'd carried her back to the cabin. He watched, eagle-eyed, as that quack Elmore checked her vital signs. He watched, unmoving, when the housekeeper came and put her back into that chaste white nightgown, ignoring any claim to modesty Francey might have. He remained all through the long hours of the day, as a storm front moved over the Mediterranean, sending the *True Blue* skidding along the tops of the waves. He remained through the long hours of the evening, when rain lashed against the portholes and wind howled along the decks. Not for a minute did he worry about the *True Blue* sinking. It would be a mercy for all if it did. Francey would never know what happened to her. And he wouldn't have to deal with the Cadre, with the deceit of everyone who surrounded him. With his own deceit.

Somewhere around two in the morning he decided he was going to start smoking again the moment he got off this boat. He didn't really know why he'd stopped, except that any addiction at all had the potential of betraying him to the enemy. He already had a powerful addiction, one to the woman lying on the bed. He was far more vulnerable through her than he was through cigarette smoke.

The sea calmed, the rain became a steady drone, and he slept, fitfully, knowing the door was locked against any intruders, knowing that for at least a few more hours he could keep her safe. When he opened his eyes again to the early-morning stillness, the bed was empty.

She was kneeling at his feet, staring up at him out of drugged eyes. Her hair was a tangled mass behind her pale face, and her hands were holding on to the seat of the chair, as if for support, as she watched him.

"Michael?" Her voice was no more than a whisper. She reached out to touch him, as if she couldn't believe he was real, he was there, he was solid flesh.

He was lost, and he knew it. In the murky shadows she wouldn't see the dark skin and hair, the added muscle. She knew him, would have known him with her eyes closed. On some level she'd probably known he was there from the beginning, no matter how drugged she was.

He could deny it, fight it. He could catch her slim white hand before it connected with his chest, put her back to bed alone and let the drug regain its control. He could leave her to the tender mercies of her cousin and his drug-pushing doctor, and she would probably be a lot better off.

But he wasn't going to. She was drugged, shocked, confused and vulnerable. And he was going to take her anyway.

Her hand was cool through the thin cotton of his open shirt, cool against his hot skin. He covered her hand with his larger one, pressing it against him, and he could feel white-hot desire leap through his veins.

That saintly, country-bred gentlewoman who ruled Whipdale Manor would have raised her son never to take advantage of a woman in Francey's condition. But then, he'd never known that mythical woman. He'd made his own ethics, his own sense of honor. Now he was about to betray it, and he didn't give a damn. He needed her more than honor.

He slid his other hand behind her, under the thick tangle of sun-streaked hair, and urged her closer. She moved willingly, kneeling between his wide-spread legs, and she tilted her head back, closing her eyes and parting her lips, waiting for him.

Such an invitation was too hard to resist, and he wasn't the man to try. He put his lips against hers, very gently, just brushing them for a moment.

She groaned, moving closer, wanting more, her hands sliding up his chest to dig into his shoulders, and he deepened the kiss, slanting his mouth across hers, dampening her drug-dry lips with his tongue before plunging it deep. She shuddered in his arms, moving closer still, her stomach pressed up against his groin, and he wanted to pull her astride him, onto his lap, opening his pants and taking her there and then.

It was a potent fantasy, but not as strong as the reality of her mouth. Whatever consciousness had surfaced beyond the drug's reach, it was being channeled into her mouth, her body. He slid his hands down, lifting her up effortlessly, and moved her over to the bed.

"Don't leave me," she whispered when he set her down, and she reached for him with something close to desperation.

"I won't," he said, knowing it was a lie, knowing he was going to leave her all too soon. He didn't bother with the row of tiny buttons this time; he simply yanked the white cotton nightgown over her head. She lay back against the pillows, her hair fanned out around her, watching him, completely unselfconscious.

Her tan had faded, she'd lost weight, and the bruises marked her body in the dim light. Stripping off his own clothes, he lay down next to her, drawing her unresisting body into his arms. "I don't even know what they did to you," he whispered against her skin, kissing the bruise on her shoulder. "I can see the marks where they hurt you, but I don't know how badly. I don't know if you're ready for this." He looked down at her, pushing her hair out of her face. "I only know I can't wait...."

She silenced him, reaching up with her mouth, catching his, kissing him, and then there was no more room for words. He touched her with his hard, dark hands and watched her body writhe with pleasure. He kissed her on her pale breasts, the bruises scattered across her peach-colored flesh; he kissed her between her legs until she arched off the bed with a strangled, inarticulate cry.

He didn't remember when he'd last had a woman. He didn't remember if he'd ever had a woman like Francey. A good woman, one who deserved far better. He knelt between her legs, looming over her in the darkness, and expected to see the shadow of fear darken her dazed face. Instead she reached for him, pulling him down to her, and he sank into her gloved tightness with a sense of coming home.

It was a reaction she didn't share. The moment he drove deep into her she stiffened, panic making her body rigid, and he wondered whether he'd been wrong, whether he hadn't gotten there in time, whether she'd been raped by those animals in the jail. She struggled for an instant, and he was about to make the supreme sacrifice, to gather what little determination he had and pull away, when she suddenly collapsed beneath him, no longer fighting.

He held himself, and her, very still, knowing he was much too big and heavy for her, needing more than numbed acquiescence from a woman who was probably too drugged to give it. He cradled her face with his hands, his thumbs brushing her cheeks, and he could feel the dampness of tears seeping from behind her closed eyes.

He cursed himself, called himself every name he could think of, but he didn't move away from her, didn't stop wanting her.

He licked the tears from her cheeks. Her eyes flew open, dazed, drugged eyes staring into his. Lost eyes, and he knew he had to move away.

And then her legs came up around him, her arms slid around his waist, and her soft mouth opened. "Make love to me, Michael," she whispered. "Now."

He couldn't control it any longer. He surged against her, tremors of need racking his body, and he covered her mouth with his. She arched up to meet him, and he could feel her own response building, shimmering within her, as her fear dissolved. Her mouth was hungry, seeking, beneath his; her body was trembling with longing, and he knew he wasn't going to be able to make it last. It had been too long, and he wanted her too much.

And then it was too late. The first spasm hit her, arching her body against him, contracting around him, and he had no choice but to follow her down that dark, limitless chasm, and it was unlike anything he'd ever experienced before. It was death and life and a blinding fragment of heaven that would have to last him forever. When he finally collapsed on top of her, his breath was coming in sobbing rasps, and he wanted to pull her into him, to absorb her into his very bones.

Slowly, slowly, his breathing calmed, his tumultuous heartbeat slowed its pace, as did hers. When he finally felt within miles of normal, he lifted his head to look at her.

She no longer seemed drugged or confused. The expression on her face, in her eyes, was very clear, very calm. "Don't leave me again, Michael," she whispered. "Don't disappear on me. Don't vanish from my life so that I doubt if you ever really existed. Don't do that to me."

It was the only thing he *could* do. The only way he could ensure she had any peace of mind. But he couldn't tell her that. "I won't," he said. "I love you." The moment the words were out of his mouth, horror washed over him. She didn't know, accepting the words with an expression of such exquisite peace that he almost couldn't regret having said them.

And then she closed her eyes, drifting, sinking back into the safe cocoon, and he knew her brief moment of lucidity would disappear into the mists of drug-shrouded memory. She wouldn't know he'd said it, not for certain.

But he would. Words he'd never said before in his life, and now that his mouth had actually spoken them, they took on a malevolent life of their own. He'd said them, he couldn't call them back, deny them. To do so would be to compound the fatal error. He loved her; he knew it. And it was going to be his doom.

She didn't move when he pulled himself from her arms, from her body, her breathing heavy and drugged. He crossed the room into her bathroom, bringing back a wet, soapy washcloth to wash the traces of his lovemaking from her body. She never stirred, even when he washed between her legs, even when he put his mouth where he'd washed. When she was once again dressed in the chaste white nightgown, her hands folded neatly on top of the covers, he told himself there was no way for her to know she'd been taken advantage of by a conscienceless brute.

But he would know, he thought, pushing her hair away from her face. He would know, in some part of his mind, some part of his body, for every waking and sleeping minute for the rest of his life. He only hoped that wouldn't be too long.

Chapter 14

Francey didn't want to wake up. The bed felt warm, safe, the covers wrapped tightly around her. She'd been through this before, waking up from a drugged sleep in the warm, sunlit cabin. And yet this time it felt different.

She opened her eyes, but the bed was still empty, just as it had been the other morning. There the similarities ended.

There was no Daniel looming over her, sounding concerned even as he planned once more to drug her. Her body felt tender, exquisitely sensitive, as if she'd spent the night making love, which was, of course, a patent absurdity, the remnants of the most erotic, realistic dream she'd had in her entire life. Her body still tingled with the memory.

But the most important change of all was that the boat was no longer moving. Kicking aside the covers, she struggled to the porthole. They were anchored in a harbor, bright sunlight washing down over the small city. Pushing open the heavy glass pane, she let the fresh salty air pour over her, clearing some of the drug-induced mists from her brain.

They kept trying to silence her questions. In the beginning they had refused to answer. When she grew persistent, someone had her immured in a filthy Spanish prison, and chances were she might never have surfaced again if it weren't for her mysterious rescuer. Now they simply kept pumping her with drugs if she grew too importunate.

She should have learned her lesson by now, she thought, pulling away from the window. But then, she'd never been that docile. She could be amazingly stubborn when someone was trying to push her, and right now she was feeling downright intractable. If people wouldn't answer her questions, she would find some other way to get her answers. She would go after them herself.

"Where do you think you're going?" Daniel materialized at the top of the gangplank half an hour later when she emerged from her cabin, his usually ruddy face pale in the bright sunlight.

Francey managed a breezy smile. "Isn't it obvious? I'm going into town. I've never been to Malta before, and as you can imagine, I'm feeling a little claustrophobic."

His hand was on her arm, above the row of bruises, and she could feel the sweat of his palm. It wasn't warm enough out for him to have sweaty palms. "I didn't even realize you were awake yet. Why don't you come and have something to eat? Your hair's still wet from your shower. Just give me a little while and I'll accompany you."

She considered yanking her arm out of his trembling grasp. But he was her cousin, her closest living relative, and she loved him. Even though he had betrayed her, she still cared about him.

"Daniel," she said gently. "I'm afraid I don't trust you not to drug my food."

He winced. "I deserve that, I know. Humor me, Francey. You can eat off my plate, drink from my cup. Give me a couple of hours, and I'll give you some answers."

She was a fool to believe him. But her alternatives weren't spectacular. "A cup of coffee," she agreed. "From the same pot you're using. And the truth."

"What I can tell you."

She wanted to argue with him. She could feel eyes on her, people watching, and she looked behind her, trying to still the little tremor of nervousness. Daniel might love her dearly, might want to protect her, but there were others who were probably more than capable of tossing her over the side of this boat. "What you can tell me," she agreed, running a hand through her shower-wet hair, turning her back to him. She'd seen that shadow again, the tall dark man. She turned back again, but he was gone. "And you can tell me how I got rescued from the prison."

"What I can," he said again.

And she had to accept it.

Michael watched her disappear into the front cabin with Daniel. It had been a close call this time, too close. She'd almost run smack into him, and all his elaborate subterfuge would have been for nothing.

Once again he wondered whether he'd done it on purpose, flirted with danger, hoping she would see him, hoping she would force a crisis. Ross wasn't there to hurt her—if she actually came face-to-face with him, there would be a hell of a blowout. And then she would leave. Get on the plane with her cousin and never think about him again, except with hatred and contempt. Wasn't that what he wanted?

Or did he want her anger, her recriminations, and then her eventual declaration of undying love, once her initial fury had passed? Was he fool enough to believe there might be a future for the two of them?

Postcoital insanity, he told himself, reaching for the pack of Turkish cigarettes he'd bought off a sailor. There were no happy endings for the likes of him. Except in front of a firing squad.

"You ready to go?" the man next to him asked, his dark eyes curious. The launch was waiting to take him back to his current identity, his current mission. Stopping the Cadre as they made one last attempt at solidifying their dubious power. Wiping the last trace of them off the face of this earth. It was the best thing he could do for Francey, that and disappearing from her life. Regrets were a waste of time. He had a job to do.

"Ready," he said. And he didn't look back.

"Witness protection program?" Francey echoed, setting the coffee cup down untouched. "I thought that was an American institution."

"It's used the world over. Invaluable, really, or no one would ever testify against powerful criminals. The man you knew as Michael Dowd was a witness to an IRA bombing. He testified, they tried to kill him, and he was sent to St. Anne and you to recuperate a bit before taking up his new life."

"He hadn't been in a car accident?"

"He'd been shot. Quite badly, but modern medicine is amazing, really. They patched him together, and right now he's living quite happily in Australia. With his wife."

"Wife?" Francey echoed.

"Quite a lovely woman. And loyal. She'd been wonderful through all this, Cardiff says. But they're quite safe and happy now. I know he regretted not being able to say goodbye to you, but things got a little dicey at the end there on St. Anne."

"Cardiff. Is that the little man?"

Daniel nodded. "He's a pretty high-up member of British intelligence. I'm afraid he got a little overenthusiastic when you went looking for Michael. You were never completely cleared of suspicion in connection with the Cadre, and he was afraid you were out to kill him. He couldn't get in touch with me, so he decided to put you out of commission for a while until he sorted things out. I'm certain he didn't realize what he'd gotten you into.''

''I imagine not,'' Francey said faintly, still trying to absorb the information Daniel was finally giving her. ''Why didn't you just tell me?''

''I told you, lives were at stake. Michael and his wife and children. Various agents...''

''Children?'' she echoed in a high-pitched little shriek.

Daniel nodded. ''Three little redheaded boys, the spitting image of their father. Their safety came first. No one thought you were in any danger, and it seemed possible that you were one of the bad guys. I tried to tell them otherwise....''

''This isn't making sense,'' Francey said, shaking her head to try to clear away some of the confusion.

''Life doesn't make sense, Francey. You've been through too much in the past few days, the past weeks, the past months. We need to get you back to the States. I've arranged for two first-class tickets for tomorrow afternoon. We'll fly to Rome, change planes, and be in New York by Sunday.''

''But—''

''Trust me, Francey. As time passes this will all seem a lot clearer. There's nothing we can do except get the hell away from here and get back to normal as soon as possible.''

''Why?''

Daniel looked confused for a moment, and he wiped his pale, sweating forehead with a white linen handkerchief. ''I beg your pardon?''

''Why do we need to get away from Malta? It's supposed to be a beautiful island, with lovely beaches. Why don't we spend a few days enjoying it? God knows I could use the sun and sea and fresh air.''

''If you want a seaside vacation, you can go back to Belle Reste,'' Daniel said.

''So someone can try to sabotage my car again?''

''Those people have been taken care of.''

"The dead men on Baby Jerome? Who killed them? Not an innocent witness who was trying to relocate."

"You ask too many questions, Francey. And you wouldn't want to know the answers, I assure you. Just believe that you'd be safe on St. Anne, or in New York, for that matter."

"But I wouldn't be safe on Malta?"

"I didn't say that."

"You didn't have to. What's on Malta that's so dangerous?"

"Nothing. Absolutely nothing. Don't you want to get home? Back to your life, your apartment?"

He was sweating even more profusely now, despite the fact that the cabin was swathed in air-conditioned cool. He looked ill, and she felt a moment's compunction. His heart wasn't in the best of shape, and if she could trust her instincts, he was as much a pawn in whatever complicated game was going on as she was.

He was right, though. None of it mattered. The man who'd been haunting her dreams, her waking and sleeping hours, was a happily married father now living the good life down under. He was exactly who he'd said he was, a decent, upper-middle-class Brit caught in circumstances beyond his control. She'd been clinging to a fantasy.

"Are you taking your heart medicine, Daniel?" she asked, trying to push her own concerns aside. "You don't look well."

Daniel managed a sickly smile. "I think I need a new prescription. The current stuff doesn't seem to have the kick it once had. Elmore's going to look into something when we get to the hotel."

"If you trust him."

"He was just following orders, Francey."

"Yours?"

"Cardiff's. If there's anyone who makes me uneasy, it's Cardiff. I'm not sure where he is—we left him behind in Spain—but he's a man with a vision. Once he decides something's for the common good, then it's damn all to the individual. You've been through enough."

Half of what he said rang true. Half was a tissue of lies. And she had no idea which half was which. "One last question, Daniel."

"Francey, the less you know, the better off you'll be."

She ignored him. "Who was the man who rescued me? Who brought me out of the prison?"

He didn't even hesitate. "Cardiff hired him after I insisted he get you out. He was an Arab sailor who does a few discreet jobs on the side for British intelligence. He got you out, brought you to the boat, took his money and left."

"Did you see him?"

"Of course. Sort of an ugly fellow, actually. It's just as well you didn't get a good look at him—you might not have come, and he would have had a harder time if he'd had to drag you."

"I would have gone with Attila the Hun."

"Well, Ahmad wasn't a far cry. Any more questions, Francey?" he asked wearily.

"A thousand. I'll wait until you're feeling better."

"Thank God for small favors. Wait till we're back in New York. Thirty-six hours, Francey, and this will all seem like a dream."

"A nightmare," she said, reaching for Daniel's coffee cup and drinking the too-sweet mixture.

"Nightmare's over, Francey. Time to wake up and start life anew. Forget the past, the people you've met. Think about the future."

Forget the past. Forget Michael. Excellent advice, as always. If only she could follow it. Her life had been on a self-destructive slide since the day she'd first set eyes on Patrick Dugan. Michael Dowd was simply part of the slide. It was past time to pull herself up.

"The future," she echoed glumly.

"In two days I'll take you to dinner at Tavern on the Green and we'll toast that future." He looked and sounded so anxious that Francey decided to dismiss her misgivings, her doubt. Daniel had done a great deal for her over the years. The least she could do under the circumstances was lie to him.

"Sounds wonderful," she said firmly. "I can't wait."

The hotel in the center of the tiny city was very small, very old and very elegant. Francey couldn't even find the name of the establishment as Daniel whisked her inside, and a moment later she gave up the attempt. After all, what did it really matter? In less than twenty-four hours she would be on her way back home, and Malta, Spain, and the last month would be nothing but a distant memory.

She and Daniel were ensconced in adjoining suites. Her marble-and-gilt bathroom was more than twice the size of her prison cell, and the hot water was unlimited. When she emerged half an hour later, her skin was pink from scrubbing, she found her bed piled with new clothes, sandwashed silks, soft cottons, all a size too small. Except that she found they fit her perfectly, were even a little loose, when she tried them on. Glancing over at her reflection in the mirror, she grimaced. Besides looking pale and haunted, she'd lost weight. Too much weight. She looked like a good candidate for Daniel Travers's rest cure on St. Anne. Even Michael Dowd had looked healthier.

She tossed her old clothes into the trash, finding a measure of comfort in the feel of silk against her skin. Maybe things would be all right if she just concentrated on the small pleasures in this life. A soft bed. Silk against skin. The scent of roses filling the air. She needed to work up an appetite, think about the taste of coffee and chilled white wine, of whipped cream and strawberries, of pungent spices.

But all she could think about was the taste of Michael Dowd's mouth on hers. The feel of his hands on her skin.

"Enough," she said out loud. Michael Dowd was several continents away, and she was the last thing on his mind. It was time to make him the last thing on hers.

She rapped on the adjoining door between Daniel's suite and hers. There was no answer. He'd said something about having a rest, and, indeed, he'd looked as if he needed sleep. While the need to know still burned in the back of her brain, for now she was going to give him what he wanted. No more questions. She started to turn away when a trickle of uneasiness danced down her spine.

The door between their rooms was unlocked. She pushed it open, calling his name softly. The room was dark, the blinds pulled against the bright Mediterranean sunlight, the sunlight Francey couldn't get enough of. "Daniel," she called again, her eyes growing used to the dimness.

He was lying stretched out on the bed, his ghostly pallor distinguishable even in the shadows. His eyes were open, just focusing on her, and his voice was a mere thread of sound.

"Get Elmore," he whispered.

"Daniel, you need a hospital," she protested, panic filling her. She'd lost too much in the past few months, the past few days. She couldn't lose Daniel, too.

"I wouldn't trust the witch doctors around here," Daniel wheezed. "Get me Elmore. He should be in the hotel somewhere. He'll have what I need, or he can get it for me. He's a . . . damned fine . . . doctor when he isn't following orders."

"I'll find him. Otherwise . . ."

"There's no otherwise," Daniel said, firm despite the faintness in his voice. "I don't trust anyone else. This old ticker of mine likes to give me a scare now and then, and with my luck, it's chosen today. By tomorrow I'll feel right as rain."

"I'll find Elmore," Francey promised, keeping the panic from her voice.

It was easier said than done. Elmore was registered, all
right, but he was nowhere in the small, elegant hotel. A
phone call ascertained that he hadn't been back to the *True
Blue,* and even when Francey asked about other doctors in
the area, the concierge refused to oblige. "Mr. Travers
wouldn't see another doctor," the elegantly suited gentleman insisted in an annoyingly paternal manner. "Let me
make a few more phone calls, and I'm certain I can track
the good doctor down."

"I'm not sure how much time my cousin has." For the
first time in almost a month an edge of hysteria was creep-
ing into Francey's voice, and she clamped down on it. If she
lost control now, she might never regain it, and she imagined a Maltese mental hospital wasn't far removed from a
Spanish prison.

The concierge allowed a faint frown of irritation to cross
his brow. Obviously he considered her to be a hysteric of
the first order, but just as obviously he didn't want to risk
having a dead rich American in one of his suites. "The
British embassy," he said abruptly, before he could change
his mind. "I expect Dr. Brady is somewhere at the embassy. He usually checks in there when he comes to the island."

"But he's not British."

The concierge lifted his hands in a dismissive gesture. "I
have no idea why he goes, Miss Neeley. I only know that he
does. Let me see if I can find him for you. The telephones
are a bit unreliable on the island, but if you'll just be patient..."

"I'll go myself." She practically sprinted across the lobby
to the glassed-in front doors, almost knocking over a well-
dressed matron in her haste. The concierge handed her into
the waiting cab, issued a few unintelligible orders to the
driver, and they were off, barreling through the crowded
downtown streets.

They arrived at the embassy an agonizing twenty minutes later, stopping at a nondescript white building that

Francey was certain they'd passed at least twice during their travels. When she questioned the driver he merely raised his hands and shrugged, and not for a moment did she believe he couldn't speak English.

By the time she stepped inside the cool, air-conditioned halls of the small embassy outpost she was ready to scream. Collaring the first bureaucrat she could find, an earnest young man in Bermuda shorts and an impeccable tie, she demanded that he produce Dr. Elmore Brady.

She half expected the response. "I'm sorry, Miss, never heard of him."

Francey took his perfect tie in her hand and yanked his head down to her level. "Then the ambassador will have to do. Maybe his memory is better than yours. And if you don't take me to see him immediately, I'll cause a scene that will be remembered throughout history. I have had enough, and I'm not willing to be fobbed off with any more excuses. My cousin could be dying, and I'm damned well not going to wait for an appointment or trust anyone less than the ambassador himself."

The young man had paled at the very mention of the word "scene," and her hand on his tie, choking him just slightly, was sufficient motivation. "Right this way, Miss..."

"Neeley. Frances Neeley," Francey said with deceptive affability, loosening her stranglehold on his school tie. Just slightly.

But the young man had obviously had the fear of God, or American womanhood on a rampage, put into him. Within two minutes Francey was being ushered into the elegant, walnut-paneled offices of Sir Henry Chapin as the ambassador himself raised his ponderous bulk from his leather chair and beamed at her.

"What can I do for you, Miss Neeley? I must say, we don't usually see such fetching young ladies, and such forceful ones, at that. Just tell me what the trouble is, and I'm certain we'll all do our best to set things right."

"If only it were that simple," she murmured, more to herself than him as she finally released the poor young man's tie. "My cousin is Daniel Travers, and I believe his doctor is somewhere on the premises. I need him, or, rather, Daniel needs him. Immediately."

"Daniel's an old friend of mine," Sir Henry boomed. "Don't tell me he's taken ill?"

"His heart. He says it's just the medicine, but I don't like the looks of him, and he says he won't see anyone but Elmore Brady."

"Understandable," Sir Henry said in his harrumphing voice. "Elmore's a damned fine doctor—wouldn't see anyone else myself, if I had the option. I'll see if he's here, though I can't say I ran across him in the past hour. Still, I don't know half of what goes on in this place, don't you know. Only been stationed here for the past six months, and it takes a while to learn the lingo, not to mention all the ins and outs. They even sent me some damned cultural attaché a couple of weeks ago to help me out. I ask you, what does culture have to do with anything? Still, they send me these charming young Johnnies and I have to do my best. At least the ladies like 'em. Tell you what, Miss Neeley, I'll pass you on to my aide. Charming fellow, name of Charlie Bisselthwaite. He'll find Elmore. Make himself useful for a change."

"I don't think..." Francey began, uneasy at being foisted off on another charming bureaucratic incompetent, but Sir Henry was already speaking into the telephone.

A moment later the door opened behind her. "There you are, Charlie. I need you to dig up Dr. Brady for this young lady here. Seems her cousin's in some kind of fix."

Somehow she knew, long before she turned around. Maybe it was the shadow of his silhouette, taller, broader, than she would have expected. Maybe it was the myth of the Mediterranean islands, and gods and goddesses playing their tricks on unsuspecting mortals. She half expected to see a gorgon when she turned, the head of hissing snakes turning her to stone.

But the reality was far, far worse. She turned, slowly, and looked up into Michael Dowd's impassive, unnaturally brown eyes.

Chapter 15

He looked so very different, and yet unmistakably the same. He was broader, stronger, more powerful looking, than the frail schoolteacher who'd come to the Caribbean. His hair was dark brown instead of auburn; his blue eyes were now a muddy brown. But even more telling than the physical changes were the differences in the way he held himself. There was a foppish quality to him, a suggestion of the dilettante that came not just from the too impeccable white linen suit and the perfectly cut, slightly too long hair, but from the slightly preening way he held himself. It was no wonder the shortsighted Sir Henry had accepted him as an ineffectual remittance man, a member of the British aristocracy forced to put up with being stationed in a nothing job on a tiny island with no political importance whatsoever.

But Francey could see, very clearly. She'd been blind, stupid, for so long that the brightness of clarity was a physical pain in her head, in her heart. The charming fop was no more real than the sweet schoolteacher. The man in front of her, watching her out of indolent eyes that showed no recognition, was a wolf. A conscienceless wild animal, one with no moral compunctions whatsoever. A man who could kill. A man who could not love.

There was no question that he was the dark, robed Arab who'd brought her out of that hellhole. No question that he'd made love to her in the darkness of her storm-swept cabin, and then left her before she awoke from her drug-induced stupor to doubt her own sanity. There was no question that he'd been sent to St. Anne to guard her, maybe to question her. No question at all that she'd been a pawn from the start, first in Patrick Dugan's hands, then in Michael Dowd's far more clever ones. She wanted to throw up.

"I believe Dr. Brady is already back at the hotel," he said politely, his voice softer, slightly more fey. "Apparently Mr. Travers is feeling better."

"Good show," Sir Henry said, his dislike of the younger man obvious. "Then why don't you see Miss Neeley back there like a good fellow? You don't have anything to do till the cocktail party tonight."

"No, thank you," Francey said quickly, unable to hide the rising panic in her voice. "I can get back there on my own."

"At least escort her to a taxi, then, Charlie."

"No!" She no longer cared whether she sounded reasonable as she scrambled out of the chair, knocking it over as she went. "I prefer to go alone." She looked up, way up, into Michael's impassive eyes. He was blocking the doorway, and there was no way she was going to bring herself to touch him. The absurd room with its walnut paneling and manor-house atmosphere was suddenly unbearably stuffy. She pulled at the neckline of her silk shirt, feeling it tightening around her throat, and struggled to catch her breath. She had to get out of there. If he didn't move, she would turn around and jump out the window.

She'd forgotten how well he knew her. "As you wish, Miss Neeley," he said politely, backing out of the doorway. "I'll be in my office, Sir Henry."

She watched him disappear. Was that message for his bombastic superior, or for her? If he thought she was ready to hear excuses, or listen to threats, he was mistaken. A confrontation was the last thing she was ready to face.

She simply wanted to get home. Away from deceit. She gave Sir Henry what she knew was a ghastly smile. "You've been very kind," she mumbled. "I won't trouble you further."

"Miss Neeley, are you feeling well?" Sir Henry rose, his bluff, hearty face creased with worry. "Let me get Charlie back, have him see you..."

She bit back the scream that rose in her throat, knowing it would only convince Sir Henry that she needed to be placed in good old Charlie's competent hands. "I'm just relieved my cousin is being looked after, Sir Henry. Thank you again."

While the old man didn't look convinced, he also looked like a man willing to believe what would cause him the least personal trouble. "If you're certain...?"

"I'm certain." She should hold out her hand to him, put the horrible interview to an end, but her palms were covered with cold sweat, and she knew they would be trembling. She backed away toward the door instead, still smiling.

"We're having a little cocktail party tonight to welcome some London men to the island," Sir Henry said. "Perhaps you'd like to join us. I could send Charlie to fetch you."

God, was the man a totally oblivious idiot? It was no wonder the sun had set on the British empire if he was a representative of the foreign service. "Thank you, but no. We're flying out tomorrow, and I think I should stay with my cousin. Goodbye, Sir Henry." She escaped before he could come up with any more idiotic suggestions.

The hallway was cool and deserted. She'd been half-afraid that Michael would be lying in wait for her, ready to pounce, but he was nowhere to be seen. Apparently he'd taken her at her word.

She passed the young man who'd first brought her to Sir Henry, and he fingered his much-abused necktie nervously as she walked by. She had a fleeting, wistful fantasy that it had been Michael she'd nearly strangled. Except with him she wouldn't have stopped short of asphyxiation.

The taxi she hadn't requested was waiting for her. The man who poked his head out the passenger side was dark, with black, friendly eyes. "Miss Neeley. I'm to take you back to the hotel."

She didn't even consider it. She asked too many questions, knew too much, showed up in the wrong places at the wrong time. She was a major inconvenience, and they'd gotten rid of her once. If she got into that taxicab, she might never see the United States again.

It was late afternoon, with the heat of the sun fading slightly. "I'd rather walk," she said.

"Miss, it's too hot and too far to walk."

"I need the exercise."

There was no mistaking the panic in his voice. "I have orders...."

She turned. "From whom?"

He looked confused, guilty, for a moment. And then he jammed the car into gear and took off into the busy streets of the tiny port city. She watched him go. She didn't turn and look back at the embassy. She knew someone was watching her, and she knew perfectly well who that someone was. She didn't have to catch him in the act to know. Indeed, he was far more clever than she'd ever imagined. She probably wouldn't see him if she turned to look. But he would be there nonetheless, watching.

He would know she hadn't taken the bait, hadn't been fool enough to get into the taxi that would take her heaven knew where. He could make of that what he wished. But if she hesitated on the sidewalk too long he might come after her. And she didn't think she could stand that.

Her slender leather sandals were part of the new clothes Daniel had provided for her, and after the first hour they began to hurt her feet. She ignored the discomfort. She needed to walk. To walk and walk and walk. To breathe in the fresh salt air, to feel the breeze on her face, to empty her mind and her heart and simply be. She paid no attention to the direction her legs were taking her. She just kept walking.

"What the hell do you mean, you don't have her?"

Niall Regan shrugged, determined not to show fear. "She wouldn't get into the taxi. She said she wanted to walk."

"Sweet heaven, and you let her? She was so damned close, and you just let her go? Why didn't you follow her?"

"She started to get suspicious. Damn it, we were still at the embassy. Anyone could have come out, started asking questions. I couldn't risk it."

"Didn't have the nerve to risk it, you mean." The voice was cool, scathing. "It's a good thing we don't have to count on the likes of you. If you'd done as you were told, things could have been finished by now. As it is, we'll have to wait until tomorrow and grab her at the airport, if we have to. I'm not happy."

Niall Regan knew that. He knew he'd chosen a stern taskmaster, and he'd always told himself the cause was worth it. Now he wasn't so certain. There had been too many deaths, too much bloody carnage simply for the sake of bloody carnage. He was used to working with fanatics, wild-eyed visionaries without the common sense to see them safely into the toilet. But the leader of the Cadre went beyond that, into the realm of certifiable insanity. And he wondered whether he could be on that plane tomorrow, in Frances Neeley's place.

"Sorry I let you down," he said meekly. "It won't happen again."

"You can be sure of that, boy-o," said Caitlin Dugan, raising the gun he didn't know she had and pointing it to his forehead. And then there was nothing but a blinding white light. Nothing at all.

There was a different concierge on duty when she walked into the dark, hushed lobby. She carried her new sandals in her hand, walking barefoot on the beautiful oriental runner, and her long gauze skirt swirled around her legs. She'd lost all sense of time, letting darkness fall around her, and it was only because she'd somehow ended up back at the hotel that she'd decided to go inside.

She walked past Daniel's door on the third floor without giving him more than a cursory thought. Either Dr. Brady had managed to stabilize him, correct his medication and bring him back to his old self, or he hadn't. If he hadn't, the alternatives were equally obvious. The hospital or death. Whatever the answer, there wasn't anything she could, or would, do about it. She didn't even know whether Daniel had lied to her or not. He might have been fed the same convoluted stories—no, that wasn't true. He told her he'd seen the Arab who'd brought her out of prison. An ugly customer, he'd called him.

One more person she couldn't trust. She closed her door behind her, very softly, and reached for the light switch.

"Don't turn it on." Michael's voice came from out of the darkness, and she froze.

She had a great many alternatives. She could scream bloody murder; she could fling herself at him in a rage; she could fall at his feet. She wanted to do all those things—and she wanted to do none of those things. So she did nothing for a moment, just took a deep, steadying breath.

"What the hell are you doing here?" she asked finally, her voice thin and calm in the inky darkness. "Come to apologize? So sorry, Francey dear, but I've lied to you, your cousin's lied to you, but it was all for the good of society...."

"Be quiet, Francey."

"I think I've been quiet long enough."

"The hell you have. What do you think landed you in that Spanish prison?" His voice was weary. He was sitting on the sofa by the French doors—she could see his silhouette. See the faint glow of the cigarette she hadn't known he smoked. "I told you to forget about me. Why the hell didn't you listen?"

"I'm listening now." She walked into the room, her bare feet silent on the thick carpet. "I'm going back to New York with Daniel...." Sudden misgivings assailed her. "Is that why you're here? Is Daniel dead?"

"He's fine. Elmore switched his medication, and he's all set to accompany you tomorrow. Assuming you're planning to go quietly."

"And if I'm not? Will someone drug me again, maybe find a Maltese prison to throw me into?"

"Don't be hysterical."

"I don't consider it hysterical of me. After all, I *have* been drugged, I *have* been imprisoned. Why not try again? I imagine this time you won't be around to rescue me. I don't quite understand why you did, Michael. Why didn't you just leave me there to rot?"

"The moment I found out where you were, I came after you."

"Why? Didn't it interfere with whatever spy game you're playing? That's what you are, isn't it? Some damned James Bond, living out Cold War fantasies?"

"Francey..."

"Why are you here, Michael? What is it you want from me?"

"I wanted to apologize."

She took a deep, furious breath. "You wanted to apologize?" she echoed in a blast of rage. "Not good enough, Michael, not by a long shot. You didn't just happen to choose St. Anne to recuperate from your so-called auto accident. You came after me. To pick my brain, to see what I knew about the Cadre. Didn't you?''

"Yes."

"It didn't matter that I'd told everybody everything a million times. It didn't matter that Patrick was dead. It didn't matter—'' She stopped suddenly, as another sick realization hit her. "You killed him, didn't you?''

He didn't even pretend to misunderstand her. "Yes."

"Of course you weren't in a car accident. You were recovering from bullet wounds. He shot you before you killed him. I watched." Her voice broke slightly in the shadowy darkness.

"Yes," he said again.

"Damn you," she said quietly.

"For what? For killing a man who was trying to turn a public occasion into a bloodbath? For killing a man who damned near killed me?''

"For lying."

"Well, in that case I'm damned for sure, because my entire life is a lie," he said savagely.

"It was your choice. I wonder what your family thinks of you. Are they proud of the life you've chosen. Or don't they even know?''

His silence gave her the answer. "They don't exist, either, do they?'' she said. "No Whipdale House and comfortable mum, no sisters and brothers and aging Newfoundlands. It was all a lie, wasn't it?''

"Yes."

She took a deep, shaky breath. "Why me, Michael? Why did you come to St. Anne? Why didn't you believe me, let me be? Why should I have lied to the investigators?''

He rose from the sofa and walked to the French doors, his back to her. She watched him in the darkness, marveling again at the difference in him. He wasn't Charlie Bisselthwaite now, or gentle Michael Dowd. He was the man on Baby Jerome. A strong, dangerous man, suddenly larger than life. "We couldn't trust you," he said finally. "Not if we took into account your family connection."

"Don't be ridiculous. Daniel is almost pathologically loyal. He likes the same stupid games you do—he'd never become involved with terrorists or an organization like the Cadre."

"I'm not talking about your cousin Daniel. His loyalty is unquestionable."

"Unlike mine," she said bitterly. "Then what the hell *are* you talking about? I don't have any other family. My mother died in a car crash seven years ago, and my father drowned when I was three. Unless you're talking about the parade of stepfathers my mother presented me with, and I hardly think I can be condemned because of them."

"No one's condemning you," he said wearily, turning to face her. She shouldn't see much in the darkness, just the shape of him, the rumpled white suit that looked so different on his Charlie alter ego, the glitter of his eyes. And yet she knew he could see her quite clearly. Her face. And her heart.

"Then why don't you explain, simply and clearly, what it is that's made you suspect me?"

"That charming Irish poet your mother married," he said. "The one who drowned in the Liffey when you were three years old. Well, he was something more than a bad poet. He had strong political leanings. He didn't drown. He died while trying to plant a bomb. And you weren't his only child."

This couldn't be happening, Francey thought. "What child?"

"A girl. Born to an Irish waitress by the name of Cassie Dugan. She named her daughter Caitlin."

It came back with sickening suddenness. The feel of the girl's tight, furious body as she shoved her away from her, the screech of tires, the ominous thump of a body striking metal. "Caitlin was my sister?"

"You were marked, practically from birth. She and the man she called her brother sought you out. You were a perfect choice, a combination of political and personal enemy, and with a comfortable trust fund to boot."

"Not anymore. I got rid of as much as I could."

Michael laughed, the sound totally devoid of humor. "Just where they wanted it to go. You really think the Children of Eire is an innocent organization? It's the Cadre. They finally got what they wanted from you. Or almost everything. Caitlin wanted your death."

"And instead I killed her." Her voice was raw in the darkness. "Didn't I? Or is that one more little surprise you have for me...?"

He moved then, crossing the darkened room to come close, too close for her peace of mind. "This time I need you to listen to me, Francey. You need to get on that plane tomorrow with Daniel. No questions, no looking back. I never existed."

"Who didn't exist? Michael Dowd? Or Charlie Bisselthwaite? Or the Arab? Or..." Hysteria was making her voice rise, and he did what she'd been waiting for. He put his hands on her, catching her arms and pulling her tight against his body. He was hot, blazing hot, and she was so cold.

"None of us," he whispered in her ear. "In a few days this will all be over. You can wipe it out of your memory, forget it ever happened...."

She yanked herself free, and her anger blazed forth. "I can, can I? It's that simple? I just wipe out blocks of my life and do a little tap dance? Next thing I know, you'll be telling me to find a nice young man, settle down and get married?"

"You should."

She slapped him. The sound was loud and shocking in the still, dark hotel room. He didn't move, and she reached out to slap him again, to goad him into a reaction.

She got her wish without her hand connecting. He caught her wrist in a tight grip, pulled her back against him and kissed her, a hard, brutal kiss that hurt her mouth. And broke her heart.

There was more honesty, more emotion, in that heated, desperate kiss than in any he'd give her before. He still held her wrist, but she slid her other arm around his waist and clung to him desperately, feeling buffeted by the winds of fate and anger.

And then he released her abruptly, flinging her wrist away, stepping back. "Goodbye, Francey," he said, biting the words off as if they pained him. And a moment later he was gone, the heavy door closing silently behind him.

She didn't move, wondering almost absently whether she was going to cry.

No tears came. No fury, no pain, no recriminations. Just a deep, thick calm, wrapping around her. Tinged with joy.

He loved her. She remembered the words from her drugged stupor, and she felt them in her heart, in his rage, his anger, his need for her. He loved her fully as much as she loved him.

And there wasn't a damned thing she could do about it. To remain on Malta would be to put her life in danger and, therefore, his. The best thing she could do was leave, to-morrow, and wait for him to come to her.

He hadn't said he would. He had told her to forget about him. He might even have thought it was possible. But it wouldn't be for him. Sooner or later, he would have to come to her. And she would be waiting.

It had never been dark in the prison cell. Bare light bulbs had glared in her eyes all night long, and the thick, stench-laden air had sunk into her lungs. She'd come to cherish the darkness. The silence. A town that closed down early. Or maybe it was later than she realized. Only an occasional car drove by outside, beneath the small balcony, and there were no voices, no sounds of street quarrels or lovers' laughter. Moving around the room, she turned off the lights, plunging it into darkness. She didn't bother to check the door. She knew she hadn't locked it, and she told herself she didn't care. She stretched out on the bed, on top of the covers, and lay very still. It was as dark and silent as a tomb, with only the fresh salt breeze reminding her that she was alive. Alive. And it wasn't until she was almost asleep that she realized why she hadn't locked her door.

It hadn't been apathy, lack of concern that the people who wanted to hurt her, the members of the Cadre, the mysterious Cardiff, might hurt her. And it hadn't had anything to do with her recent intense hatred of locks and keys.

It had to do with the deep-seated, unshakable hope that Michael Dowd would change his mind, come once again to her in the shadows, and make her feel alive.

Their plane was due to depart from the tiny Maltese airport at one-thirty in the afternoon. They were to change in Rome, then fly straight on to the United States without stopping, passing time zones and governments without even being aware of them.

Francey threw out the sand-washed silk clothes she'd walked the streets in, threw out the sandals that had carried her away from the embassy. She dressed without thinking, not noticing the texture of the silk this time, not noticing the flattering drape of the cloth. She left the hotel room without a backward glance, meeting Daniel in the lobby and accompanying him out to the airport in complete silence.

He still didn't look well. Whatever drugs Elmore had given him hadn't done the trick, and his color was just as bad as it had been before. He kept rubbing his upper arm in an unconscious gesture, and occasionally he stumbled. By the time they'd managed to check in for their flight at the tiny airport, he was sweating profusely in the cool, air-conditioned atmosphere.

"Boarding in half an hour, Miss Neeley," the flight attendant announced.

"Damned island," Daniel muttered as he sank into a chair. "The runway's too small for my jet. I hate flying commercial airlines. I hate it."

Francey tried to dredge up some sympathy and failed completely. "It can't be that long a flight to Rome. If you want, you can wait there for your jet while I go on ahead. I have no problem with flying commercial airlines. I simply want to get home."

"I'm coming with you," Daniel said, wheezing slightly.

"Why? So I don't get into any more trouble?" she asked tartly.

He shook his head, closing his eyes in sudden weariness. "I haven't done well by you, Francey. When your mother died, I promised I'd watch out for you, make sure you were all right. I've failed at that, failed miserably."

"You did your best," she murmured soothingly, the hard knot of her anger buried deep inside. It wouldn't do any good to accuse Daniel of betrayal. His motives, his beliefs were his own.

"I should have told you, warned you..." he said, rubbing his upper arm.

"Yes," she said. "But it's past that now. Shouldn't I be looking ahead? Shouldn't both of us?"

He sighed. "He told you, about Caitlin, didn't he? I'm glad. I wish I'd felt I could, but I promised your mother..."

"Let's not talk about it now," Francey said, putting a soothing hand on his arm, feeling the faint tremors. "She's gone, there's nothing she can do to hurt us anymore."

Daniel opened his mouth to speak, but instead a look of intense surprise passed over his face. He clutched his arm again, tightly. "Francey," he gasped. And then he pitched forward onto the tile floor.

Chapter 16

The man known by many names, including Michael Dowd, had been furious when he'd walked into Sir Henry's office and seen Francey's slender back. He'd been in a white-hot rage, so intense he was barely rational. How someone would have been shortsighted enough to let Francey Neeley come to the British embassy, how all their fail-safe systems could have shorted out, was a matter of complete mystery to him. He'd been a fool to think he could ever get away with it, simply fade out of her life without seeing her again. He was too old a hand at this game to have wasted his time on false hopes. But he couldn't rid himself of the blind rage that had swamped him as he saw the shocked recognition in Francey's eyes.

He couldn't understand why she hadn't denounced him. Why she hadn't launched herself in a furious attack, or at the very least told that old fool, Sir Henry, that he was no more a cultural attaché than Oliver North had been. Because she'd known. He understood her very well, better than he knew himself. And in her shocked, hurt eyes he'd

seen a sudden wealth of comprehension. She knew everything, or just about. Knew the limits of his betrayal.

And she'd simply walked away. Without a word of re-
proach or threat. Simply curled in on herself and vanished.

She didn't know he'd followed her. He hadn't lost his
touch enough for her to notice he'd been shadowing her as
she walked aimlessly through the old town section, down by
the waterfront, up past the rich houses of the expatriates,
skirting the cafés and bars that were bright and warm with
humanity. She didn't know his watchful shadow had kept
any number of men from trying to strike up a conversation with the aimless wanderer.

He'd waited until she neared the hotel, slipped ahead of
her in the shadows and waited for her in her room. He
didn't know what he'd hoped to accomplish. He certainly
hadn't wanted to touch her again. Had he?

But of course he had. He'd come within inches of taking
her to that wide, empty bed and making sure nothing
fogged her memory of what it was like between them. But
something had stopped him. Maybe his last remnants of
decency. Or maybe just the dazed pain in her beautiful
brown eyes.

He'd left her before he could touch her again. And then
he'd turned and walked to the nearest bar and proceeded to
get just as drunk as he could afford to.

It didn't make the next day any better. He didn't have a
headache or a hangover—his body was too well controlled
to be prey to any such weaknesses. He showed up at work
a fashionable forty-five minutes late, as his alter ego,
Charlie, always did, and managed to look languid and unconcerned as he waited for his carefully constructed cover
to come crashing down around him.

He had no idea what she was going to do. Whether she
would leave with Daniel, quietly accepting that it was over.
He'd told her the truth, or most of it, about her sister to

shock her into acquiescence. But with Francey, nothing was a certainty.

There was no phone call. No outraged summons from Sir Henry, demanding an explanation. Not even a word from Daniel, warning him of the upcoming debacle. Nothing at all.

He was more than accustomed to the frantic tedium of waiting for all hell to break loose. He told himself that this was no different from keeping watch outside a terrorists' hideout, but he knew otherwise. For the first time in his life his emotions were involved. And in a matter of hours the first woman he'd ever loved would send his mission into oblivion. Or she would disappear from his life forever. And he didn't know which would be worse.

He spent the hours shuffling papers on his artfully messy desk, drinking very strong coffee and flirting with any woman who happened to walk by his open office door. Her plane was due to leave at two-thirty. If he could just ignore the clock until after that he would be fine.

But for the first time in his life his iron will faded. At a quarter of two he looked at the thin gold watch that belonged to a Charlie-type person and knew he had just enough time to make it to the airport. Not to stop her. But to watch her fly away, out of his life forever.

The ambulance was just pulling out when he arrived at the airport, and it charged past him, lights flashing, siren keening. He barely noticed it, so intent on finding Daniel and watching the plane take off that he almost didn't see the car following the ambulance. Almost didn't see Francey's pale, frightened figure in the back seat, sandwiched between two large men.

He didn't waste his time cursing; he jerked the wheel, heading after the ambulance and the gray car. Charming Charlie the indolent fop had disappeared. The man who'd taken his place had no name, no identity other than Cougar, only one purpose in life, and the willingness to use any means to get it. He'd recognized Dex, the man to the left of

Francey. And he knew with a cool clarity that he wouldn't be able to get her away without killing on her behalf.

"I wish you'd let me ride in the ambulance," Francey said, squirming slightly. The two airport officials on either side of her were very large, cramping her on the small back seat of the Fiat.

"Sorry, miss, but you'd just be in the way," the kinder looking man on the right said. "Your cousin's suffered a massive heart attack, and the paramedics are doing their best to stabilize him. They don't need the likes of you getting in their way."

She thought she could hear the charming trace of Ireland in his voice, and she had to stifle her instinctive, distrustful reaction. She was so desperate to get away from the life her cousin had chosen, from lying, deceitful men. The airplane had been so close, freedom just a few steps away. If she'd been able to leave she truly believed she could have turned her back on Michael Dowd—or whoever the hell he was—forever.

But Daniel's collapse had changed all that. Through the exigencies of fate she was being drawn back into the spider's web of deceit. And there was no longer any way she could retreat.

The car took a sharp right, and Francey looked up, the first inklings of dread washing through her as she watched the ambulance continue barreling straight ahead. "Why aren't we following them?"

"We're taking a shortcut," the kindly man said. "They'll be going to the emergency entrance, and you'll need to go to the business office, fill out papers and the like. You know hospitals—bureaucracies like all the rest. Don't worry, we'll get there in good time."

She didn't believe him. He had such a broad, trustworthy face, such warmth in his blue eyes and ruddy smile, such concern in his voice. She wanted to believe him so badly, and she knew she'd made a major mistake in getting into the car with him. Not that he'd given her any alternative. The two men had come up on either side of her as the paramedics were loading Daniel into the ambulance, and she'd been too frightened and upset to put up more than a cursory argument.

"We're in trouble, boy-o," the previously silent driver announced in a voice thick with Ireland. "Someone's following us."

"Lose him," the man said briefly, patting Francey's limp hand.

"What's going on?" she asked, knowing full well she wasn't going to like the answers.

But no answers were forthcoming. "You want to finish her now? You know what happened to Niall—we wouldn't want to displease the powers-that-be."

"Killing her now would be the height of stupidity," the kind man said. "If whoever's following us has backup, we'll have nothing to bargain with. And if we get back with her already dead, the boss will cut our throats. Just shut up and drive." He turned and gave Francey an affable smile. "Sorry about this, miss."

"You're the Cadre."

"And you're not very careful. This time you don't have the Cougar to keep you safe. You're on your own, and no one's going to rescue you this time."

"I wouldn't count on that, Dex," the driver said, his voice tight with panic. "Who the hell do you think is following us?"

Francey tried to swivel around, but Dex clamped a hand on her arm, holding her in place while the silent man on her other side stared out the back.

She heard the crack of glass. The man slumped down beside her. A moment later she heard the whine of a bullet, and the driver swerved off the road, cursing, stopping at an angle on the side of the roadway.

Her seatmate had fallen in her lap. She pushed him away from her, and her hands were wet and sticky with blood.

She wanted to scream, but she had no breath in her. Dex had grabbed her arm and pulled her from the stalled car. A moment later she was clasped against his body, a human shield, and she could feel a cool steel gun barrel against her temple.

The car that had followed them pulled ahead, stopping in front of the car, blocking their exit. The driver was already running, disappearing into the distance, but the man holding her was made of sterner stuff. He wasn't going to run away.

"Hey, Cougar," he shouted toward the dark car with the smoked windows. "You want to strike a bargain?"

Francey watched, numb, as the door opened. She knew who would step out, and yet she couldn't quite believe it. Once more he looked completely different. Charlie had vanished. So had Michael Dowd, and the dream lover from the boat. This man was closer to the drunken Arab who'd brought her out of purgatory, though this time it looked as if he were there to deliver his own taste of hell.

He didn't even glance at her. All his attention was focused on the man holding her. The hand digging into her arm was sweaty, and the gun trembled against her temple. He might very well kill her by accident if Michael wasn't careful.

"What kind of bargain?" Michael asked in a voice that bordered on indifference.

"You want the lady?"

"I want the lady." It was spoken softly, but Francey felt a chill slide down her backbone.

"Then you'll have to bargain. I want your car. I want you to put the gun down. And I want you to step back while I drive away. I'll leave her safe and sound in the next town."

Michael smiled. "Don't waste my time, Dex. Let her go."

"In the next town. Or I swear I'll blow her brains out right now."

"And then I'll kill you."

"I don't mind dying for the cause," he said nervously. "I just don't like losing."

"Too bad," Michael said gently. "You're going to do both."

Dex was shivering behind her, and cold sweat was soaking through his clothes, through hers. Francey didn't move, couldn't move as she watched with numb fascination. Dex held the gun, the hostage. And he was terrified of the man confronting them. So terrified that he was bound to make a lethal mistake. Yet she felt only a passing interest in whether her life was going to be forfeit in that mistake.

"I'll give you the girl," Dex said hoarsely. "Here and now. You let me take the car, get the hell out of here...."

"No."

"I'll disappear. No one will have to know...."

"The Cadre will find you," Michael said. "You know they will. And you know how they deal with traitors."

"I'm not a traitor!" Dex said desperately. "I just know when the odds are against me. Cougar, let me go."

"Let the woman go."

She could feel his indecision. The gun at her temple wavered for a moment, but a moment was long enough.

Dex fell backward, his sweaty hands slipping from her, and a second later she heard a whine and pop, the delayed report from Michael's gun. She stared down at the man at her feet, the pool of blood.

"You killed him," she said in a harsh whisper. "He was going to let me go. He was starting to release me...."

"He was about to shove you at me and then shoot us both." Michael was cool and matter-of-fact. "Get in the car and let's get the hell out of here."

"He might not be dead...." She started to lean down, to touch Dex's fallen body, when Michael crossed the space that separated them and hauled her upright.

"He's dead. Trust me. Now get in the car."

"I'm not going anywhere with a murderer." The moment the words were out of her mouth she regretted them.

His face was cool, handsome, absolutely expressionless. For a moment she wondered whether he would hurt her. And then she knew he wouldn't. No matter what he'd done, what crimes he'd committed, why he did what he did, one thing had been constant. He'd been trying to help her.

"Get in the car," he said again from between clenched teeth. "Or I swear to God I'll knock you over the head and drag you there."

So much for not hurting her. She moved stiffly, her body radiating outrage and indignation. "I'll get in the car," she said, "because I have no other way of getting to Daniel. But I don't want to have to talk with you, look at you, or have anything to do with you."

"You'll get in the car because I'm not giving you any other option. I imagine the driver's long gone, but that doesn't mean he won't be back. There's nothing I'd like better than to find some nice quiet jail cell and put you back there until this blows over, but I don't think I have that option. So get in the damned car and stop arguing."

Francey got in the car.

He climbed in beside her, and he seemed huge, overpowering, in the cramped space as he put his gun on the seat between them. It smelled of smoke and what she imagined was cordite, and it was lethal, black and ugly.

He glanced over at her, huddled by the door. "Put on your seat belt."

It was suddenly too much. "I've been kidnapped, shot at, nearly raped, imprisoned, bombed, had my car sabotaged, and you tell me to put on my seat belt? Why don't you give me a lecture about safe sex while you're at it?"

Only by a slight stiffening in his shoulders could she see that her barb had hit home. Ignoring her, he reached over and yanked the seat belt across her lap. "Do me a favor," he said softly. "Keep your mouth shut or I'll gag you."

She almost told him to try it. But some last-minute wisdom stopped her. He was a man who was more than capable of doing just that. He'd just killed two men—why would he balk at a little bondage? Ignoring him, she leaned back against the seat and closed her eyes, willing the inner trembling to subside. Daniel would make things better. She just needed to hold on till Michael brought her to the hospital, then disappeared into whatever fantasy he was living out. Surely she could keep herself together that long.

The car started with a jerk. He was driving fast, probably much too fast for the narrow island roads, but she refused to open her eyes and look. She was already intimidated by his presence, the size of him, the heat of him, the sheer animal intensity of him. In the shadows the night before he'd been disturbing. In the daylight he was overwhelming. Her only defense was to try to withdraw into some safe place of her own making. She'd been able to do that in prison, but that particular gift was failing her sorely. She knew why. She could hide from anything in this life. Anything but Michael.

She had blood on her dress. He hoped she hadn't noticed, but he couldn't count on that. Francey could be far too observant when she wanted to be, and right now she had nothing to gain by hiding from the truth. She'd hidden from reality when they'd been in the Caribbean, but the last weeks had brought life crashing down on her. Even if she wanted to, he doubted she could keep the truth from intruding.

She'd shut him out when she'd shut her eyes. Which suited him just fine for the present. He didn't want to talk to her, either. What could he do, offer excuses, apologies, explanations? None of them was good enough.

He had that sick, angry feeling inside that he always got when he had to kill. It didn't matter that he'd had no choice. It didn't matter that he could have killed the driver but had let him escape. It didn't even matter that he knew the history of the two men he'd killed, the crimes they'd committed, the innocent lives they'd ended. He'd learned long ago that nothing could assuage the burning inside, the hollow, empty feeling.

Once upon a time he'd hoped that Francey could. That tiny kernel of purity in her had been like a beacon. As long as he could keep her safe, then there would be a haven for him.

He knew now that that had been a foolish, romantic longing. There was no haven for him anywhere, and particularly not with her. She'd seen him kill. She knew his lies. And she knew he'd come to her bed when she was too drugged and shocked to have any conscious say in the matter.

It had been a taste of heaven, and one of the worst mistakes of his life. He'd hoped actually making love to her would wipe out the obsession. Nothing could be as good as the fantasy that he'd built up over the weeks.

But it had been. Better than the fantasy, better than any reality he'd ever known. He'd been able to turn his back and leave, knowing it was saving her, knowing he was being noble, self-sacrificing, and his one selfless act might somehow atone for his countless sins.

But she'd been brought back into his life time and time and time again. The more he fought it, the more he hurt her. As long as the Cadre existed to spin its murderous webs, then he and Francey were going to be caught in them. He had to stash her someplace safe while he finished with them. And then he could finish with Francey.

"Where are we?" She'd opened her eyes finally, staring around her with growing rage. "We should be at the hospital by now."

"We're not going to the hospital." They were taking a narrow road that ran along the sparsely populated western side of the island. The sea was beyond, gray and angry. It matched his soul.

He waited for her to start screaming at him, fully prepared for her to launch her body at him. She stayed very still in that distant corner of the front seat. "What about Daniel?" she said finally.

"Daniel will either recover or not. Your presence won't make a difference. In case you haven't noticed, the Cadre wants you dead. If you're at the hospital, they'll come after you there. They won't stop until they get you."

"For God's sake, why? Patrick is dead, and probably Caitlin, too. I didn't kill Patrick, you did. And I didn't mean to kill Caitlin. I was stupid enough to give them a lot of money. What more do they want from me? Why should one idiotic American female matter so damned much?"

"She shouldn't. But the leader of the Cadre has an obsession, and the members follow orders without question." He turned inland onto a narrow, winding drive. Francey didn't appear to notice.

"Why should the leader of the Cadre be so determined to kill me? Was he Caitlin's lover? Does he want revenge for her death?"

There was no reason not to tell her. He'd already told her too much. The more lies she was fed, the more she went ferreting for the truth. Maybe he could placate her, shock her into acquiescence, with enough of the truth. "Caitlin Dugan didn't die that night in New York."

He hated the expression that sprang into her eyes. "She didn't? She's still alive? Why didn't you tell me that last night? What happened to her?"

"I don't know the details," he said sourly. "I was otherwise occupied, taking out your murderous lover."

"We weren't lovers," she said automatically, and he didn't know whether he believed her or not. Or why it mattered. "But if she's alive," she went on, oblivious to his reaction, "then I could see her. Reason with her. There must be some humanity still left in her. No matter how monstrous she is, she's still my family. I can't believe that she couldn't call off the leader of the Cadre...."

"Caitlin Dugan *is* the leader of the Cadre," Michael said flatly.

The color and animation drained from her face. "She's trying to kill me?"

"She always was. And she won't stop until you're dead. Or she is." He pulled up outside a decaying villa, but she didn't even notice, still intent on him.

"So you're going to kill her?"

He didn't bother to deny it. "Yes."

"I can't let you do that."

"You're not going to have any say in the matter. My mission is to deactivate the most ruthless group of fanatics ever to be born on English soil. To intercept a shipment of arms and money, and to wipe out the last remaining members. The Cadre won't let themselves be taken prisoner. If we don't kill Caitlin, she'll kill herself rather than let herself be taken."

"Then let her," Francey said with sudden fierce passion. "Wipe out her organization, destroy their evil, but don't kill her. Not for her sake. But for yours. Promise me, Michael."

God, he wanted to. He would have given years off his life to offer her that assurance. "My name isn't Michael," he said coldly. "And I have no promises for you."

The light went out of her eyes. She gave up on him then, he knew it without question. Before, a part of her heart had belonged to him. Now it was wiped out, one more casualty of the Cadre's far-reaching destructiveness. One more casualty of his own empty way of life.

"Get in the house," he said, turning off the engine and pulling the key. He wouldn't have put it past her to try to make a run for it.

She didn't. Instead she looked down at her hands lying limp in her lap, at the blood on her silk skirt. She touched the stains that were rapidly turning brown in the hot, dry air, and she shivered. "Damn you, Michael," she whispered, staring at her hands.

"You can curse me to your dying day," he drawled, forcing a casual tone. "But at least that'll be decades away, and not tomorrow. Out of the car, Francey, or I'll carry you."

She looked up sharply then, and he could see the intensity of her emotions burning just beneath the surface. Hatred for him, without any question. He accepted it.

Without a word she opened the car door, sliding out and standing in front of the tumbledown villa. "What is this place?"

"A place to hide. No one outside the organization even knows of its existence. You'll be safe here."

"The organization? Now why doesn't that fill me with confidence?"

"The only one you have to fear in the organization is Ross Cardiff, and he's still in Spain. Assuming he managed to swim to shore." The moment the words were out he regretted them.

"What do you mean by that?" she demanded.

"I threw him off the *True Blue*. Last time I saw him, he was floundering around in Mariz harbor."

The light had come back into her eyes. "You did that for me?"

"Hell, no. I did it because he'd screwed up the mission by his rash actions."

"Didn't I do the same? By coming after you, asking questions? Why didn't you throw me to the sharks?"

"You'd already been there," he said flatly. "Don't get sentimental, Francey. I'd been looking for an excuse to get the drop on Cardiff for a long time. You simply provided it."

"I see."

"You'll find food in the kitchen area. There's no power, but the kerosene lamps are cleaned and ready. No telephone, either, and you'll be at least twenty miles from the nearest neighbor, so I wouldn't try to make it on foot if I were you. Someone will come to collect you as soon as it's safe."

"You're not leaving me here."

"You have no choice in the matter."

"The hell I don't," she said, as all her hard-won control suddenly short-circuited. And she leaped at him, her fury and rage and pain centered directly on him.

Chapter 17

Michael put up his hands to stop her, to keep her not from hurting him, but from hurting herself. He caught her wrists in his hard hands, but the feel of her flesh beneath his was a torment he wasn't able to resist. He yanked her body hard against his, and she stared up at him, wild-eyed, furious, for a long, breathless moment. And then slowly, deliberately, he dropped his mouth to hers.

She jerked spasmodically, trying to reject him, but he was too strong, too determined. He pulled her arms tight around his waist so that her thin, panting body was plastered against his. She could stop him, he knew, by using her knee, by kicking him; she could distract him enough to stop him kissing her. But she didn't. Her arms tightened around his waist, her head tilted back beneath his, and if she didn't kiss him back, she didn't deny him access to her open mouth.

She let him kiss her, an angry, passion-filled kiss that ravaged her mouth even as it ravaged his soul. When he lifted his head to look down at her, he didn't know what he expected.

She looked dazed, wary, but not ready to give up fighting. "What are you doing?" she asked, her voice husky.

He found to his complete amazement, after all they'd been through in the last bloody hour, that he could smile. "That was supposed to be a kiss. If you didn't recognize it, I must not have been doing it right."

For a moment she didn't say anything. "Then maybe you'd better try it again."

He caught her face in his hands, and when his mouth touched hers this time, he was lost. She kissed him back, sliding her arms up his back, clinging to him, her fingers digging into the loose cotton shirt.

He had to get back to town. Things were moving quickly; he needed to stash Francey and get back to the others. He needed to shove her away from him, get in the car and drive away without looking back.

But he couldn't. He lifted his head to look down at her, knowing he should say something, anything, to get her away from him.

"What's the matter?" she whispered huskily. "You only like drugged women?"

She was turning feisty in her old age. "Were you drugged that night? I thought you were normally that passive."

Withdrawing her arms from around him, she slid her hands up the front of his shirt to the open neck. And then she yanked, hard, ripping his shirt open. "I think I've been passive long enough."

He caught her hands in his, knowing he should put her away from him. Instead he hauled her into his arms, picking her up and starting into the cool dark interior of the half-ruined villa.

He slept at the end of the house, on a king-size bed surrounded by paneless windows. The breeze from the ocean blew night and day, and the place was clean, bare, stark. He set her down on a mattress covered only by a white sheet, and he knew he should turn and run.

She didn't move, just watched him, her eyes huge in her pale face. Her mouth was red and damp from his own mouth, and it made him hard just looking at it.

How many times had he justified his actions by telling himself it was the last time? He would never see her again, so this once was all right? He was telling himself that same thing once more. In a few hours he might be dead. If he wasn't, the Cadre would be, and there would never be another reason for their paths to cross. She would be free of him. It might take her a while—he was pragmatic enough to realize that—but sooner or later the sheer normalcy of life would take over. She would find someone to love, to marry, to have babies with.

She would get over him a lot faster if he turned and walked away right now, without a backward glance. He'd tried so damned hard to be noble; if he gave in now, all that effort would have been wasted.

"No," she said clearly, not moving from the bed.

So she was going to make it easier for him. "No?" he echoed quizzically, unable to resist. "Then why did you rip off my shirt?"

She rose from the bed, and he knew he was in trouble. The bed was huge, white, pristine, behind her, and she was small, frail, wounded. And far too determined. She slid her hands up under his ripped shirt, her skin hot against his flesh, and he groaned quietly.

"I mean, no, you're not leaving," she said, low and determined. "You're not disappearing again, leaving some soulless bureaucrat to pick up the pieces. You're staying here with me."

If her hands reached his nipples he would be lost. "I'm a soulless bureaucrat," he said, trying to back away.

"No, you're not. You're the man who loves me. And you're not going to leave me again."

He'd known the words would come back to haunt him. He knew he should deny them, dismiss them. But her hands slid up, covering him, and he needed her out of that bloodstained dress, he needed her naked, stretched out on his big white bed that had been so empty for so long, and there was no way he could fight them both.

"Take off your dress," he said.

She smiled then. Not a look of triumph, more an expression of relief. And mischief. "Make me."

It came apart easily under his big hands, far more easily than his alter ego Charlie's custom-tailored linen shirt. In a moment she was standing naked in front of him, her head thrown back in defiance as she waited for him to touch her.

And then she didn't wait. Moving closer, she pushed his ruined shirt off his shoulders and onto the floor. She reached for his leather belt, unfastening it deftly and pulling it from the loops with a tiny whispered sound. He let her do it, holding himself perfectly still, giving her control.

He waited, wondering whether she was going to have the nerve to unfasten his trousers. It took her a moment, and then she swayed against him, reaching out to touch him through the linen trousers.

He wondered whether the extent of his arousal would shock her. And then he no longer wondered anything, as her deft, curious fingertips traced the rigid outline of him behind the row of buttons.

He covered her hand with his, pressing her harder against him, and he made a low, guttural sound of need in the back of his throat.

She was struggling with the buttons, her hands shaking with arousal and frustration. Holding her hand still against him, he kissed her hard, pushing her back against the mattress, falling with her, half covering her. He fumbled with the buttons himself, finally shucking out of his pants, and then he pushed her up higher on the mattress, cradling her head with his arms as he lay beside her.

"Damn Charlie and his buttons," he said wryly, brushing his lips against hers.

"Who is Charlie?"

"No one. An illusion. A means to an end. He's not here."

"Who is? Who are you?"

He closed his eyes for a moment, wishing he could find an answer. Wishing he even knew. "The man who loves you," he said finally.

She smiled then, a radiant expression. "That's enough," she whispered. "For now."

She was awake this time, shiveringly, blindingly awake. Her flesh trembled with sensitized awareness as he ran his mouth across her stomach, and her nipples tightened fiercely when he suckled them. She was hot, damp, tight, when he sheathed himself in her, too soon and not soon enough, and she climaxed immediately, convulsing around him, her eyes wide with shock.

It took all his rapidly vanishing self-control to keep from following her. If this was his last time with her, possibly his last time on earth, he was going to make it last. He waited for the contractions to lessen, and then he surged against her, hard, fierce and hungry.

If he'd worried that he was too much for her, she immediately disabused him of the notion. She arched her hips up, pulling him in deeper, and her mouth was hungry, seeking, beneath his. He rocked against her slowly, wanting to bury himself in her tight, needful body, and the bed bounced beneath them, a gentle counterpoint.

And then it wasn't slow at all. It was fast and hard and furious, the bed pounding beneath them, her hands clawing at his back, her mouth full of anguished entreaties, and he wanted to give her more, more, give her everything she asked, everything she didn't ask. He wanted to give her his life, his soul, to pour everything into her and exist only in that moment. He waited, stretching out the moment until he could no longer bear it, waiting for the wave to hit her once more. She made a sound, part scream, part sob, as her body shattered once more, and this time he let himself go, shaking to pieces in her arms, disappearing to the kind of place only a man with no name could reach.

She reached for him when he finally pulled away, but he placated her with a gentle kiss on her damp brow, and she smiled, her eyes closed, foolishly trusting. He found a sheet somewhere and threw it over her sleeping body. He took an abstemious shower, leaving enough hot water for Francey, and went to the kitchen to make himself a cup of instant coffee before leaving.

He knew he was just prolonging the inevitable. He knew the longer he waited to get dressed the more likelihood there was of her waking up. But he couldn't make himself go.

It was earlier than he'd thought, just after seven. He wasn't due to meet the others until after midnight. He had more than enough time to just sit and watch her while she slept.

But he wasn't going to do it. If he watched her, he would pull the sheet away from her and join her back on the bed, and every time he touched her it got harder and harder to leave her.

"You're going, aren't you?"

He hadn't even realized she was there. He turned in the dimly lit kitchen, his face carefully blank, even when he saw her.

She was wrapped in the sheet he'd thrown over her. Her sun-streaked hair was a tangle behind her pale face, her eyes large and beseeching, and he could see the marks he'd left on her only too clearly. The lovemarks on her neck and shoulders, and other places beneath the heavy white sheet. And the pain reflected in her eyes.

"I have a job to do," he said, deliberately calm and noncommittal.

"Were you going to say goodbye?" she asked. "Or were you just going to slink away in the night like the rat you are?"

It made him smile. Francey when she was calm and loving was a potent package indeed. Francey when she was angry was somehow reassuring. The truth was there in her eyes, that she loved him enough to be mad. Perhaps it might provide balm for his wounded soul during the long, empty years ahead. And perhaps it would be a torment all its own.

He wasn't going to tell her that. He was trying to pull the tattered remnants of Charlie back around him. "You were sleeping quite soundly. I didn't want to wake you."

"Like hell," she said, coming closer. "You keep leaving me, Michael, or whoever you are. And I keep turning up like a bad penny. When are you going to realize that we're meant to be together?"

All trace of amusement fled. "We're not. Don't be absurd, Francey. Do you really think there are happy endings for the likes of us? For you, maybe. I'm doing my damnedest to ensure that. But not for me. Not with you."

She came right up to him, vibrating with intensity. She smelled of flowers; she smelled of sex. She smelled of him. "You're wasting your time. There is no happy ending for me if you're not part of it."

He cupped her face with his hands, brushing his mouth across her soft lips. "Then, Francey," he whispered, "there's no happy ending for you, either."

He walked away from her without another word, and she let him go, the feel of his mouth still warm on her lips, the feel of his body still imprinted on hers. She wanted to call after him, to plead with him, to fling herself at his feet and beg. But she didn't move.

He'd left a cup of coffee on the scrubbed wooden counters. She took a sip, but it was cold, and she shivered. She heard the car drive away, and her hand tightened around the coffee cup. Charming Charlie would be back at work, probably squiring someone to an embassy cocktail party, and his boss, Sir Henry, would look down his nose at him and mutter deprecating remarks.

And then, sooner or later, he would leave and turn into...what had Dex called him? The Cougar? And before long, possibly before the morning, her sister, her dear, murderous sister, would be dead.

He would disappear. She knew it. And despite her pledge, this time she wouldn't find him. If he wiped out the Cadre, there would be no more threat to her. He would simply vanish. And she would have no way of finding him ever again.

She drank the cold coffee after all, for the dubious comfort of putting her mouth to something he'd put his mouth to. She left the kerosene lamp burning as night darkened around her and the wind whipped through the half-ruined building. She moved slowly back to the bedroom, the sheet trailing around her like a ruined toga, and it wasn't until she was sitting cross-legged on the bed in the dusk-laden darkness that she saw the man in the window.

He was sitting there, watching her with bland, unreadable eyes, and she knew him immediately. The last time she'd seen him it had been outside the café in Mariz, Spain. And suddenly the warm Mediterranean breeze was icy cold on her skin.

"I wondered when he was finally going to remember he had a job to do," Ross Cardiff said affably. "This is quite unlike him—he's always put his mission first. You've been the ruin of him, young lady. The sordid finale to a fine career."

She wanted to pull the sheet tighter around her, away from his prying eyes, but she let it stay loosely around her shoulder. For one thing, she knew instinctively that he had no lascivious interest in her, or any other woman, for that matter. For another, she didn't want to show how completely unnerved she was by his presence.

"Why do you say his career is ruined?" she finally managed to ask, her voice cracked and dry, showing all the fear she'd hoped so desperately to disguise.

He put his other leg over the windowsill and stepped into the room, and Francey knew where Michael had gotten the inspiration for Charlie the fop. The little man in front of her carried himself the same way. The only difference was the intensity in his gaze, the sheer malevolence beneath the bland smile. "It's down the toilet, my girl. But then, he knows that better than anyone. He's going to be a little too careless, tonight, or soon after. He's going to be courting death, all thanks to the influence of a good woman."

"Don't be ridiculous, he's—"

"Women like you make me sick," he said, overriding her protest. "He was doing fine, just fine, until he ran into you. I was against his going to St. Anne, but then, he never did listen to me. Never could accept that I had his best interests at heart. He was weak but determined, and there you were, a sweet little damsel in distress. The first woman he trusted in his entire life."

"What's wrong with that?"

"I'll tell you what's wrong with that," Cardiff hissed. "People like the man you call Michael can't afford to trust. Because trust is always betrayed, by accident or design, and in his line of work, that will kill you. He's been a dead man since he met you, and he knows it. That's why he wants you out of the way."

"Is that why you had me stashed in a Spanish prison? To save him?"

Cardiff smiled, reaching out a small, well-manicured hand to touch her hair. "I already knew it was too late. I was just playing for time. And indulging in a particular weakness of mine. A taste for revenge." He yanked on her hair, hard, then released it. "If I'd known Michael would come racing to the rescue like a tarnished Sir Galahad, I would have had you killed outright and risked your cousin's suspicions."

He moved away from her, wandering over to the window with a dreamy expression on his face. "Maybe I'll rape you," he murmured. "It's the closest I'll ever get to him, and there might be some sort of vicarious thrill in it. And in knowing I've done it."

I will not panic, she told herself, her fingers clutching the sheet. Panic won't help. "You don't strike me as the sort of man who's interested in raping women."

He smiled sweetly. "I'm not. But I'm afraid I have rather a . . . thing . . . for Michael. Not reciprocated, of course. He is rather determinedly hetero. But then, life is full of disappointments, isn't it?" He shrugged. "Get your clothes on."

"Why?"

"You have an appointment."

The man didn't look crazy, even if his words seemed over the edge. Surely he could be reasoned with. "Look, Mr. Cardiff, I'm sorry if I jeopardized your mission. I want the Cadre wiped out just as much as you do, and I promise I'll stay here and keep out of the way. I won't interfere at all."

"But you don't understand, my dear." Ross patted her hand gently. "You're part of the deal."

"The deal?"

"With your sister. I don't just deliver up the British government's well-laid plans for wiping them out in return for my tidy little sum of money. I also present Caitlin Dugan with a far from virgin sacrifice to appease her family pride and bloodlust."

For a moment Francey couldn't breathe. Suddenly it all made sense. "You're a traitor."

Again he shrugged. "Every man is out for his own benefit. I'm a pragmatist. Of course, the Cadre have promised me a prominent role in the new order, but I'm not holding my breath. They'll be wiped out sooner or later, quite possibly sooner. Michael is a phenomenal agent, an absolute killing machine. He's quite beautiful in action. He might very well prevail tomorrow morning. In which case I've covered my tracks quite effectively, and while I'll enjoy giving him an official reprimand for going off on his own, I believe I'll give him an opportunity to continue the good work he does for us."

"The killing, you mean." She was numb, sick with horror.

"They don't call him the Cougar for nothing. He's quite lethal." He tapped his neatly shod little foot. "Hurry up, there's a love. Caitlin's waiting for us, and she *is* an impatient one."

"And if I refuse."

"Then I'll kill you in his bed, quite bloodily, and leave it to him to find you. I imagine you know he's quite foolishly sentimental where you're concerned. If you have to die—and believe me, Miss Neeley, you do have to die—then you might do your best to make it easier on the lad. After all you've meant to each other.''

"You're a pig."

"Spare me. I've been called any number of creative things, and I have a very thick hide. Your choice, Miss Neeley. At my hands, or your sister's.''

She closed her eyes for a moment, conjuring up Caitlin Dugan's hate-filled face. She had no hope of making her see reason. The best she could do was buy herself some time.

She wouldn't show him how frightened she was, how much she wanted to throw up. She put a bright, angry smile on her face. "I think I'm in the mood for a family reunion,'' she said with false brightness.

"A wise decision,'' Ross Cardiff said calmly. "I never was particularly clever with my hands. Clumsiness can be so painful.''

"Cardiff's here, mon.'' Cecil's phony Caribbean accent was still getting on his nerves, but for the first time Michael ignored it.

"Bloody hell. How did he get here so fast? I thought we had another couple of days at least.''

"I'm not sure. But he was chatting up Sir Henry, and the two old biddies were getting on like a house afire.''

"When was this?''

"This afternoon. He left the embassy around five, and he hasn't been seen since.''

"He's not staying there?''

"That remains to be seen. At least he hasn't been anywhere near the Cadre. Everyone's holed up at the old army barracks way out on the peninsula, thinking they're bloody invisible. Stupid fools.''

"What the hell is he up to?'' Michael peered through the dark. His nerves were hopping beneath his skin. He always felt this way just before everything all blew to hell. He hadn't been involved in anything of this magnitude in a long time, and his instincts, his reflexes, were off. He was going to die in this one. He knew it full well. And he didn't really give a damn.

"Beats me," Cecil murmured. "I tell you, I was spooked as hell to hear he'd shown up. At least he's out of the way for now."

"Who says?"

"One of my contacts. He was seen driving out to the eastern end of the island just before sunset. No one lives out that way, just a few abandoned villas, and the road's not much better than a goat track. He'll probably get lost looking for the Cadre's hideout and not be seen until all the shouting's over and he can come out and take credit for it and . . . what's the matter, mon? You look like you've seen a ghost."

"The eastern side of the island? Are you sure?"

Cecil shrugged. "I trust my contact. Why?"

Michael rose, surging upward. He didn't waste time with rational thought, weighing the alternatives, or anything else. His instincts kicked in, and he went with them. "Francey," he said abruptly.

"So they'll keep each other company," Cecil said easily.

"Like hell," Michael said, his voice as cold as ice. "He's going to kill her."

Chapter 18

The night had grown cold, far colder than Francey would have expected as she stumbled behind Ross Cardiff's small, immaculate frame. She found if she kept a modest three paces behind, no further, he would leave her alone. If she tried to fall back, he would put those soft, manicured hands on her, and hurt her, and she knew if he did it one more time she would start screaming and never stop until he did kill her, and then what good would this midnight trek have done anyone?

At least Michael wouldn't find her in his bed. The image Ross had conjured up had been horrifying, for Michael's sake, not hers. If it came right down to it, she would go over a cliff rather than let them use her to hurt him. He'd already said goodbye, dismissed her from his life. If she died, he would mourn, there was no doubt of that. But he'd managed to shut off his emotions with a cold efficiency that astonished her. He would probably be just as efficient in dealing with her loss.

If she was going to die. She wasn't prepared to accept that, not yet. That was the other thing that sent her off into the night with a man who was either mad or intensely evil or both. She was still ready to fight. For her life. For Michael's life. And for the future that he didn't believe in.

They'd driven at first, bouncing over unpaved dirt roads in a late model Range Rover that Cardiff barely knew how to drive. He ground the gears, stalled out, skidded on the loose gravel and generally proved himself incompetent. That weakness went a small way toward improving her equanimity. She almost went so far as to offer to drive for him, then thought better of the notion. He was a man on the very edge, and a woman's mockery might just drive him over.

They'd been walking for the last half hour. Cardiff had stashed the car behind a small outcropping of bushes, and the two of them had taken off down a narrow spit of land leading away from the island. The place was desolate, deserted, a setting for ghosts. A fitting place to meet her sister once more.

Francey's only shoes were a pair of flats she'd worn for traveling. There was blood on them, Dex's blood, and she'd wanted to leave them behind and go barefoot, but thought better of it when she saw Cardiff's expression. He would like nothing more than to drag her barefoot through nettles, or whatever the Maltese equivalent was.

She had no idea they were getting close until they passed the first lookout. The whole affair was ridiculously melodramatic, with passwords and such, like little boys playing soldier. The watch was a young man with a mop of curly dark hair and bright, irrepressible eyes. "They're waitin' for you," he said, gesturing ahead into the impenetrable darkness. "That's the one?"

Cardiff smirked. "The very one."

"Heard they did for Dex and Petey. Her highness is in a rare taking, I promise you." His glance swept her, cool and unconcerned. "Rumor has it they're sisters. They don't look much alike, do they?"

"Particularly not now," Cardiff said with a hollow laugh. "Keep an eye out, lad. They're not planning to come until dawn, but things might change. Cougar's never been one to follow orders.''

The young man didn't look as though he cared for Cardiff's orders, either, or the condescending tone they were delivered in, but he nodded anyway. "Better get along with you now. She wants her pound of flesh, she does.''

Francey considered diving into the bushes.

"Don't even consider it, Miss Neeley," Cardiff said, putting his soft, slimy hand on her arm once more. "Teddy here's an excellent shot, and I happen to know he's equipped with the finest of British military equipment, including heat-seeking bullets. I've seen to it myself. You wouldn't get two feet.''

Francey swallowed the scream that tickled the back of her throat. "I'm getting tired," she said in a flat, unimpressed voice. "Do you suppose we can get on with it?''

"A cool one," Teddy said admiringly. "Sorry I'm going to miss all the fun.''

Francey shivered.

Cardiff didn't release her again. The two of them continued onward in the dark, past the ruined remains of what seemed like an old army outpost. She could smell the sea, the clean fresh fragrance of salt, and in the distance she could hear a rustling sound that might be the wind in the trees that she couldn't see. Or surf crashing on rocks.

The light blinded her. Sudden and shocking, it blasted into their faces, and she stumbled backward, breaking free of Cardiff's grip as she put an arm up to her face.

"It's about time," Francey knew that voice. Faintly husky, like her own, with the charming lilt of Ireland overlying it. Enriched with the sound of murderous contempt. "You *are* a stupid bugger, Cardiff. Did you get lost along the way?''

Cardiff was fool enough not to be frightened. He'd underestimated her sister, Francey knew that immediately. Francey didn't. The moment she heard that voice a flood of memories came rushing back. All of them evil.

"I'm not a boy guide, Caitlin," he said stiffly. "I've brought you the woman. The rest is up to you."

"You're not interested in watching?" The voice was silken, insinuating. "I underestimated you, Cardiff. I thought your tastes were a bit more sophisticated."

Cardiff shrugged. "I want the money, Caitlin, and then I'm leaving. I've told you, there's no guarantee that the Cougar will stick to the plan. He's always been too independent, and I value my skin enough not to stick around."

Francey could see nothing but Cardiff in the brightness of the artificial light. "Boys," Caitlin Dugan said, "pay the man."

Francey saw it coming; Cardiff didn't. She opened her mouth to scream a warning, but it was too late. The gun was silent, wielded by unseen hands, a deadly, snicking sound beneath the rush of surf and wind. Cardiff's bland face creased in sudden surprise as the bullet entered his brain. "Damn," he said faintly. And died.

"Fool," Caitlin Dugan said. "Stupid bloody English bugger." And she stepped into the pool of light.

Except that she didn't step, she lurched. And with sudden sickening horror Francey understood Cardiff's amused remark that they no longer looked alike.

In the hours since she'd learned Caitlin wasn't dead, she hadn't had time to figure out how she'd managed to miss that huge, oncoming car. Obviously she hadn't. The vibrant, determined young Caitlin who'd dragged her across Manhattan in a vain effort to save Patrick was gone, replaced by a malevolent hag with a ruined face and body. Her body hunched to one side, her arm hung useless, her leg a withered stick. The left side of her face had been smashed, distorted in a cruel parody of healing, leaving the unmarked right side of her face an even greater contrast. If Caitlin had hated her legitimate half sister before, her reasons had increased a thousandfold.

"Sister dear," Caitlin hissed, hobbling over to her. "What a joy to welcome you to our humble encampment."

Francey had always been taller than Caitlin, but now she towered over Caitlin's hunched body. She tried to summon up pity, regret, some distant feeling of emotion for the warped soul that was her sister. But the smell of death was all around her as the woman looked up at her out of bright, malicious eyes that were eerily like her own, and it was all Francey could do not to shudder.

"Get it over with, Caitlin," she said flatly. "You've brought me here to kill me, so have done with it."

"I wouldn't think of doing anything so tame," she crooned. "I have great plans for you."

"I'm certain you do." She kept her voice cool as she clenched her bloodstained silk skirt in her fists. "I won't be much fun, I'm afraid. I'm squeamish, and I don't like pain. You won't have any trouble making me scream and cry. If you're going to think of all sorts of nasty things to inflict on me, why don't you get started? You heard Cardiff— Michael's coming. He's going to be quite a distraction for you."

Caitlin smiled. The teeth on the left side of her face were gone, increasing the ghastliness of her expression. "But, sister mine, that's part of the plan. I agree, it would be child's play to torture you. Instead, we're going to sit and have a nice sisterly conversation while we await your sweet Sir Galahad. And he'll come, I promise you. Not at dawn, as he'd planned. But alone, and very soon. You see, I made certain that he'd get word about you. The chain of information is so lengthy that by the time he gets word, he'll trust it implicitly. And he'll come for you. I can't wait."

She sounded like a child on Christmas morning. "What then?"

"Why, then you both die. Slowly, painfully. And I can start concentrating on more important things. My people are getting impatient with me. They follow me because they're afraid not to, but I know they don't understand my decisions. I don't bother to explain— I know what I'm doing. And getting rid of the two of you is imperative if we're to continue our life's work."

"Your noble calling," Francey said with contempt.

But Caitlin wasn't disturbed. "Hoping I'll jump the gun, dearie? Not on your life. I'm looking forward to your lover's expression when he shows up and sees you."

No one bothered to remove Cardiff's body. The bright lights were turned off as Francey was dragged to the burned-out shell of a building where Caitlin made her headquarters, and as her eyes grew accustomed to the dark she could see the weaponry, poised and ready, the motley group of men with sullen eyes and angry mouths. Someone shoved her down on the far side of a small campfire, and when she tried to move she heard the unmistakable warning click of a gun.

She still wasn't ready to die. When the time came she would face it, fighting all the way. But she didn't want to die for nothing but a madwoman's vengeance. She wanted a chance, one last chance, and she was going to do her damnedest to get it.

Caitlin sat next to her, watching her with gleeful anticipation, probably waiting for her to blubber and beg. She would do that if it would help, but Francey doubted her sister would react with anything more than amusement. Together they waited, Caitlin avid-eyed, Francey with numb dread.

At one point Francey must have drifted asleep, waking up with a jerk. "I must say, I'm in awe of your sangfroid," Caitlin said. "I doubt I'd be able to doze if I were waiting for judgment day."

"I've done nothing to be judged."

"Your life is an affront!" Caitlin shrieked suddenly. "All that money, that comfort, that safe, fat American life, while your father was bleeding to death on the soil of Ireland."

"Planting a bomb, wasn't he?" Francey said with a disdainful sniff. "Better him than innocent victims."

She almost died then; she knew it. If it hadn't been for the sudden distraction of the tall shadow at the edge of the fire, she would have breathed her last breath beneath Caitlin's clawlike fingers.

"I'm here."

The blind fury on Caitlin's face vanished in a ghastly parody of a coquettish smile. "How sweet of you to drop in," she murmured. "I gather you got my invitation."

He stepped into the circle of light thrown by the fire, and Francey stared up at him in shock. Once again he was a different man. Dressed all in black, with some sort of camouflage paint on his face, he looked like a savage. Cold, emotionless, brutal, he was a stranger, and far more dangerous than all the sullen killers who milled around Caitlin's ramshackle camp.

He didn't even glance in her direction; all his attention was focused on Caitlin Dugan. "It was delivered. What do you want?"

"I've got what I want. You and my sister. I have a taste for vengeance, Cougar, and you've more than earned it. You killed Patrick, you killed my baby brother, and you killed two other loyal soldiers on that little island."

"Don't forget Dex and his friend."

"Oh, I'm not forgetting. I figure we have plenty of time. You see, we know about your plans. We know you have twelve men waiting at Delbert Beach planning to intercept the arms shipment we've been waiting for. They won't dare come to your rescue—the mission is more important than the lives of two people, isn't it? Of course, they don't know that the arms have already arrived, along with a generous donation from some of our more militant, anti-British Middle Eastern friends. The British government didn't win any new friends with their participation in the Gulf War, Cougar, and that's greatly helped our cause."

"I imagine it has." His voice was low, cool. "What makes you think your information is correct?"

"Because it came from the top of your particular food chain. I don't suppose you noticed Ross Cardiff lying over there."

"I've seen a lot of dead men in the past few days, Caitlin. I admit I wasn't curious enough to investigate."

"He's been helping us out. Of course, he was doing it for money, not for politics, which made him a liability. But he's the one who makes the plans, you're simply the lackey. By the time your hand-picked little strike force realizes the shipment isn't coming, we'll be long gone." She cackled. "Of course, we'll leave your bodies behind. You would like a hero's burial, wouldn't you? Maybe you'll get to be buried next to your true love."

He still didn't look at Francey. She was listening to everything with numb horror, her eyes glued to Michael's tall, dangerous form. He walked closer, moving past her to squat in front of Caitlin, his back to Francey. If she hadn't been so mesmerized she wouldn't have noticed the knife he somehow managed to push toward her in the dirt as he concentrated on her murderous sister.

"What if I told you, Caitlin Dugan, that you were as big a fool to trust Cardiff as he was to trust you? That despite his title, no one paid the slightest bit of attention to him? That we know when the arms were delivered, and there aren't twelve men waiting on Delbert Beach, but more than one hundred of the most highly trained operatives the British government and their allies can afford, and they're damned close? What would you say to that?"

Francey managed to slide the knife under her skirt without attracting any attention. The men surrounding them were all mesmerized by the confrontation between the two powerful forces.

Caitlin's expression didn't waver. "I'd say you were bluffing. An act of desperation, knowing you can't save her."

"Even if I tell you the arms were delivered by a rusty fishing trawler out of Morocco on Thursday morning between 3:00 and 5:00 a.m.?"

Francey didn't need to hear the ominous rumble of voices surrounding them to know that Michael was right. "We'd best get out of here, Caitlin," someone spoke up.

"I'll do the deciding!" Caitlin shrieked. "Can't you see he's lying?"

"How would he know when the arms arrived, or how they got here? You were a fool to believe the traitor. We're leaving."

Caitlin lurched to her feet. "The first man who tries to leave is a dead man. Take him." There was a moment's hesitation as no one moved, and she screamed again. "Take him, damn you!"

To Francey's surprise, Michael didn't fight. Four men surrounded him, and she suspected if it came down to it, they would need all four to restrain him. But for now he wasn't resisting. "Let her go, Caitlin," he said evenly. "She didn't kill Patrick or your brother. She's never done you any harm. You've got me to play with—let her go."

"Her existence did me harm!" Caitlin staggered past him to grab Francey, hauling her to her feet. "The only reason I haven't killed her is because I want her to have the pleasure of watching you die first." She was drooling slightly, and her clawlike fingers were digging into Francey's arm. "And you *will* die, both of you. We have plenty of time. If you have a hundred soldiers surrounding us, where are they? We have guards stationed all around, and none of them has called in anything suspicious."

"None of them has called in at all," a voice spoke up. "Teddy was supposed to check in half an hour ago, Diurmud twenty minutes ago. We can't raise them on the radio."

Again the rumble grew louder. "We're out of here, Caitlin. We've followed you through thick and thin, but this goes beyond what's sensible. We're taking the arms and heading out. We're—"

The sudden explosion was deafening, blinding. Francey was thrown to the ground, something large and heavy crushing her. For a moment, stunned, she didn't move, and when her mind cleared, she realized she was in the midst of a battle zone.

Michael had vanished. Of the four men who'd surrounded him, two lay on the ground writhing in pain. The other two didn't move at all.

Francey tried to move, tried to push the dead weight off her, when suddenly that crushing burden came to life. And it was no dead weight at all; it was her murderous sister Caitlin, scrambling to her feet with insane fury, dragging Francey with her.

Francey reached beneath her for the knife Michael had slipped her, but she was hauled to her feet before her hand could connect with her one hope of salvation. "Looking for this?" Caitlin cackled, holding the knife aloft.

"Let me go, Caitlin. You don't really want to kill me. You know you don't."

"Of course I want to kill you," Caitlin said with mad cheeriness, dragging her away from the raging battle. "Since I was five years old and learned of your existence I've wanted to kill you. I'm not going to give up my last chance."

"You could escape. Everyone's busy. . . ."

"I don't want to escape. Not if it means letting you live." She held the knife up to Francey's throat, and she was far, far stronger than her sister could have imagined. "Some things are worth dying for, and this is one of them. Come along, sister dear."

"Where are you taking me?"

"Out of the range of rescue. Not that the Cougar will waste his time. He's got more important things to do. I must admit, that was a bit of a disappointment. I thought he'd be more heartbroken at the thought of losing you. Take a bit of advice from me, dearie. Men aren't worth it."

"You're crazy, Caitlin," Francey said, trying not to stumble as Caitlin dragged her along. "You know that, don't you?"

"Yes, dearie. I know that."

Francey knew now that the rustling sound was the surf, crashing on the rocks. There were no trees around the old army barracks, only a rocky promontory with the pounding waves below. The battle raged onward, but they were moving farther and farther away, and no one would even notice they were gone.

A moon had risen, dancing through the angry clouds, and as it peeked out she could see the ocean, the sharp cliff. Francey tried to struggle, but Caitlin simply pushed the sharp blade of the knife against her neck, and she could feel the first traces of blood slide down her skin. "Are you going to die with me, Caitlin?" she asked when they finally reached the edge. "Are you going to throw yourself over with me?"

"Don't be ridiculous," she cackled. "I'm not defeated yet. You're going over the side alone, with my knife buried in your throat, and then I'm out of here. I have the money, I have the luck of the Irish, I have—"

"You have nothing, Caitlin." Michael's voice came from out of the darkness. "You're a dead woman."

"Michael," Francey whispered, and she felt Caitlin grow very still as she clutched Francey to her.

"Perhaps. But I'll take her with me."

In the darkness Francey could see him. He had a gun; she knew that. She also knew he was capable of shooting Caitlin, of killing her quickly and efficiently, before Caitlin could finish with her.

With sudden, sickening clarity she realized that she wasn't going to let that happen. She'd seen Michael's face when he'd killed Dex. She'd seen the bleak, soulless look of a killer, and she knew without a doubt that with each additional death more of the man she loved was lost. And if he killed the madwoman holding her, then he would be gone for good.

"Let her go, Caitlin." His voice was calm, but Francey could see his desperation, could feel it.

"Not on your life. I know about you, Cougar. Know that you won't kill me. You don't kill women, no matter how much they deserve it. It's your weakness, Cougar. And it's going to bring you down this time."

Francey saw the faint movement of the gun. The gun that would end Caitlin's life. And Michael's.

And then she didn't think at all. She kicked out, wrapping her foot beneath Caitlin's sticklike leg and pulling. Her sister collapsed, her hands clawing for support that wasn't there. And then she was gone, over the cliff, smashing onto the rocks below.

Francey turned and sank to her knees, sobbing. Caitlin's body lay on the jagged rocks, still and unmoving, and there was no doubt she was dead. Francey waited for Michael to come to her, to draw her into his arms and comfort her. But when she looked up, he was gone.

And in the distance, the battle raged on.

Chapter 19

"I don't like the idea of you going out there alone," Daniel fretted. "Can't you wait till I'm out of the hospital?"

Francey reached over and patted his frail hand. She'd spent the past two weeks by his hospital bed, the enforced quiet going a tiny way toward healing her own wounds, but she knew full well that Daniel wasn't going to be up and around for a long time. "I need some time alone, Daniel. Just peace and quiet and sunshine. Belle Reste will give me that. With the Cadre wiped out I'm in no danger. Even you admit that."

"I'm afraid it will bring back painful memories. He's gone, Francey. We both know it."

"I'm surprised you even admit he existed in the first place." The pain had become a constant companion now, almost a comfortable friend, and she scarcely noticed its intensity.

"I'm the only one who'll admit it."

"Cecil admitted it. When he brought me out of that inferno and left me here at the hospital. He's the one who told me he'd died."

"Buried with full military honors," Daniel said. "Just like that little rat Cardiff."

"But he wasn't really Charlie Bisselthwaite," Francey said, leaning against the hospital bed.

"He wasn't Michael Dowd, either. We've gone over this time and time again, Francey. I don't even know who he was. He'll rest just as easily in Charlie Bisselthwaite's grave as anyone else's."

"If he's dead."

"Don't fight it, Francey. Cecil wouldn't have lied to you."

"No one tells the truth," she said flatly. "He's not dead."

"Is that why you want to go back to St. Anne? Are you hoping he'll show up? I would have thought life had knocked such romantic notions out of your head."

"You'd think so, wouldn't you?" She didn't deny it.

Daniel shook his head wearily. "You're an enigma to me, Francey. You have that madwoman buried on Irish soil, at great expense, when the creature would have murdered you. I have my accountants go to a great deal of trouble to get your trust fund back from the Children of Eire, and you simply hand it over to another organization. At least this time it was a legitimate one, but you might consider that you need to earn a living."

"I have enough to tide me over."

"Francey, he's not coming back."

She took a deep, shaky breath and smiled at Daniel. "I know. I'm just not ready to accept it."

The tiny island of St. Anne was just as she remembered it, the climate temperate, the trade winds blowing. The car she rented was a sedate American station wagon with excellent brakes and air conditioning, and she experienced only a moment of overwhelming grief when she glanced over at the tarmac where she'd first seen the man who called himself Michael Dowd.

She drove directly to Belle Reste, using the brakes sparingly. It wasn't until she faced the reality of the empty house that she knew she'd been fooling herself. Some small, crazy part of her had dreamed that Michael would be there, waiting for her. But when she walked through the empty, closed-up house and found no trace of him, she finally lost the iron-hard composure she'd held on to for so long.

The deed arrived in the mail, notarized, witnessed, signed and sealed. With his usual magnanimity, Daniel had given her ownership of Belle Reste and its twenty acres of beautiful waterfront, with a short note.

"Don't refuse—it's the only thing I can do to assuage my conscience. I should have warned you. For old time's sake I'm sending you another wounded bird. I'm counting on you to heal him. All my love, Daniel."

Francey accepted the gift with apathy. Accepted the upcoming intrusion with the same numbness. She had no interest in wounded birds or in taking care of others. She was too busy searching in vain for her own healing.

She was down at the beach when he arrived. She'd done her hostessly duties, making up a room at the opposite side of the house for him, arranging for a taxi to pick him up at the airport. She would cook for him and be unflaggingly polite until he finally left her in peace. But that was all.

She saw him from a distance, coming down the long set of wooden steps that led to the beach, and he couldn't have been more removed from Michael. The sunlight was blinding, but she could make out a tall, jeans-clad figure, with a rumpled khaki shirt and longish, curly blond hair and mirrored sunglasses. Just her luck, she thought. An aging hippie.

Her heart lurched to a sudden stop. There was something familiar about the way he held himself. Something heartbreakingly familiar about the set of his shoulders, the controlled grace of his walk. She didn't move as he approached her, too terrified to do anything but force herself to breathe.

He stopped in front of her, pushing his sunglasses up on his forehead, and he had the most beautiful green eyes she'd ever seen in her life. They were wary, watching her as if he wasn't quite sure of his reception.

"Who the hell are you?" she said.

"You aren't going to believe this," he said in a voice stripped of his faintly British accent and sounding more like Oklahoma, "but I was christened James Mackintosh Bond."

She shook her head. "And who are you today?"

"The same man I'm going to be for the rest of my life. Michael Cougar."

She considered it for a moment. "I like it. What do you do for a living?"

"I'm out of work, I'm afraid. I quit my last job, and my prospects aren't promising. I thought I'd take some time off, spend the next couple of years lying on a beach and finding out whether I really exist."

"That sounds like a good idea," she said carefully. "I happen to own a large section of beach."

"Convenient," he murmured. "What do you think of the name Francey Cougar?"

"Utterly ridiculous."

"I knew you'd like it."

She was in his arms, and he was solid and real and warm and there. She clung to him, fighting back the tears, and his arms were tight around her, holding her so fiercely that she had no more doubts. "I thought you didn't believe in happy endings?" she muttered against his warm chest.

He tipped her face up to his, and his beautiful green eyes were shining with love. "I'm counting on you to convince me."

"With babies and fights and old age?"

"With all those things," he said. "I love you, Francey. I always will."

And with his words, freely spoken, the last of her sorrow lifted and sunlight filled her soul. "Not happy endings," she said. "Happy beginnings. I just want to know one more thing."

"Are you certain you want the answer?"

"Positive." She cradled her head in his, pressing her nose against his. "What the hell color eyes are our children going to have?"

He grinned then, the first unshadowed smile she'd ever seen on his face. "Let's do our best to find out, shall we?" And scooping her up in his arms, he started up the winding wooden steps to the house.

* * * * *

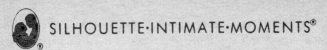

SILHOUETTE·INTIMATE·MOMENTS®

COMING NEXT MONTH

#433 UNFINISHED BUSINESS—Nora Roberts

When sexy, successful Vanessa Sexton returned to her hometown for some rest and relaxation, she didn't expect to run into Dr. Brady Tucker—the only man she'd ever loved. He had broken her heart years ago—how could she ever let him back into her life now?

#434 WAKE TO DARKNESS—Blythe Stephens

Curtis Macklin's investigation of a shot in the night offered him an opportunity he couldn't pass up—the elegant Yvonne Worthington. Certain she would lead him to his fiancée's murderer, he came to her rescue. But vulnerable Yvonne had lost her memory, and suddenly Curtis's priorities changed. He had to keep her safe from the bad guys . . . and himself.

#435 TRUE TO THE FIRE—Suzanne Carey

Revolutionary leader Gabriel Sanchez could handle many things. Unfortunately, protecting Miranda Burton was not one of them. She could never fit into his dangerous world, so being true to his cause meant rejecting love as a luxury he couldn't afford—or could he?

#436 WITHOUT WARNING—Ann Williams

Michael Baldwin—alive? Blair Mallory couldn't believe her childhood sweetheart had survived the boating accident ten years ago. Now Michael was back and wanted to avenge his father's death. But this Michael wasn't the same man Blair once knew—this dangerous stranger was tough and mean and oh, so sexy. This man, without warning, could steal her heart once again. . . .

AVAILABLE THIS MONTH:

FREE GIFT OFFER

To receive your free gift, send us the specified number of proofs-of-purchase from any specially marked Free Gift Offer Harlequin or Silhouette book with the Free Gift Certificate properly completed, plus a check or money order (do not send cash) to cover postage and handling payable to Harlequin/Silhouette Free Gift Promotion Offer. We will send you the specified gift.

FREE GIFT CERTIFICATE

ITEM	A. GOLD TONE EARRINGS	B. GOLD TONE BRACELET	C. GOLD TONE NECKLACE
# of proofs-of-purchase required	3	6	9
Postage and Handling	$1.75	$2.25	$2.75
Check one	☐	☐	☐

Name: _____

Address: _____

City: _____ State: _____ Zip Code: _____

Mail this certificate, specified number of proofs-of-purchase and a check or money order for postage and handling to: HARLEQUIN/SILHOUETTE FREE GIFT OFFER 1992, P.O. Box 9057, Buffalo, NY 14269-9057. Requests must be received by July 31, 1992.

PLUS—Every time you submit a completed certificate with the correct number of proofs-of-purchase, you are automatically entered in our MILLION DOLLAR SWEEPSTAKES! No purchase or obligation necessary to enter. See below for alternate means of entry and how to obtain complete sweepstakes rules.

MILLION DOLLAR SWEEPSTAKES
NO PURCHASE OR OBLIGATION NECESSARY TO ENTER

To enter, hand-print (mechanical reproductions are not acceptable) your name and address on a 3" × 5" card and mail to Million Dollar Sweepstakes 6097, c/o either P.O. Box 9056, Buffalo, NY 14269-9056 or P.O. Box 621, Fort Erie, Ontario L2A 5X3. Limit: one entry per envelope. Entries must be sent via 1st-class mail. For eligibility, entries must be received no later than March 31, 1994. No liability is assumed for printing errors, lost, late or misdirected entries.

Sweepstakes is open to persons 18 years of age or older. All applicable laws and regulations apply. Sweepstakes offer void wherever prohibited by law. Prizewinners will be determined no later than May 1994. Chances of winning are determined by the number of entries distributed and received. For a copy of the Official Rules governing this sweepstakes offer, send a self-addressed, stamped envelope (WA residents need not affix return postage) to: Million Dollar Sweepstakes Rules, P.O. Box 4733, Blair, NE 68009.

✂ SI2U

ONE PROOF-OF-PURCHASE
To collect your fabulous FREE GIFT you must include the necessary FREE GIFT proofs-of-purchase with a properly completed offer certificate.

(See inside back cover for offer details)